Buried
in the
Stacks

Also available by Allison Brook

Buried
in the
Stacks

A HAUNTED LIBRARY
MYSTERY

Allison Brook

**CROOKED
LANE**

NEW YORK

Chapter One

"The blue-cheese burger and fries are calling to me, but I'm going with a small salad, no bread," Angela said, glancing up from the lunch menu with a sigh.

I shot my best friend a look of disbelief. Angela was tall and slender, and I'd never known her to watch her weight. "Don't tell me you're on a diet."

"Of course not. But . . ." She glanced around the Cozy Corner Café to make sure no one in the busy lunch crowd was listening. "After work, Steve and I are going to the Clover Ridge Country Club to sample their desserts." Her eyes glowed as brightly as the diamond in her engagement ring. "If they're as yummy as the prime rib and chicken florentino we had there Tuesday night, Steve agrees, the country club goes to the top of our list! The dance floor's large and the view is awesome."

She frowned. "The only problem is, it's *sooo* expensive, even on a Sunday night. Which we'd have to settle for anyway, since their Saturday nights are all booked up till early September, and Steve and I want a June wedding. I told Mom the cost wouldn't be so high if we cut down on the guest list. We don't have to invite every third cousin we haven't set eyes on in years. But my mother insists—"

Angela stopped when our waitress came to take our order, and then, as soon as she sped off, segued into their honeymoon. Steve wanted to go to Cuba while Angela thought a Caribbean cruise would be nice and relaxing. I found myself tuning out, something I'd never done before. But who was this clone of my best friend sitting across the table discussing her wedding plans ad nauseam?

I was overjoyed that Angela and Steve had finally made the big move to get engaged. They'd been dating exclusively these past five years, with a few time-outs—usually lasting a week or two—after a big blowup over some silly issue. Both of them were outgoing, warm-hearted, and well suited to each other. Still, I never expected Angela to become obsessed with every detail of her wedding. She usually had no patience for formality of any sort and left such matters to her mother. Now the only subject on her mind, the only topic she cared to talk about, was her upcoming nuptials.

"Carrie, don't forget we have a date next Wednesday evening."

I stared at Angela.

She stared back. "You haven't heard one word I've said in the past five minutes."

"Sorry, I . . ."

Angela laughed. "Oh man, I've been running at the mouth again, haven't I? I never thought I'd get so caught up in all this wedding business." She stopped and rapped her knuckles to her head. "I'm so dumb. Here I go blabbering on, totally insensitive to—geez, not giving a thought to your feelings."

"What about my feelings?" I cocked my head, trying to understand what she was getting at.

"You know. Maybe you're wishing Dylan would move things along, and I'm making it worse."

I burst out laughing. "Dylan and I are so far from anything serious. With the kind of work he's been doing, we've hardly spent any time together. This past week was supposed to be his last with the insurance company—only now his boss has him off chasing after a stolen painting in Louisiana."

"Then you won't mind going shopping for my wedding gown as planned?"

"Are you kidding? I wouldn't miss it! Besides, as maid of honor, it's my job to help choose your gown."

"I'm hoping we'll find something really cool, so when Mom and Steve's mother check it out, I can tell them it's what I want. Phyllis dresses even more conservatively than Mom. If it were up to the two of them, I'd get married in a turtleneck gown."

We were still laughing when the waitress brought us our order. I bit into my turkey and avocado sandwich on eight-grain bread and smiled as I munched away. As soon as we finished eating, I called for our check, and we made our way to the cashier.

"They say we'll get more snow tonight," Angela said as she slipped on her gloves.

I pulled my woolen hat over my ears. "I'm so glad Dylan has Jack Norris plowing me out whenever it snows. The minute it stops coming down, he's at it, regardless of the time. Last week it was after three in the morning when I heard the plow."

We walked the few blocks back to the library where we both worked—Angela at the circulation desk, me as head of programs and events. We cut through the parking lot and entered the library's back door. Smoky Joe, the library cat, who really belonged to me, came bounding over to rub his face against my leg.

"Missed me, did you?" I asked, patting his furry gray head.

"He's probably hungry," Angela said.

"Are you kidding? I fed him before we left. And God knows how many of the librarians have their own stash of treats. Not to mention the coffee shop patrons who feed him a piece of whatever they're eating—despite all the signs I've posted that say 'Please don't feed the library cat.'"

Angela and I stopped by the ladies' room and agreed that we'd talk later. Finally, I headed to my office with Smoky Joe at my heels.

"You got two calls while you were out to lunch," Trish reported as I hung up my parka, then poured some more kibble into Smoky Joe's dish.

I glanced at the messages, both from people scheduled for programs in the next few weeks, and turned on my computer. There was an email from my Great-Aunt Harriet:

> The condo is lovely, though the kitchen is small. Your uncle insists that's a sign we should be eating out lunch and dinner while we're down here, but we'd both gain weight if we did anything of the sort. The weather is lovely. Mid-seventies today and tomorrow. We met a few neighbors while sitting around the pool. One of the men is on his library board at home in Ohio, so you can imagine the conversation he and your uncle got into.
>
> I hope all is well at home. Please stop by the house to see if my plants need watering. As you know, we've asked our handyman to check on the house every few days, but I bet he forgets to water the plants.
>
> Love from Uncle Bosco and me

I smiled, glad that my great-aunt and -uncle were enjoying themselves. Aunt Harriet had told me they'd often discussed spending part of the winter in Florida, but until this year they had never actually done it. Though I wasn't an orphan, my parents were divorced and living in other states. Harriet and Bosco had been my anchor here in Clover Ridge, Connecticut, since last May, when I'd shown up at their door and moved in with them for the next five months.

"I almost forgot," Trish said, breaking into my thoughts. "Sally asked me to tell you to stop by when you have a free minute."

4

"That doesn't sound urgent."

Trish laughed. "You should know by now—an invitation to her inner sanctum usually means she wants you to do something."

"I must be blocking out all those times she's had me do something not specifically spelled out in my job description." I picked up the DVD on my desk. "I'll start the movie, then find out what's on Sally's mind."

I headed downstairs to our large meeting room, smiling and greeting whomever I passed on the way. Though I'd only been head of programs and events since mid-October, the room already held memories for me—most of them happy, with one tragic exception when a retired homicide detective had keeled over and died while he was discussing one of his cold cases. I loved my job, which entailed providing the Clover Ridge Library's patrons with worthwhile classes and entertainment.

I was pleased to see that most of the seats were occupied. I slipped the DVD into the player and gave a brief talk about the film, which dealt with the Second World War. I turned out the lights, thinking ahead to the fall, when the work on our new section would begin. Instead of this long, narrow windowless room, we'd have an auditorium with stadium seating, as well as more rooms for more programs. Most of the library would be closed to the public during the construction period, but the results would be worth all the hassle.

I climbed the stairs to the main level and crossed the large reading room on my way to the director's office. Patrons, browsing through magazines and newspapers, occupied most of the comfortable chairs and sofas scattered about the room. My attention was drawn to three people, huddled in a corner, whispering to one another. The two men and one woman were shabbily dressed. When the younger of the two males burst out laughing, two women sitting at a nearby table scowled at him.

"Shh," one woman hissed.

"Mind your own business," he muttered.

The women sniffed and glanced at each other. I waited a moment to see if things would escalate, but thank goodness nothing more was said. Still, the incident was disconcerting. Clover Ridge Library patrons were usually civil toward one another.

I thought no more of the hostile exchange as once again I wondered what Sally wanted me to do. It was mid-January, and our monthly schedule of activities was running smoothly. Twice she'd made suggestions for new programs, but neither had proven feasible. And then there were her occasional "requests." Last month she'd had me conduct a choral group when the director was out with the flu. The idea had terrified me since I'd never done anything like it before in my life, but it had proved to be a fun experience. What's more, many patrons made a point of telling me that they'd enjoyed the concert tremendously.

"Come in!" Sally called when I knocked on her door. She greeted me with a big smile.

Uh-oh! "Hi, Sally. Trish said you were looking for me."

She waved her hand. "Nothing important. Everything running smoothly?"

"As far as I know."

"Good. Why don't you take a seat?"

Double uh-oh! I sat down and faced Sally across her desk while she rifled through some papers. "Okay. What would you like me to do?"

A blush spread from her cheeks to her ears. "Now you can always say no, but I am hoping you'll agree to be our next Sunshine Delegate."

I blinked. "I'm not sure what that is exactly."

"It would be your responsibility to send a card or flowers to anyone on the library staff who falls seriously ill or loses an immediate member of his or her family. You'd have a small bank account at your disposal. Gayle Morrison in the children's section has been our Sunshine Delegate these past two years. You might want to talk to her, see what gifts and cards she's sent and how much she spent on them."

"Hmm. I'd like to think it over. Can I let you know by the end of the day?

Sally's eyes widened as if I'd taken her by surprise. "Of course. That sounds fair, I suppose."

"Okay. Talk to you later," I said, and closed her door behind me. I started across the reading room, when I heard a familiar voice.

"Well, aren't you the take-charge working woman!"

I grinned at Evelyn Havers, who had manifested and was keeping pace at my side. Today my ghostly friend was wearing a black pencil skirt, a baby-blue twin sweater set, and low-heeled suede pumps. Not for the first time, I wondered where she kept her rather extensive wardrobe.

"I've learned to think over Sally's requests before I commit," I said. "She issues enough decrees that I've no choice but to follow."

"Being the Sunshine Delegate is no big deal. There are maybe twelve of you on staff, and you're a healthy, hearty bunch. If you buy three cards and four gifts a year, it's a lot."

I laughed. "I'm not worried that taking the job will be a time suck. I simply don't want to give Sally the idea that I'm a pushover for all of her suggestions."

Evelyn shot me a look of admiration. "You're a quick study! It's true. Once Sally realizes a person's reliable and responsible, she piles on the obligations. Oh no!"

I stopped in my tracks. I'd been paying attention to our conversation—making sure that no one was close enough to decide I was going gaga and talking to myself—instead of noticing the atmosphere in the reading room. I suddenly became aware of the raised voices coming from the far corner. Rudy Philips, a retired

patron who spent afternoons in the library reading financial publi-
cations, was berating the grubby-looking dude who had caused a
ruckus only minutes earlier.

"You don't own this chair," the troublemaker shouted back at
Rudy. "I happened to notice it was vacant so I sat down."

"As I explained, I got up to check something on a computer in
the other room. I left my jacket and my notepad on my seat."

"*My* seat!" the dude taunted. "Well, it ain't *your* seat if you're not
sitting in it. Your things are over there on the table where I put 'em,
safe as can be."

"Everyone knows it's common courtesy not to move other
people's—"

"What's the problem?" I asked, doing my best to sound calm.

"Hi, there, Carrie. I left my seat for five minutes and came back
to find this young man"—Rudy wrinkled his nose—"who could
stand to take a bath, occupying my chair. He had the nerve to move
my possessions to that table."

I turned to the intruder, expecting a tirade of abuse, but instead
saw his lips pressed together in silent protest as he glared over
my shoulder at someone or something. I spun around in time to
see the older couple he'd been sitting with earlier, mouthing him
instructions.

"You can have your old seat," he grumbled as he got to his
feet.

"Thank you." I pointed. "There's a vacant seat."

He ignored me and joined the couple, who were heading for the
main exit of the library that faced the Green.

I continued on my way back to my office. I was surprised to find
Evelyn still at my side. Usually when we were interrupted, she took
off for places unknown. Her normally unflappable expression was
gone. She looked upset.

"Trouble's brewing," she said darkly.

"I hope that guy doesn't come back any time soon," I said. "He caused a commotion earlier too." I wrinkled my nose. "And Rudy's right. He smells."

"I venture to say you'll be seeing a lot more of him and his friends."

"What makes you say that? Who are they?" I asked. "I've never noticed them in the library before."

"Doris and Henry Maris are the older couple. Nice people. They used to own a store in town. It did well until Henry started to mishandle money. A few people took advantage of him. Turned out, he had early-onset dementia. They lost the store and couldn't keep up with their mortgage, so they moved away to live with their son, but that didn't work out." Evelyn sighed. "Doris could get a job in town, but she feels she has to keep watch over Henry."

"And the troublemaker? What's his story?"

"The young man's name is Jimmy Belco. He's always been restless and unable to focus. His family left the area, and Jimmy's too rambunctious to keep a job." Evelyn pursed her lips. "They're homeless."

I shivered. "It's scary to think that middle-class people can suddenly not have a place they call home."

"It happens—to single mothers, veterans, people with problems," Evelyn said drily. "Anyone who has trouble keeping a decent job. Jimmy and the Marises spend the nights in the shelter just outside of town. They have to vacate the shelter by ten in the morning and can't return until five in the evening."

"And so they come to the library to keep warm."

"Right. I overheard part of their conversation earlier today. They had been hanging around the large mall outside of town until Jimmy got into one too many fights. He's been banned from the mall, and the Marises feel obliged to keep an eye on him."

"Clover Ridge is a solid middle-class community," I said. "I never realized we had a homeless population."

"Well, we do. Mostly made up of people who once lived here. After Doris and Henry moved in with their son, Tom, he and his wife divorced. She got the house, and Tom could only afford to rent a small apartment and was unable to take his parents in."

"How sad," I said.

"Very," Evelyn agreed. "Sally's going to have her hands full with this latest problem." She sent me a sad smile. "And I'm afraid you're going to be in the middle of it as well."

Chapter Two

Two hours later, after Gayle gave me the lowdown on being the Sunshine Delegate and told me the job was no biggie—she'd sent out a few cards and bought all of four gifts in the two years she'd been Sunshine Delegate—I called Sally to let her know I'd be happy to accept the position.

She exhaled a sigh of relief. "Good girl! I'm coming over now with the Sunshine Delegate charge card and paperwork."

Wow! My own library charge card! I *was* coming up in the world. Sally breezed into my office, dropped the items on my desk, and breezed out again, clearly delighted to have solved her problem. I stopped by the three scheduled programs in progress, then did paperwork until the clock's hands pointed to five o'clock.

I put my desk in order and then went searching for Smoky Joe. I found him in the children's room, sitting beside Marion at her desk. She wore a guilty expression, so I suspected she'd just given him a forbidden treat. I scooped him up and brought him back to my office, where I put him into his new carrier. He squawked a bit as I carried him out to my car in the parking lot.

"I know it's confining, but it's for your own safety. You only have to stay in the carrier until we get home."

"Meow!" was Smoky Joe's unhappy response.

Darkness had fallen, and the January wind chilled me to the bone. It was late Friday afternoon, and I was lucky to have both Saturday and Sunday off. Sally had offered to introduce the jazz musicians performing Sunday's concert since she and her husband would be attending anyway. And she'd asked Trish, one of my part-time assistants, to work that afternoon though Trish rarely worked on weekends. Now I wondered if my sudden extra vacation day was meant to soften me up so I'd say yes when Sally asked me to take the Sunshine Delegate job.

Other than my Sunday plans to visit my cousin Randy's family, the weekend was one huge void. My boyfriend, Dylan Avery, was still out of town, working on his last case for his employer before starting out on his own. Angela was deeply involved in her wedding plans. My great-aunt and -uncle were enjoying Florida's warm weather, and my father, with whom I'd recently reconciled after years of estrangement, was in Atlanta being trained for his new position with the company that Dylan would soon be leaving.

I drove halfway around the Green, admiring the shops and galleries that, like the library, were once large residences built a century or two ago. A few, like my aunt and uncle's house, were still private homes. I drove up the rise to the end of their long driveway and stopped in front of the detached garage.

"Be right back," I told Smoky Joe and headed for the kitchen door.

Brrr! The chill of the empty house ripped right through my zipped-up parka. I filled the watering can I'd left on the counter and watered the plants in the kitchen and dining room. I took a fast look around. Everything appeared to be in order, so I locked the door and returned to my car.

I drove slowly to my cottage, which was located on the Avery property a few miles outside of town. Back in October, soon after I'd gotten the position of head of programs and events at the library,

I'd answered Dylan's ad. I was able to afford it because the rent he charged me was ridiculously low. Shortly after, I discovered that Dylan had been my brother's friend when Jordan and I had spent summers on the family farm when we were little. Now Dylan and I were dating. Because of his job, we'd been apart a good part of the time, but I hoped that would soon change when he set up his own investigating office here in Clover Ridge.

Back at the cottage, I opened a can of tomato soup and made myself a tuna salad sandwich. Not a very appetizing dinner, I had to admit, but I wasn't very hungry. Smoky Joe, on the other hand, chowed down his dinner like a hungry wolf and begged for a few treats. I wandered into the living room and flipped through TV channels and then decided to settle down with the novel I was reading instead. My only interruption was Dylan's phone call an hour later. We chatted about nothing in particular for half an hour or so before hanging up.

Saturday morning I went to the mall to buy presents for Randy and Julia's kids and discovered great sales going on in all the stores. I ended up buying a doll for four-year-old Tacey, a book for her older brother, and a sweater and a blouse for me. My father called to say he was settling into his new apartment in Atlanta. Jim sounded excited. and I was happy for him. I was glad he had a normal job like other people, instead of scheming to pull another heist that could very well land him in jail.

The next day, I was taking full advantage of a quiet Sunday morning in my bathrobe, browsing through the newspaper and sipping a second cup of coffee, when my cell phone rang. It was Sally. I hoped she wasn't about to ask me to work that day because Trish couldn't come in as scheduled. I wasn't about to disappoint my cousin Randy and his family.

"Good morning, Carrie. I'm calling to let you know Dorothy Hawkins is in the hospital."

"Sorry to hear that. What happened?"

"Her husband just called. She was shopping at the supermarket last night. As she was putting her packages into the car, she slipped on black ice and fell. Turns out she twisted her ankle, cracked a few ribs, and suffered a concussion. Fred said she'll have to stay in the hospital for a few days."

"That's too bad."

Dorothy, the reference librarian, was the one staff member with whom I didn't get along. Nobody did, except Evelyn, who happened to be Dorothy's aunt. Dorothy had a sour disposition. What's more, she made it her business to ferret out people's secrets, which she threatened to expose if they didn't do her bidding. She had it in for me especially because she'd taken it into her head that *she* should have been named head of programs and events when the position had become available in the fall. Right now we shared an uneasy truce.

Sally cleared her throat. "I know visiting Dorothy in the hospital must be the last thing you want to do, given your history, but as our Sunshine Delegate, it would be a nice gesture. She's close by—at South Conn—and you needn't stay more than half an hour. Unless you have other plans, of course. In which case, a flower arrangement or basket of fruit would be in order."

"No, I don't mind stopping by to see her," I found myself saying. Evelyn, who seemed to be the only "person" in the library who cared for Dorothy, would appreciate the gesture.

Sally released a deep breath. "Thanks, Carrie. If you stop by the library, you can pick up the mystery she put on reserve. It just came back this morning."

"Of course. And I'll bring her a small fruit arrangement."

"She'll like that. I know how difficult Dorothy can be, but she means well—most of the time."

You should know, I thought, as I headed to my shower. Dorothy and Sally had been good friends until Dorothy had tried to coerce Sally into giving her my position.

Forty-five minutes later, I set down an ample supply of food for Smoky Joe and set out for South Conn Hospital. I'd been there a few weeks ago to visit my father, who had gotten himself into a spot of trouble. More than a spot, actually. I found myself smiling when I thought about Jim Singleton. He seemed really excited about his new job. I hoped that meant he'd given up his larcenous ways for good.

My cell phone jingled. When I saw it was Dylan, my heart beat faster.

"Where are you off to?" he asked.

"How did you know I was in the car?" I asked.

He laughed. "I'm an investigator, remember?"

"How could I forget."

"Which is partly why I'm calling."

Oh no! "Don't tell me. Mac has you working a new case."

"Absolutely not. I told him I wouldn't take on anything new under any circumstances. But we got a new lead on the case I thought I was finishing up. Turns out the crime ring is much larger than we'd thought. Several heists have been planned and executed by a hierarchy of thieves. We're working with a few police departments now."

I groaned. "How long will that take?"

"No idea yet, babe, but I told Mac I'm here only 'til the end of the month. That's a promise. And I'll do my best to make it home next weekend."

"You'd better," I said vehemently. "I miss you."

"I miss you too."

I slowed down as I joined the traffic approaching the Green that was the heart of the village of Clover Ridge. "Would you believe me if I told you I'm on my way to visit Dorothy Hawkins in South Conn?"

Dylan whistled. "Is she sick, or did she get into a fistfight with someone at the library?"

I laughed. "Neither. Seems she slipped on some black ice last night at the supermarket."

"On Saturday night? She and her husband must lead very dull lives."

"Sally didn't mention if he was with her when it happened."

"But why the visit? I know you're the new Sunshine person or whatever, but couldn't you have sent her something instead?"

"I suppose, but I know it would please—" I stopped before I uttered Evelyn's name. Dylan had no idea that I had a relationship with a ghost. I planned to tell him one day, but certainly not during a phone conversation. "Sally," I finished lamely. "She thought it would be a nice gesture. Since I have the time, I agreed to go."

Dylan chuckled. "Not a bad move, come to think of it. You'll be scoring points with your boss. Always good to have those on hand when you need to ask for a favor."

"I don't mind going to the hospital for a short visit."

I heard chatter in the background. "Gotta go, "Dylan said. "Talk to you later."

When I reached the Green, I stopped at the boutique food market for one of their elegantly wrapped food baskets, then pulled into a spot behind the library and made for the circulation desk, where Angela checked out Dorothy's mystery for me. The lineup of patrons prevented us from saying little more than to agree it was pretty darn ironic that as soon as I'd become Sunshine Delegate, I was obliged to visit Dorothy in the hospital.

My thoughts were with Evelyn as I returned to my car. By now she must have heard the news about Dorothy's accident and was probably worrying about her favorite niece. When I came into work tomorrow, I'd be able to give her a full report on Dorothy's condition.

Going to the hospital before noon proved to be a smart move. I had no trouble finding a parking space in the large lot that would be filled with circling cars in a few hours. I asked for Dorothy's room number at the reception desk, then took the elevator up to the third floor. It was the same floor my father had been on—clearly the section for injuries and accident victims.

The door to 315 was open. Still, I knocked as I entered, smiling at the woman in the first bed and her two visitors. Beyond the curtain divider, Dorothy was lying in the bed by the window. Though the shade was up, allowing the pale sun to light up the room, her eyes were closed.

"Dorothy," I said softly.

When she didn't respond, I figured she was asleep. I sighed with relief. My duty done, I set the cellophane-wrapped basket and book on the nightstand and tiptoed out, careful not to disturb her.

I was halfway across the room when she called out so softly I barely heard her. "Who's there?"

"It's me, Carrie." I retraced my few steps and looked down on her. Her eyes were still closed.

"Why are you here?"

"I'm the library's new Sunshine Delegate. I'm sorry you fell and hurt yourself. I've brought you some fruit and Sue Grafton's *Y is for Yesterday*. It came in this morning."

"Thank you." She surprised me by saying, "Please sit down."

I sat down on the chair beside the window. Dorothy pressed the button that raised the head of the bed, grimacing as she struggled to partially sit up. She had a cast on her twisted ankle. I knew she was in pain, because there was little the doctors could do to help her cracked ribs mend.

"Can I get you anything? Call a nurse?" I asked.

She gestured to the pitcher on her tray. "Just some water, please."

"Of course."

I filled a cup halfway and studied her as she drank thirstily before holding out the cup for me to fill again. No sign of the disdainful sneer that was her usual expression. Her shoulder-length black hair, which until today I'd seen only in a neat pageboy, was tangled and disheveled, and her face, devoid of her trademark fuchsia lipstick and pencil-thickened eyebrows, looked ashen. Dorothy was in her early fifties, but today she appeared younger and vulnerable.

"Do you know how long they'll be keeping you here?" I asked.

"Probably a few days. I'm not sure."

Not sure? Dorothy makes it her business to know everything about everything. But maybe her medication was making her dopey.

"I suppose they're giving you something for your pain."

She huffed. "I wish. My doctor said they can't give me pain meds because they might affect my breathing. Then I could develop pneumonia and die."

"Oh." Her gloomy answer left me speechless. I racked my brain, trying to come up with something else to say, when a woman burst into Dorothy's half of the room, bringing a whiff of Chanel No. Five in her wake. She was slender and blonde and elegantly dressed in a mink jacket over a pale pink silk blouse, leather pants, and high leather boots. The area suddenly seemed crowded.

"Dorothy, dear, I just heard! Well, actually, Fred called me last night, but I couldn't come see you a minute sooner. Tammy had me on the phone for an hour, terribly upset about a problem she's having at work, and needed my opinion—not that I know beans about the kind of financial deals she arranges, but she values my insight into relationship dynamics. Then Gerald asked me to sew a button on his favorite suit before he left for an important brunch meeting. Finally, I drove to the mall, ate the tiniest of lunches, and bought you this yummy box of chocolates! Now, where shall I put them?"

"Carrie, this is my sister, Frances Benning. Frannie, Carrie Singleton. Carrie works in the library with me."

"How very nice to meet you, Carrie, but I go by Francesca, as Dorothy well knows." She placed her small, well-manicured hand in mine. I was enthralled by her coral-colored nails that glittered with sparkles.

"Nice to meet you too," I said, marveling at how different the two sisters in front of me were. Francesca seemed so bouncy and full of life, while Dorothy was dark and gloomy and as sour as vinegar.

Francesca perched on the edge of the bed and shook her head in mock dismay. "I don't know why you had to go food shopping on a Saturday night. All that black ice. I hope you're considering suing the store. Gerald would be happy to start a suit on your behalf. Just give him a call when you're up to it."

Dorothy chortled. "I'm sure he'd be very happy. By now your husband must have lawsuits against every business in town."

"Now, Dorothy, he's only thinking of what's best for you. If you slipped and fell because the supermarket didn't clear the parking lot properly—"

"I don't want to talk about it!" Dorothy said.

Francesca glanced at her diamond-studded watch. "Just look at the time. I must be going. We have early dinner plans, and I've so much to do before we meet our friends. Heal quickly, Dot. I'll try to stop by again."

She bent down to kiss Dorothy's cheek, but Dorothy pushed her away.

"Love to Fred." To me, she called out, "Nice meeting you, Carrie."

When she was gone, Dorothy lay back against her pillows and shook her head. "There goes my little sister, Frannie."

"She's very pretty," I said.

"And doesn't she know it. Marrying Gerald has made her even more of a phony and a snob. I wonder which of them decided to turn Frances into 'Francesca.'"

"You two seem very different," I said.

"I believe in living within one's means. My sister thinks she's royalty and deserves to live in a castle."

"How are you feeling, my love?" a man's voice said suddenly.

Dorothy and I turned to the man who, I assumed, was her husband, Fred. He was of medium height, balding, and had a pleasant demeanor. In his hand, he held a bouquet of mixed flowers in a cellophane wrapper.

"Not much better," Dorothy answered. She turned her head quickly when Fred tried to kiss her cheek. Was that a look of terror in her eyes?

"Hello, I'm Carrie Singleton," I said, to cover up for what I thought was an awkward moment.

"Nice to meet you." Fred reached across the bed with his right hand, and we shook.

He looked down at the long-stemmed flowers. "I suppose I'll have to go find a vase for these." He chuckled. "I'm sure the nurses must have a collection of vases, with so many patients receiving flowers."

I stood. "I think it's time I—"

Dorothy gripped my wrist. "Stay awhile. Please, Carrie."

"Of course." I sat down.

Fred smiled at Dorothy. "I'll be right back. Anything you'd like me to get you in the café?"

"One of their blueberry muffins would be nice. Lightly toasted and buttered."

"Be back when I'm back," Fred said cheerily as he took off.

I glanced over at Dorothy's roommate. Her visitors had left, and she was dozing as her TV droned on. "You seem upset, Dorothy. What's wrong?"

She grabbed my hand. "Please, Carrie, don't leave me alone with him."

"You mean Fred? You're afraid of your husband?"

She bit her lip. "He knocked me down outside the supermarket. He wants me dead."

I stared at her, wondering if she was delusional. I'd been involved in a few homicide cases and knew only too well that people did actually murder other people, even in a small town like ours. Accordingly, I was aware that people often pretended to be nice, when their motives were less than genuine. But my ability to sniff out the bad guys was developing. I didn't get the impression that Fred Hawkins was anything but the sweet guy he appeared to be.

"Dorothy, I know you suffered a trauma when you fell. And lying in a hospital bed makes some patients loopy and confused."

"I'm not crazy, if that's what you're getting at."

That was more like it! It was a relief to have the old Dorothy back. "I didn't say you were."

"Just stay with me until Fred comes back, and I'll convince him to go home."

"All right," I said, not wanting to upset her further.

Dorothy closed her eyes. A minute later she was fast asleep.

Chapter Three

Two hours later, I was on my way to Randy and Julia's home, still wondering if Dorothy's fear had any real basis. I had no problem calling John Mathers, the Clover Ridge chief of police, to tell him what she'd said. John and I were now friends after a bit of a rough start. But I'd since helped out in a few homicide investigations, and I knew he would take my concerns seriously.

But the longer I thought about it, the more I was convinced that Dorothy had gotten things wrong. I assumed that Fred had been with her when she'd gone shopping at the supermarket the previous evening. Perhaps he'd tried to help her up when she was slipping, and she had misinterpreted his actions.

Or maybe she'd been disoriented by her concussion or stay in the hospital. Or she associated me with murder cases. But whatever the reason, I had no business assuming someone was out to kill Dorothy Hawkins.

I chuckled. Not that I couldn't imagine a line of people wanting to throttle her. She was a most unpleasant person and had irritated or offended every staff member of the library at one time or another. Even though there might be several people who wanted to off Dorothy, I was convinced her mild-mannered husband, Fred, wasn't one of them.

Julia's directions to their house were excellent, and ten minutes after I'd set out I was turning into their development. I hadn't had fond memories of my cousin Randy, who used to tease me when my brother and I had spent summers at the Singleton farm, but our adult relationship was based on fond affection. Julia, his wife, was a doll, and I hoped we'd become better friends. I adored their studious eight-year-old Mark, but four-year-old Tacey was my favorite, partly because she was the only other person in Clover Ridge who could see Evelyn Havers in her ghostly form.

I parked in Julia and Randy's two-car driveway and reached in the back seat for the cake and the toys I'd bought for the kids. I had no sooner used the knocker than the front door flew open.

"Cousin Carrie! Cousin Carrie!" Tacey shouted. "You're finally coming to visit me at my house."

"Of course!" her father said. "I told Cousin Carrie she had to come visit us or else."

"Or else what, Dad?" Mark asked.

After I untangled myself from Tacey's embrace, I hugged the others in turn. It was wonderful knowing I had relatives who cared about me, something I'd only discovered at the late age of thirty.

"Chocolate cake for all of us," I said, off-loading the box to Julia. "And something for you, Mark." I handed him the electronic toy. "And for you." I gave Tacey the book I'd bought her.

"I'll read it with you later," I told her.

"I can write my name," Tacey said. "I'll write it in my book so everyone will know it's mine."

"Good idea," Randy said. He put his arm around my shoulders. "Come inside and take off your jacket."

"Wow! Thanks, Cousin Carrie," Mark said.

Julia took my jacket and hung it up in the hall closet. "Would you like a brief tour of the house?" she asked.

"I'd love it."

"Living room, dining room," Julia said, pointing to one side of the hall, then the other.

"What a lovely home you have," I said. The décor was modern—simple and tastefully done in taupe, with accents in teal and burnt orange.

"The family room and the kitchen run along the back of the house."

Except for the sofa, loveseat, and the large TV mounted on the wall, the family room was crammed with toys. Tacey took my hand as we went upstairs to see the four bedrooms and two baths.

"Isn't my room pretty?" she asked.

"Beautiful," I said, admiring the canopied bed and the large wall mural of fantastic animals done in cheery pastels.

"And here's the guest room. For when you stay over," Tacey said as we entered the room across the hall.

The queen-sized bed had a purple and beige patterned quilt that went very well with the beige carpet. And the master bedroom was something else entirely. The bedspread and shams were a deep red with swirls of yellow and green. I would have sworn they'd be garish if I weren't admiring them in person. The bathrooms too were unique. The kids' bathroom was painted a bright yellow and gave the feeling of being in a boat, while the gray and white master bathroom was elegant and classical.

"Your house is beautifully decorated," I told Julia. "Your decorator is extremely talented."

Julia giggled. "My decorator thanks you."

For a minute I didn't get what she was telling me. "Oh! You did this yourself. You *are* very talented."

"That she is," Randy said, appearing on the scene. He slipped his arm around Julia's waist. "I convinced Julia to take a few interior decorating courses and work for a company before setting out on her own."

"Last year I decided to go for it after checking out the school systems within a half hour's drive and discovering there were no vacancies for early primary teachers."

"I didn't realize you used to teach."

Julia nodded. "For three years. Before Mark was born. I enjoyed teaching, but I *love* decorating houses. I was lucky to get a part-time job with Markham Designs here in town. Right now I work two days a week. I'll be putting in a full week when Tacey starts kindergarten in the fall."

I was filled with admiration for Julia. Much as I'd always liked her, I'd always viewed her as just Randy's wife and Tacey's mom. I knew she wanted us to be good friends, and I was determined to do my part in making this come about.

Dinner turned out to be a very casual event, which suited the five of us just fine. Julia and Randy were easy-going parents, and both Mark and Tacey were well-behaved and used to holding up their end of the conversation. I was surprised when our appetizer turned out to be ceviche, but the kids finished their portions of shrimp, scallops, and calamari marinated in lime sauce in record time. They each ate most of their avocado salad and meatballs and pasta, then dashed off—Tacey to watch TV and Mark to play with his new electronic game.

We three adults finished our main course at a more leisurely pace.

Randy said, "I heard Dorothy Hawkins took a bad fall at the supermarket last night. Cracked a few ribs."

"And injured her ankle. I visited her at the hospital this morning."

"I didn't know you were such great pals," he said. "According to Uncle Bosco, she pulled a few dirty tricks when you started your new position."

"That she did. Since then we've struck a truce. Not that we're great buddies. I visited her on behalf of the library staff."

"She's nobody's favorite," Randy said. "We have friends who live on the same block. They tell us Dorothy's filed complaints with the town against some of their neighbors for various offenses." He laughed. "I wouldn't be surprised if someone tried to knock her down last night, hoping she'd stay down for the count."

"Randy!" Julia exclaimed. "What a thing to say! We've had enough murders recently to last us till the next century. Besides, Dorothy is a very capable research librarian. She helped me get books from other libraries that I needed for my decorating classes— books they usually don't lend out."

"She is an excellent research librarian," I agreed. "If only she had a sweeter disposition." *And didn't blackmail people into doing what she wanted.*

"Well, I hope Dorothy recovers soon," Julia said. "But I'm upset by another library matter that hits closer to home."

"What is it?" I asked.

"I've noticed that several homeless people have taken to hanging out in the library. I've no complaints if they stay in the reading room, but they get bored and wander around. When I picked up Mark the other afternoon, a scruffy-looking guy was talking to him and his friend. Neither Marion nor Gayle was in sight."

"I'm sorry to hear that," I said. "They both must have had something important to take care of in the office. They make it a point not to leave the children alone."

"Regardless, I don't plan to bring Mark or Tacey to any more programs unless I can stay with them the entire time."

At that point both Tacey and Mark came into the dining room, asking when cake was being served. We cleared the table, and Julia made coffee.

After we had our dessert, I helped Julia clear the dishes. I stopped in the bathroom before my drive home. Tacey was waiting for me when I stepped outside.

"Can you bring Miss Evelyn when you visit us again?"

I knelt down and held her close. "Honey, Miss Evelyn can't leave the library. You know that."

Tacey nodded. "I know, but I want her to come to my house."

"I'm sure she'd love to."

Tacey sighed. "I haven't seen Miss Evelyn in a long, long time."

"Maybe Mommy will bring you to the library soon. Then you can see her."

"I hope so."

I hugged everyone goodbye amid promises to get together again very soon. I drove home slowly, my head filled with various thoughts: Dorothy's fear of her husband, the disruptions the homeless people were causing in the library, Tacey missing Evelyn.

It had taken Tacey awhile before she had realized Evelyn couldn't eat the cookies she kept offering her. Julia had been concerned that her daughter had an "imaginary friend," but once Tacey realized that I also saw Evelyn and I explained that Evelyn was on a different plane and couldn't eat our food, she stopped mentioning Evelyn in front of her mother. Still, Tacey wanted Evelyn to visit her in her home. Interesting how the mind worked, even in a four-year-old girl.

I turned onto the private road that ran through the Avery property. As I drove past Dylan's manor house on my way to my cottage, I was overcome by a longing to see him. In the short time we'd been a couple, our relationship had gone through a rocky phase, but now we were back on an even keel. Soon Dylan would be living in Clover Ridge on a permanent basis. I hoped our relationship would deepen and that eventually we would get married—a totally new concept for me. Up until recently, I'd doubted that, given my dysfunctional background, I'd ever be part of a loving family like Julia and Randy's—able to raise happy, healthy kids like Mark and Tacey. But falling in love with Dylan and getting to know my father and seeing him in a different light had given me hope. Maybe I'd end up being "normal" after all.

Chapter Four

Evelyn was waiting for me when I unlocked my office door Monday morning. "How is Dorothy? Is she in pain? Please tell me everything. I need to know how she's doing."

I'd never seen Evelyn this agitated—wringing her hands as she paced the short distance between my desk and the one Trish and Susan shared. "Yesterday morning I overheard Sally telling Gayle that she had to spend a few hours working at the reference desk because Dorothy had taken a bad fall and was laid up in the hospital. Later on, when Max was setting up the chairs for the concert, Sally mentioned you'd gone to visit her. What happened, Carrie? How did she end up in the hospital?"

"She's all right, but it was a bad fall. She has a badly twisted ankle, some cracked ribs, and a bit of a concussion from hitting her head. Nothing fatal, though . . ."

"Though . . ." Evelyn urged.

"Dorothy acted kind of strange when her husband came into the room. As though she were afraid of him. She told me he'd pushed her to the ground outside the supermarket . . . that he wanted her to die."

To my surprise, Evelyn burst out laughing. "Fred kill her? That's difficult to imagine. He adores Dorothy, though most people can't understand why."

"When I met him in the hospital, he struck me as genuinely thoughtful and caring toward Dorothy. I didn't pick up any hostile vibes. Still, it's not like Dorothy to be easily frightened."

Evelyn nodded in agreement. "It must have been the drugs talking. As I remember, Fred always treated her better than she deserved."

"But what about her fall?" I asked. "She got pretty banged up from simply falling on some ice."

Evelyn cocked her head at me. "My dear, people can break all sorts of things when they fall down on ice."

"She said there was an icy patch," I said.

"And knowing my niece, she was in a hurry, as usual." Evelyn tittered. "And she is something of a klutz."

Clearly, Evelyn's spirits were much improved, so I ventured to say, "We would have heard by now if Fred had managed to finish her off in the hospital, so it's safe to assume she's alive."

"Let me know how she's progressing, Carrie," Evelyn said, frowning to let me know she didn't appreciate my little joke.

"Will do," I promised as she vanished from sight.

The phone rang, demanding my attention. It was a patron named Carol Dixon, who had just returned from a trip to Vietnam and Cambodia and wanted to offer a slide show one evening in the library.

"Nice to hear from you, Carol. We're pretty well booked up for the next few months," I said.

"Could you check to see if you have a free evening in April or May? My husband and I would love to share our experience with our friends and neighbors."

I'd learned it was best to take care of calls like this on the spot whenever possible. "I'd be happy to check the calendar. I can call you right back, or you can hold if you prefer."

"I'll hold, if that's okay."

Carol and Stanley Dixon. Their names sounded familiar, so I knew Trish or Sue must have mentioned them. I riffled through the cards of past presenters and the invaluable comments that Barbara, my predecessor, had left me. There it was: "Well-informed if a bit stuffy. Might be best to limit the next program—and there will be a next program—to an hour."

Next, I pulled up the schedules for March and April. There was a six o'clock slot available on a Thursday in late April. That meant an hour's presentation since a craft class was scheduled in that room at seven thirty.

"I can offer you a six o'clock slot for one hour in late April," I told Carol.

I gave her the date, to which she readily agreed. When she asked for a fee of three hundred dollars, I explained that the library didn't pay patrons who shared their experiences such as this, and asked her to please fill out the form that she could download from our website and send it to me.

I answered some email and made a few phone calls until Trish joined me, followed by Smoky Joe wanting his mid-morning feeding. Trish's eyes gleamed with excitement as she hung up her coat.

"War zone in the reading room!" she announced.

"Oh no! Not Jimmy Belco from the shelter again."

"Yep. He and a pal got bored looking through the same magazines they've probably seen one hundred times already. They crumpled up sheets of paper they took from the wastepaper basket and started lobbing them at each other. Patrons got pissed and complained, and things got out of hand." Trish glanced at me sideways. "Sure you didn't hear the noise?"

I shook my head. "I think this room is soundproof."

"Max and Pete came running from wherever they were working and broke it up. Sally called the police. It's not in our custodians' job description to break up fights."

"No, it isn't," I agreed. "Did someone come down from the station?"

"Danny Brower arrived just as they got things under control. I figured it was time to stop being a looky-loo and earn my keep." Trish grinned. "You don't want your right-hand gal turning into a slacker, do you?"

I chuckled. "Fat chance of that happening."

I brought Trish up to date on what needed to be done, then left to check on the aftermath of the incident in the reading room.

Patrons milled about in small groups, conversing in low tones. I caught sight of Danny Brower, the police department's rookie officer, leading Jimmy and another young guy out through the front entrance. As far as I could tell, they weren't in handcuffs. I was about to enter Sally's office, when the door swung open, and out walked the older homeless couple who had been with Jimmy Belco the day he'd gotten into a shouting match. Doris and Henry Maris. Henry seemed befuddled, as if he wasn't sure what was happening. His wife, on the other hand, was clearly upset.

Though we'd never spoken, Doris must have known that I worked in the library, because she latched onto my arm. "Please help us!"

"I don't know how I can."

Her grip grew tighter. "Sally says Jimmy can't come back here, but you have to help make her understand. Jimmy's a fine young man and doesn't mean to start trouble. He promised to behave, only he has a short attention span—"

"I'm sorry, but I'm sure Sally explained the situation," I said, cutting short her plea. "The library's for patrons who want to read or take part in our programs. Jimmy's been upsetting the other patrons."

"It's because we brought Trevor," her husband said. "We promise not to bring Trevor here again,"

"Yes, Henry, that's right!" Doris said. "It was a mistake letting Trevor come with us." She turned to me. "But he had nowhere to go today, and Jimmy swore they'd behave."

I wanted to hug them both and tell them everything would be all right. Only nothing in their lives was all right. "I wish I could help, but there's nothing I can do."

I ducked into Sally's office, leaving Doris and Henry murmuring to each other.

Sally was sitting at her desk, holding her head. "I need an aspirin."

"Where is Danny taking them?"

"I have no idea," Sally said as she rummaged through her drawers. She pulled out a bottle of aspirin and swallowed two without the benefit of water. "I feel sorry for all of them—having no home to call their own—but they're not welcome to hang out in the library if they can't behave."

"Were they all once Clover Ridge residents?" I asked.

"I don't know about Trevor, but Jimmy and the Marises were. Jimmy has a severe case of ADHD. He had trouble getting through high school, then holding down a job. He moved to Florida with his parents a few years ago but eventually came back here, working occasionally and sleeping in the shelter."

She shook her head. "Doris and Henry are as middle class as you and me. At least, they were until Henry's decline, when they lost their store and had to sell their home for a song because they couldn't pay their mortgage. They went to live with their son, but that didn't work out. And suddenly they had nowhere to go."

I nodded. "So I've heard."

Sally let out a deep sigh. "It must be so humiliating, having to live the way they do now. In that awful place, with no sense of privacy. People who were their neighbors staring at them." Sally closed her eyes and grimaced. When she opened them, she sent me a meaningful glance.

"How did your visit go yesterday?" She gave a little laugh. "I promise you, when I asked you to be our Sunshine Delegate, I had no idea that Dorothy would be your first case."

"It went okay. She's in pain from her cracked ribs and twisted ankle. And her head aches. I met Dorothy's sister and Fred, Dorothy's husband." I decided to omit Dorothy's wild accusations. "I think she'll be staying in the hospital a few more days. Are you thinking of visiting her? I'm sure she'd like to have more visitors."

I'd said it mostly as a joke since I knew the two women weren't as friendly as they'd once been. Still, I was surprised when Sally reared back in her chair as if I'd asked if she planned to come to the library tomorrow dressed in a bikini.

"I'd visit her in a shot, except I have tons of work to wade through in the next few weeks. And you did say she's on the road to recovery."

"Looks like she is," I said, though I knew nothing of the kind.

"It sounds like Dorothy will be well enough to come back to work in a week or so. I'll send her a get-well card, of course." Sally stood.

My cue to leave. I exited Sally's office, puzzled by her reaction. It struck me that she intended to avoid direct contact with Dorothy. Not that anyone else on the library staff had offered to visit Dorothy. Still, Sally was the director. Our boss. I shrugged. At any rate, I'd fulfilled my duty as Sunshine Delegate where Dorothy Hawkins was concerned. I'd paid a visit and dropped off a basket of goodies. Surely, I wasn't expected to call her or visit her again. I'd see Dorothy Hawkins soon enough, when she was back at work and up to her usual tricks.

* * *

My office phone rang the following morning just as I was coming in from setting up coffee for the new political discussion group.

"Hi, Carrie. It's Dorothy."

"Oh. Hi." I drew in a deep breath. "How are you feeling?"

"Lousy. My ribs hurt when I take a deep breath. Good thing I don't find anything funny around this place. Laughing would be agony."

I didn't know how to respond, so I said nothing.

"I called to thank you for bringing me the basket and the Sue Grafton mystery. I was too zonked out on Sunday to even notice them."

"Well, enjoy them," I said.

"Thanks. I will." Dorothy sighed. "I'd love to get out of this place. It's driving me bonkers."

"When can you leave?"

"Not for a few days. After that, I have to stay home until the doctor decides I can put weight on my bad ankle. I dread having to sit around the house with nothing to do."

"I'm sorry to hear that," I said in my Sunshine Delegate voice.

"I hope you'll stop by the house and maybe bring me another mystery. Something by Anne Perry or Krista Davis. Or both."

"Of course."

"I have to go. I'll call you when I'm home."

So . . . apparently disconnecting from Dorothy, the wounded, was not going to be as quick and easy as I'd thought.

Chapter Five

Tuesday and Wednesday passed peacefully enough. The temperature outside stayed in the low twenties, but there was no sign of snow in the forecast. The reading room had remained free of incidents and disruptions ever since Jimmy Balco had been barred from the library. Doris and Henry Maris continued to pass their days reading or dozing in the reading room except for the short time they spent in the computer room.

Thursday afternoon I noticed Doris gazing longingly at the coffee shop. I wondered if she was hungry. Although the shelter provided an early breakfast and dinner when the residents returned, there was a good chance that the Marises didn't spend the little money they had on lunch.

I walked over to her and smiled. "Hi, Doris. I don't think we've ever met officially. I'm Carrie Singleton, the head of programs and events here at the library."

"I know." Doris gave me a ghost of a smile. "Harriet and Bosco's grand-niece."

"That's right. I'm about to take a break in the coffee shop. I love Katie's pecan chocolate pie, but I dare not eat an entire piece on my own. Care to share one with me?"

Doris's expression turned wary. I was afraid she was going to tell me to keep my charity to myself, so I quickly added, "I can't resist that pie, but I *have to* lose five pounds. They're the most difficult pounds to lose."

Inwardly, I released my breath when she grinned. "You young girls. So nice and slender. You don't have to lose even a pound. But I suppose you stay that way because you watch how much you eat."

"Shall we?" I asked.

Doris glanced at her husband, dozing in the chair next to her.

"He'll be fine," I said. "We won't be long."

Smoky Joe chose that moment to appear. Doris bent down to pet him. "Such a lovely cat," she said as she stood. "I had to give my Mittens away when we moved in with my son and daughter-in-law."

We sat down at one of the small tables in the coffee shop, and Katie Rollins, who now ran it, came over to wait on us. She was a robust, pleasant-looking woman in her mid-forties, and she clearly liked her new job. The selection at the coffee shop was more extensive now because Katie brought in baked goods that she made at home. I understood that patrons and a few of the library staff were placing orders with her for her cookies, cakes, and pies.

"Good afternoon, ladies. What can I get you?"

"We're going to share a piece of your delicious chocolate pecan pie," I said. "And coffee for me. Doris, coffee or tea?"

"Tea, thank you," Doris said.

"Oh, and a few of your chocolate chip cookies to go," I added as Katie was leaving. "For your husband," I said to Doris.

"Thank you," she said. "Henry will love them."

Katie left, and I had no idea what to say next. I couldn't very well ask how it felt to suddenly lose your home and your business and spend your nights in a shelter.

"Do you like working here in the library?" Doris asked me.

"I love it. After college I spent the next seven years living in various places and never settling down. And then last May I came to stay with my aunt and uncle. Uncle Bosco got me a job in the library. I was here when my predecessor had to leave, so Sally offered me the position. I was very lucky." I smiled. "I think I'm just beginning to realize how lucky I was."

"Luck," Doris said. To my surprise, she patted my hand. "Make sure you make the most of your good luck because you never know what's in store for you."

Katie brought over two steaming mugs and returned immediately with two pieces of pie on separate plates. To my eye, they didn't look like halves of one piece, but rather like two generous pieces.

"To die for," I murmured as I lifted the first forkful to my mouth.

"This is delicious," Doris said after she tasted her pie. "Thank you for inviting me to join you."

I told Doris about my favorite double-chocolate brownie recipe, and she mentioned a few of her own. Katie brought over a bag. "The cookies you ordered."

I moved the bag across the table to Doris. It felt heavy, and I knew there were a lot more than a few cookies inside the bag.

I glanced at the clock. "I'd better get back to work, or Sally will have my head." When Doris started to get up, I told her to sit there as long as she liked.

"Thank you, Carrie, for being so kind."

I smiled, touched by her gratitude and wishing I could do more. At the cash register, I glanced down at the bill. "You forgot to charge me for the cookies," I told Katie.

"My treat. I feel awful for the Marises. I even feel bad for that Jimmy Belco. I've a nephew like that. A well-meaning lad, but edgy and irritable and can't keep a job. My poor sister and brother-in-law do their best to keep him out of trouble."

On the way back to my office, a gentle waft of air riffled my hair as Evelyn appeared at my side. "That was kind of you—treating Doris to coffee and dessert."

"Kind?" I felt frustrated. "Doris was hungry. I wish I could do more."

"You will do more, Carrie. I'm counting on it." She disappeared as quickly as she'd come.

The library phone was ringing as I entered my office. Susan Roberts, my assistant who worked late afternoons and a few evenings, reached for it. "Hello?"

I grinned, thinking how A-type Trish would have greeted the caller: "Good afternoon. Programs and events. Trish Templeton speaking." But I'd quickly learned to appreciate Susan's creativity and her solutions to problems by viewing them in her own unique way.

"Oh, hi, Dorothy. How are you? Sure. She just walked in. I'll put her on."

Susan and I exchanged grimaces as I reached for the phone.

"Hi, Carrie. Fred brought me home yesterday, and I'm bored to tears. Do you think you could drop off a few mysteries for me after work? I finished the Grafton, and I don't have anything to read."

"Sure," I said and asked for directions to her house.

She told me, then added, "Please see if the latest Charles Todd and Ann Cleeves mysteries are available. If they aren't, I'd love to read the first Maisie Dobbs book by Jacqueline Winspear. I've been meaning to start the series, and now I have the time."

"I'll check."

"Much appreciated," she said and hung up.

Susan laughed. "So now our least favorite staff member thinks you're her personal assistant."

"I don't mind. She's home now, and this should be the end of my duties as Sunshine Girl—at least where Dorothy's concerned."

Susan handed me a paper. "I finished working on the graphics for the April–May newsletter and started a list for possible new programs.

"Hmm," I said, reading aloud. "A group reading by a psychic. Interesting. Plant a vegetable garden in the spring for the elementary school crowd." I turned to her. "That's Marion's department, not ours."

"I know. But I thought it was a good idea."

"So it is. And a visit to the old cemetery at night. I like that. An ongoing poetry workshop. A Jeopardy or trivia evening." I smiled at her. "These are all great ideas, Susan. I'll run them by Sally, see what she says."

"And look! I've been working on the Valentine decorations." She held up a colorful sketch of red hearts and a cupid with a bow. "Of course this will be a collage and three-dimensional. What do you think?"

"I think you're very talented and we're lucky to have you."

"I'll work on these the next few evenings at home, and we can put them up next week." Susan winked. "After all, Valentine's Day is only a few weeks away."

"Ms. Roberts, are you implying something by that comment?"

Susan was grinning when she left to check on the adult programs in progress while I read the newsletter she'd been working on. Her selection of photos and her own little sketches were spot on and creative. Not for the first time, I wondered if she shouldn't be working at a job that made better use of her artistic abilities.

At four o'clock, I took over from Gayle at the hospitality desk. All of us took turns hosting the desk where patrons signed up for various programs. I enjoyed having the opportunity to chat with our visitors and learn which programs and events they enjoyed and which they didn't much care for. Susan took my place at five. Smoky Joe appeared suddenly and rubbed against my leg.

"Time to go home, buddy, and don't you know it. But first I have to pick out a few books for Dorothy."

I plucked the latest Vera mystery by Ann Cleeves from the new books section and the first two Maisie Dobbs books from the stacks and carried them to the circulation desk.

"I thought you preferred to read on your Kindle," Angela said as she was about to check them out.

"These are for Dorothy."

Her lips twisted into a grimace. "Oh."

I laughed. "You're as bad as Susan. The doctors sent Dorothy home, and she's bored. She asked me to drop off a few mysteries for her to read."

"In that case, I'll check them out to her." Angela reached behind her. "I'll put them in a library cloth bag. She can return it when she comes back to work."

"Thanks, Ange. I'll tell her."

Dorothy and Fred's home was only a five-minute ride outside of town. A large SUV straddled the middle of their two-car driveway, so I parked in front of their small colonial-style home.

"I promise not to stay long," I said to Smoky Joe, who meowed his dissatisfaction from the new carrier, which he still didn't much like. I felt guilty each time I placed him inside it, but he had to travel in the carrier to and from the library and the vet's for safety reasons. Still, I felt relieved when he resumed his grooming. Maybe he was getting used to the carrier, after all.

I grabbed the sack of library books and followed the cement path to the Hawkins's front door. I rang the bell and waited. Nothing. I rang it again.

When no one answered the bell to let me in, I knocked. I waited another minute, during which I decided to leave the books and take off, when an apologetic Fred opened the door.

"Ah, Carrie! So sorry. We were talking and didn't hear the bell. Come in, come in!"

I followed him into the small hall, past the staircase, to the den at the back of the house.

"I don't know what's wrong with you! That man is the last person you want to get involved with. He's crooked through and through. Don't you remember—?"

Dorothy, reclining in a lounge chair, an afghan draped across her lap, was arguing with a good-looking man in his mid-forties. She stopped mid-sentence to greet me.

"Hi, Carrie. Sorry we didn't hear the bell. I've been trying to knock some sense into my brother's head. Carrie, meet Roger Camden. Roger, Carrie works with me in the library."

We nodded to each other. Roger eyed me speculatively. *A Romeo type.* He was so obvious, I almost burst out laughing.

"Sit down, Carrie. I promise this won't take long," Dorothy said.

"Well, I—"

"Can I get you a cup of coffee? Tea?" Fred offered.

"I'm really not—"

"Carrie loves her coffee. Make her a cappuccino with lots of cinnamon." Dorothy nodded to me. "Fred can't boil a hard-boiled egg, but his coffee's to die for."

I was about to insist I was only here to drop off the library books she'd asked for, when Roger stopped staring at me and returned to the conversation I'd interrupted.

"Dorothy, you're being short-sighted. Ernie's admitted to having pulled a few dodgy deals in the past, but he swears this project is clean and aboveboard. And time is of the essence. We can't sit on this too long. There are other investors—"

Dorothy roared with laugher. "Right. Other investors. They're lining up to hand over their money. People don't change,

Roger. You're the one that's *short-sighted* when it comes to Ernie Pfeiffer. Have you forgotten what he pulled on your own aunt and uncle? They had to go to court to get back some of what he stole from them."

"Did you say Ernie Pfeiffer?" The words tumbled out before I could stop them. *The man who had tricked Evelyn and her husband out of most of their money.*

Roger was about to respond to his sister. Instead, he closed his mouth and frowned at me.

"Sorry. I don't mean to interfere in your private discussion, but I recognized the name."

"Don't tell me Ernie's bamboozled you out of money in the short time you've been living in Clover Ridge," Dorothy said.

"No, I met him in the hospital last month. He was my father's roommate." *And thinks of you as the Dragon Lady.*

Dorothy waved her hand dismissively. "Unfortunately, he lives next door to us. You couldn't wish for a worse neighbor. He refuses to take care of his property. If he mows twice in a summer, it's a lot."

"Yes, he mentioned he was your neighbor." *And that you tried to sue him several times.*

Fred came in, carrying a steaming mug of cappuccino, which he set on the table in front of me. I sipped. Heavenly!

"Thank you—this is delicious."

"Told you," Dorothy said. She turned to her husband. "It's bad enough that Roger's all gung-ho about Ernie's next scam, but I don't know why you want us to get involved."

Fred smiled at Dorothy. "Because, dear, I think it's a safe way for us to make some money. Roger's checked out the proposal very carefully. He even called the bank that's involved. It's all above-board and looks to be a safe investment. We should go for it."

"I don't think so." She cast a baleful eye at him. "Let Roger go ahead and throw away his money if he wants to, but don't include us."

42

Fred cleared his throat. "The thing is, I told Roger I'd cover part of his investment—just until it starts paying, that is. And if you agreed, of course."

"I see." Dorothy turned to look at her brother. I watched his ears redden under her stare. "And how much are we talking abut here?"

"Thirty thousand each," Roger said. "I only need ten to cover my share."

"Sorry, Roger, I don't approve. And we don't have ten thousand dollars to join another loan that somehow never got repaid."

The blush spread to Roger's cheeks. "I'll pay you back everything, as soon as the first money comes in."

"Money for your kids is one thing. A gamble on one of Ernie's schemes is another." Dorothy pursed her lips. "In fact, I think I'll call that man and give him a piece of my mind."

Chapter Six

Roger's hands formed fists as he loomed over his sister. "You are the cruelest, most selfish person I know." He stomped out of the room.

"Roger, don't go. She doesn't mean it," Fred said, chasing after his brother-in-law.

Dorothy turned to me "Sorry you had to witness that, Carrie. If my brother put half the effort he wastes on get-rich schemes into getting a decent job, he'd be a wealthy man. Poor Fred is dazzled by anything Roger suggests because my brother is a math whiz and was a football hero in high school."

I stared at her, so self-confident and sure of herself. So very much Dorothy once again. "But Dorothy . . . about Fred."

"Yes?"

"I don't understand. When I saw you in the hospital, you were terrified of him."

"Of Fred?" she scoffed. "Why would I be afraid of my husband? You met him. He's the sweetest man around."

"He does seem very nice, but in the hospital you said he knocked you down outside the supermarket. That he wanted to . . . kill you."

"Really? I said that?" Dorothy looked truly puzzled.

I nodded. "Uh-huh."

"I can't imagine saying any such thing. It must have been the meds talking."

"Don't you remember? You told me you were afraid of Fred."

"I remember slipping on the ice as I was putting the groceries in the car."

"Was Fred with you?"

Before she could answer, Fred returned to the living room, shaking his head. "Roger's beside himself. I hope he doesn't get into an accident, driving in that state."

Dorothy turned her attention to her husband. "Now, Fred, don't you go worrying about Roger. He'll calm down. That boy has to learn not to expect us to bail him out when he wants to get involved in some hair-brained scheme."

Fred shrugged. "I thought it sounded like a fine proposition. But perhaps you're right." He glanced at my half-empty mug. "Would you care for another cappuccino, Carrie?"

"No, thank you."

"But I'd love a cup of lemon tea," Dorothy said.

"Coming up, my love."

Fred disappeared into the kitchen and I stood, having decided that my Sunshine visit was now over. Dorothy was on the mend, and she didn't appear to be in any danger from her husband, despite what she'd said in the hospital.

"I brought you a few mysteries from the library. They were checked out to you, so please return them when you come back to work."

"Thank you so much," Dorothy said. "I've set aside the book I finished, so you can put it back into circulation."

She pointed to the bookcase across the room. As I went to get it, my glance landed on several vases on display. They varied in color, size, and shape, but on closer examination, each was striking in its own right.

"What beautiful vases!" I exclaimed.

45

"Thank you. My vase collection is my pride and joy. Some of them are antiques." She cocked her head. "More valuable than you'd imagine. Carrie." Dorothy's voice softened as she spoke my name.

"Yes?"

"I want to thank you for visiting me in the hospital and for stopping by today. It's meant a lot to me."

I shrugged. "Well, I am the Sunshine Delegate."

Dorothy smiled. "We both know you didn't have to visit me in person, regardless of Sally's orders."

I grinned at her. "That's true."

"I admire you, Carrie Singleton. You have more gumption than most people in this town."

"Well, thank you, Dorothy," I said, touched by the only kind words I'd ever heard her utter.

Fred brought Dorothy her tea and walked me to the door.

"Thank you for visiting today," he said. "I know you two have had your differences, but I can tell—Dorothy feels a special link to you, Carrie."

I suppose it's because she knows I'm in touch with her Aunt Evelyn. "She seems to be feeling better."

"She is. The doctor wants her to stay home another week, and then she should be strong enough to go back to work."

* * *

Evelyn pursed her lips as I related the events of my visit the next day. We were downstairs in the supply room, where I'd gone to retrieve some typing paper.

"So, Ernie Pfeiffer's up to his old tricks. And he has the gall to prey on my family!"

"Not if Dorothy has anything to say about it. She said she was planning to call him and give him a piece of her mind."

Evelyn sighed. "Good for Dorothy! She's the only one of my sister's children with a lick of sense. Frances is a social climber. She probably wishes she were living two hundred years ago, so she could be the lady of the manor. And poor Roger." She sighed again, more deeply this time. "Spoiled growing up and never developed a back-bone. He'll try any quick scheme to make a buck. It's a good thing his wife is a guidance counselor at the high school, or I don't know how they'd be feeding their four children."

"Dorothy's feeling better and should be back at work soon. She claims she's not afraid of Fred and never was."

"See? I told you," Evelyn said. "Being injured and in the hospital can do something to the mind. At least I can rest easy about her."

I locked the supply closet, and we started up the stairs. As we reached the main level, we heard angry voices coming from the reading room.

"Oh, not again!" I said. "I can't believe Jimmy Balco had the nerve to come back here after being banned."

A crowd of angry patrons was standing around a person who was trying to speak. When I got closer, I saw that the person being mobbed was Doris.

"I most certainly did not take—"

"Yes, you did!" a white-haired man insisted. "I saw you staring at Leslie's pocketbook."

"What's going on?" I asked the woman beside me.

"*She*—that homeless woman who comes here every day—stole Leslie Todd's wallet."

"Really? Are you sure?"

The patron glared at me. "Leslie got up to talk to a friend. When she came back, her wallet was gone."

"But why does she assume that Doris Maris took it?"

The patron wrinkled her nose. "That's her name?"

"Yes. Doris and her husband used to live in the neighborhood. I don't think—" What did I think? I hated to think that Doris was a thief, but I knew nothing of the situation.

"Anyway, this *Doris* was sitting across from Leslie. People said she kept giving Leslie the eye."

Before I could respond, Sally appeared and led Doris and the small woman who'd been gesturing wildly into her office. Another woman insisted on joining them.

"Oh, good! The police have arrived!" my informer exclaimed.

I turned. Sure enough, Lieutenant John Mathers had entered the library. When he spotted me, he drew me aside.

"What's up, Carrie? Sally called and said a woman's wallet was stolen. Witnesses claim they saw who took it."

"I know, but I have my doubts."

"Where's Sally? In her office?"

"Yes. With the two women involved."

In two strides, John was halfway to Sally's office. Without thinking, I followed him. As he entered the office, I caught sight of Henry. He had a look of terror on his face. He tried to catch the attention of a man speaking to two women by tapping on his arm. When the man noticed him, he drew his arm away. I walked over to him.

"Henry, are you looking for Doris?"

He nodded.

"I'll bring you to her." I took his arm and opened the door to Sally's office. "Doris is in here."

The office, though considerably larger than mine, was crowded with seven of us inside. Leslie, the woman who'd been robbed, was speaking nonstop in a shrill tone.

"I didn't take your wallet," Doris said. "I didn't. I swear I didn't."

"I saw you watching her," the other woman said to Doris. "As soon as Leslie got up, you must have grabbed her wallet." She looked at John. "Open *her* pocketbook. See if it's there."

"You can look if you want," Doris said, unzipping her pocket-book. "See? Nothing. Just as I said."

"You must have hidden it somewhere. So you can get it later," Leslie said.

"They should never let the likes of you in our library!" her friend said with a sneer.

Doris sent me a look of anguish. I moved closer and took her hand. The two women glared at me.

John asked the two women for their names.

"I'm Leslie Todd and this is my friend Marcy. Marcy Faraday."

John looked at one, then the other. "I intend to get to the bottom of this. Mrs. Maris does not have the missing wallet in her possession. We must consider that there might be another explanation."

The two friends started to speak at the same time. John raised his palms. "Please allow me to finish. Mrs. Todd, where was your pocketbook when you went over to talk to your friend?"

"I left it on my seat."

"Did you leave it open or closed?"

"Closed, of course."

Henry cleared his throat. "Excuse me, but I'm quite sure you left it open."

Six pairs of eyes turned to stare at him.

"You're just saying that to protect your wife," Leslie Todd said.

Henry blinked, and for a moment I thought he'd lost his train of thought. "No, I'm certain. You unzipped your pocketbook to search for something. You retrieved a tissue and handed it to *her*." He pointed his finger at Marcy Faraday. "Then you stood suddenly and dashed off, I don't know where."

"Right. You gave me a tissue," Marcy said as she remembered, "and then you noticed Grace Parris heading for the exit. You said you wanted to talk to her about getting you and Larry tickets for Sunday's show."

49

"If you left your pocketbook open, it could have fallen on its side, and your wallet might have slipped out," I said.

"I don't remember seeing it on its side when I returned," Leslie said.

"Did you look under your seat?"

"I thought we did," Marcy said.

John headed for the door. "Why don't the three of us take another look? Perhaps we'll manage to put this matter to rest."

Doris and Henry remained in the office with Sally while I followed John and the two women to the section of the reading room where they'd been sitting. Most of the crowd had dispersed, though a few patrons stood in one corner talking. John asked the gentleman now occupying the seat that Leslie had been in to stand, and the two men peered under the chair while Leslie and Marcy searched the surrounding area.

"It's not here," Leslie said. She glanced at Sally's office, then at John. "Maybe we have the wrong person. The husband knew that I'd left my pocketbook open. He must have taken my wallet. You should have frisked him, Lieutenant."

An idea suddenly struck me. Smoky Joe had taken to batting objects around the cottage. Which meant he was probably doing that here in the library. "I think we should expand our search. Leslie's wallet might have dropped to the floor, and then Smoky Joe might have batted it into a corner."

"If that isn't the most far-fetched idea I've heard!" Marcy said.

"I think it's worth a shot, don't you?"

We didn't even have to ask for help as five patrons who had been watching us search spread out and peered under shelves and into corners. I even looked behind the counter of the coffee shop.

After several minutes passed, I was beginning to think that my suggestion was a waste of time after all, when an elderly man came running into the reading room, waving a wallet in his outstretched hand.

"I found it! I found it!"

We gave him a round of applause.

He presented it to Leslie with a bow, which earned him more applause.

Leslie hugged him and thanked him profusely before stowing the wallet in her pocketbook.

"Where was it? Where was it?" patrons demanded.

"Could you believe? It was in the children's room, under a chair."

"Smoky Joe," I murmured to John.

As though on cue, the mischievous feline appeared, bushy tail in the air, and rubbed against my leg.

Everyone burst out laughing. By now, Doris, Henry, and Sally had stepped out of her office. I was greatly relieved to see Leslie approach them and offer what appeared to be a sincere and heartfelt apology.

"A very unpleasant experience for Doris and Henry," Evelyn said.

I nodded in agreement. "They've been made to feel unwelcome. At the same time, the patrons feel threatened by their presence."

"Something has to be done, and soon," Evelyn said.

Chapter Seven

S ally must have felt that something had to be decided about the homeless people camping out in the reading room, because she called a meeting of the department heads at noon the following day. Without Dorothy, there were five of us: Marion Marshall, the children's librarian; Harvey Kirk from computers; Fran Kessler, Angela's boss at the circulation desk; Sally; and me. We gathered around the oval table in the conference room. Sandwiches, cookies, and urns of coffee and hot water for tea were set out on the smaller table at the far end of the room.

"Help yourself," Sally invited as she sat down at the head of the table.

"Oh my. Big doings," Harvey murmured.

"I bet I know what it is," Marion said.

I had my suspicions but said nothing as I reached for a turkey and avocado sandwich on rye. When everyone was seated and munching away, Sally began her address.

"I know you've all heard about what happened yesterday. One of our patrons, Leslie Todd, left her seat in the reading room to speak to another patron. When she returned, she realized her wallet was missing. Other patrons claimed that Doris Maris, a woman from the homeless shelter, stole it. I was forced to bring in the police to resolve this matter.

"It turns out that the wallet hadn't been stolen, after all. It was discovered in the children's room. I'm assuming Smoky Joe, our library feline, had batted it around until it ended up there."

"There's a good reason why patrons are—" Harvey began until Sally held up her hand.

"Please let me finish what I have to say. Then I want to hear all of your thoughts and feelings, and hopefully we'll find a resolution to this matter.

"No one was to blame in this case, but perhaps patrons were quick to blame a homeless person because a few of them have been spending a good part of every day in our library. Mostly they sit and read or even doze, but there was one young man who caused a few disturbances and had to be barred. Our policy is to allow people to spend time in our facility. We do not prevent people from sitting in the reading room unless they disturb other patrons." Sally looked at each of us.

"Yesterday neither Doris nor Henry Maris did anything inappropriate, yet Doris was accused of stealing. Clearly, their presence and that of other homeless people is upsetting our patrons. We have a situation that I hope we can resolve so that it benefits everyone involved."

"But Doris and Henry Maris aren't patrons, are they?" said Fran.

"Their shelter is located in our district. And even if it weren't, we wouldn't limit their time spent in the library unless they exhibited disruptive behavior."

Marion frowned. "I don't know if I'd use the word 'disruptive,' but occasionally they'll come into my section when Gayle or I am reading a story to the children. Aside from their distracting the children, I don't feel comfortable having them in our room."

"My cousin said a scruffy-looking man was talking to her son and his friend when she went to pick them up. Now she won't let her children come to library programs unless she can stay with them," I said.

Sally grimaced. "That won't do. Clearly, we have to set limits."

"Who's going to watch them and make sure they remain in the reading room?" Harvey Kirk demanded. "Every day an older gentleman wanders into the computer room. He sits down at a computer, is clearly confused, then asks me to help him. A young guy used to come and hog a machine until I told him he had to leave. He complained that he couldn't get on the porn sites."

"I hate to be the one to say it, but they're unkempt. They smell," Fran said.

Suddenly, everyone was speaking at once. Sally raised her hand and established order. "All right. What I'm hearing is that you wish we didn't have this problem, but we do. The question is, what can we do about it. Any suggestions?"

I thought a moment. "Is there any other place where they could stay during the day? Someplace warm and comfortable?"

"Most of them go to the mall," Fran said. "They wander into the stores and shops. If they cause a ruckus, the security guards are called to escort them out to the center corridor."

"They probably get bored just sitting around," I said.

Everyone turned to stare at me.

"They wouldn't be bored if they got a job," Harvey said.

"A few of them work," Sally said. "Unfortunately, they don't make enough money to rent an apartment, and so they have to stay in a shelter. A few own cars and sleep in them during the warmer months, but it's much too cold now."

"Too bad there's not a place where they could stay and be comfortable during the day. Where they could read, watch TV, or play board games," I said.

Marion said, "At my last civic association meeting, a neighbor mentioned she'd joined a group that was starting up a day program for the homeless. A few residents got together to buy an abandoned house right here in town. It's rundown and needs lots of repairs, so I doubt it will be ready for use any time soon."

"Well, that's encouraging," Sally said. "Meanwhile, we'll be more vigilant these next few months. The problem will ease up when the weather turns warmer."

"Only to be repeated next winter," groused Harvey.

"Maybe the new day program will open before then," I said. I turned to Marion. "Can you text me the phone number of the person who's involved in the group? I'd like to attend one of their meetings."

"Of course."

Sally brought the meeting to an end. As I stood to leave, she said, "Carrie, I'm glad you're going to find out more about this day program for the people living in the shelter. If the group needs a place to meet, this conference room is available most evenings. They're welcome to hold their meetings here."

"Thanks, Sally." I smiled at her, glad to know that she was as concerned about the homeless people as I was.

* * *

Saturday morning, Dorothy surprised all of us by hobbling into the library on crutches.

"What are you doing here?" I asked as I took her pocketbook and the canvas bag dangling from her shoulder and accompanied her to the reference desk. "I thought you were supposed to stay home for another week."

She made a face. "I couldn't bear to stare at the walls in my house one minute more. I was turning into a shrew."

Turning into? "Did Fred drive you here?"

"No." She grunted as she positioned herself in her chair behind the desk. "I told him I could manage very well on my own, and he was free to go back to work."

I set her pocketbook and bag on the desk. "Well, let me know if you need anything."

"There is one thing—the books you brought me to read are in the canvas bag. Please return them for me."

"Will do." I set off to the circulation desk to do her bidding.

"Dorothy's back," I told Angela as I handed her the three mysteries and the bag.

"Aren't we lucky?" Angela said. I laughed and turned to leave, when she said, "Hey, you doing anything this evening?"

I made a face. "And what should I be doing with Dylan still away, you on your wedding-go-round, and my aunt and uncle in Florida?"

"Want to join Steve and me for dinner tonight at that new pub? We hear they have great burgers."

"Sure. As long as it doesn't turn into another strategy session about wedding plans."

"It won't. I promise. Though we still haven't decided on our honeymoon. We're considering Hawaii and—"

"Surprise me!" I said, making a beeline for my office.

"We'll pick you up at seven," she called after me. "Be ready!"

The day moved along faster, now that I had plans for the evening. I couldn't wait for the following weekend, when Dylan was scheduled to fly home.

At five minutes to five I locked my office door and went in search of Smoky Joe. I found him lounging in the children's room, receiving the royal treatment from two little girls. Their mothers were trying to get their daughters to stop petting the cat and put on their jackets as my spoiled feline purred happily away.

"Come on, Smoky Joe. Time to go home," I said.

He ignored me, so I reached down and scooped him into my arms. Both girls sounded a complaint.

"See, even the kitty cat has to go home," one mother said.

Reluctantly, the girls stood and got ready to leave the library.

"Goodbye," I said. "See you all soon."

"You're getting heavy," I told Smoky Joe as I positioned him over my shoulder. I walked past the reference desk to see if Dorothy needed any assistance, but she had gone for the day.

Chapter Eight

"So, when are you and Dylan thinking of tying the knot?"

"Steve!" Angela punched her fiancé's shoulder. "You don't say things like that. Not appropriate."

"Sorry, Carrie," the unrepentant Steve said to me. He turned to Angela, "Do we add that to your very long 'not appropriate' list?"

"We do."

I gazed across the table at the two of them, grinning at each other like two people madly in love. They *were* madly in love, and the upcoming wedding was putting them in full romantic mode. They were both tall and slender with dark curly hair and flashing brown eyes and would make a handsome couple when they exchanged their vows in front of friends and family in a few months.

I sipped my beer then declared, "You guys will have beautiful children."

"Carrie!" Angela admonished me. "Now you're getting ahead of yourself."

I grinned and bit into my avocado cheeseburger. "But to answer your question, Steve, Dylan and I have no plans to get married any time soon. We just started going out in late November, and we've been apart most of the time since then."

"But he'll be starting up his own agency soon—right here in town," Angela said. "Then you can see each other as often as you like."

"That's what I'm hoping."

"Do you want to get married?" Steve asked, suddenly serious. "I mean, not everyone wants to these days."

An image of Julia and Randy popped into my head. "Of course I do. And I'd love to have kids. But not right now." I grimaced. "My parents' marriage wasn't a happy one. I'm only now finally getting away from its impact on my life."

"Think of your aunt and uncle, how happy they've been together," Angela said.

I smiled. "Coming to Clover Ridge last May and living with them *was* a rebirth of sorts. As for Dylan and me—we've lots going for us, but we'll have to see what unfolds."

Our conversation turned to other topics.

"Fran told me about your meeting this morning about the homeless," Angela said.

"It's a tough situation for the library, but even tougher for the people who end up sleeping in a shelter. I did some research this afternoon. Many of them have mental issues or addiction problems."

Angela shivered. "Then there are folks like Doris and Henry Maris. How can people like them manage to shut their eyes at night in a place like that?"

"Shelters can be dangerous places," I agreed. "And Henry is becoming senile if he isn't already. He needs care and attention." I made a mental note to discuss the Marises with Uncle Bosco as soon as he and Aunt Harriet returned home. Hopefully, he'd have an idea, some way to help them.

The waitress came to clear the table and asked if we'd like to see the dessert menu.

"Of course!" Angela said before I could object.

We ordered two desserts to share—a slice of chocolate pecan pie and a serving of chocolate bread pudding. I hadn't planned to, but I ended up eating at least my third of each.

When the bill came, Steve insisted on treating me. He winked at me. "You're my Angie's bestie, which means now you're my bestie too."

I thanked him and hugged them both. We drove home, chattering about nothing important. I arrived back at my cottage feeling cared for and befriended—a relatively new feeling for me and one I cherished. I called Dylan and went to sleep early, dreaming of a dessert party in the library. Not a bad idea for a special occasion!

I spent Sunday morning going through email and straightening up the cottage. There wasn't much for me to do since Mrs. C, who cleaned Dylan's manor house, also cleaned the cottage and changed the linens. She also ran my clothes through the washer and dryer, which she then folded and put away in ready-to-wear condition. All of these indulgences left me few chores to see to besides shopping for food, making meals, and looking after Smoky Joe.

Marion texted me her neighbor's email address, and I shot off a message to the woman, saying I'd heard about the plans for the day program and would love to attend the group's next meeting. I included my cell phone number. Five minutes later, my phone's distinctive jingle sounded.

"Hi, Carrie. This is Reese Lavell, Marion's neighbor. I'm so glad you're interested in the day program project we're calling Haven House. We sure can use more volunteers."

"Hi, Reese. I am interested in attending your next meeting. When will that be?"

"We'd planned to meet next Thursday evening in the house itself, but it turns out the town says we can't because of health and safely rules."

I grinned. For once things were working out well. "We could meet in the library. The conference room holds about twenty people."

"That would be great! We've numbered between fourteen and seventeen at the two meetings we've held so far."

"The library closes at nine thirty."

"In which case, we should start at seven thirty. I'll notify the others. Thanks so much, Carrie! You've been a big help already."

"See you next Thursday evening," I said, pleased that the library was able to offer its services to a worthy enterprise like Haven House.

*   *   *

I was feeling cheerful Monday morning as I lifted Smoky Joe's carrier from the car and brought him into the library. The sun was shining, there was no snow in the week's forecast, and Dylan had called the night before to tell me he'd be flying home late Friday afternoon.

As soon as I released Smoky Joe, he dashed off to visit with patrons. Or to beg for a treat in the coffee shop. He was definitely gaining weight, and I suspected that Katie and some of her customers were feeding him. Maybe I'd ask Evelyn to observe him and tell me who the guilty parties were so I could ask them politely *not* to feed the cat. I smiled. How Evelyn hated to spy—as she put it—but I'd stress the fact that I was concerned about the little fellow's health.

I wasn't ready to settle down to work, so I decided to stop by Sally's office to tell her that the group initiating the day program for the homeless would be meeting in our conference room Thursday evening and that I planned to attend. As I walked across the reading room, it occurred to me that once the program went into effect, the group could set up a liaison with the library. We could send them some of the books, magazines, and tapes that we were discarding instead of selling at our annual book fair.

I raised my hand, about to knock on the door, when I became aware of shouting coming from inside the office. First one woman's voice, then another. Sally and Dorothy were arguing, but I couldn't quite make out the words. I stepped back as the door flew open and Dorothy stormed out—as quickly as one could exit on crutches.

"What was that all about?" I asked Sally.

She shook her head. "That woman! She's a menace to everyone she knows."

"Oh." Clearly, she wasn't going to tell me why they had been arguing.

"Did you want something?"

I gave a start. It wasn't like Sally to be so brusque. "I wanted to tell you I contacted Marion's neighbor about the day program being set up for the homeless. They'll be meeting here next Thursday night, unless there's a problem."

Sally turned to her detailed schedule stretched across her bulletin board. "No problem," she declared.

"Thanks. I'm planning to attend. I have some ideas how the library could help out with this project."

"Good thinking. I look forward to hearing your ideas on the matter."

I was clearly dismissed. "Okay, then. See you later."

I headed back to my office, puzzled by what had just happened. Angela had told me that Dorothy made it her business to gather dirt about everyone she worked with. Probably everyone she knew. Before she returned to work, she'd had plenty of time to do research via her computer at home. Had she unearthed something that had happened in Sally's past before coming to Clover Ridge, something Dorothy had tried to use as leverage to get what she wanted?

I shuddered. My job was the one thing she wanted more than anything else.

Evelyn appeared as I was finally settling down to work. Today she wore navy trousers and a pale blue sweater set. "Morning, Carrie. Enjoy your weekend?"

"It was okay. Did you happen to hear what Sally and Dorothy were arguing about just now?" I asked.

Evelyn looked affronted. "I most certainly did not. I don't go around listening in on private conversations."

I scowled at her. "Well, maybe it's time that you did. Sally was upset when I spoke to her afterward. I think your niece is up to her old tricks."

Evelyn drew back her shoulders. "I don't feel comfortable spying on people."

I met her gaze. "Do you remember, when I first took this position, you told me you thought you were meant to help me, but you weren't sure how?"

"Ye-es," she reluctantly agreed.

"I believe you're meant to help me solve mysteries and problems that arise in the library. In the past, you've held back on sharing information because you were afraid that Dorothy was involved."

Evelyn nodded slowly. I was well aware of her divided loyalties—to the library and to her niece, both of whom she loved. I needed to convince her that the library required and deserved her support.

"The library has been through a lot of turmoil these past few months and doesn't need any more problems. I'm asking you to be observant. Be on the lookout for anyone that causes trouble." I fixed my gaze on Evelyn. "And that includes Dorothy. Right now I sense she needs watching."

"I will," Evelyn said as she vanished. It made me sad that she couldn't wait to get away from me, but I knew I'd done the right thing by convincing her to overcome her scruples about spying, especially on her favorite niece. A few times in the past, she'd neglected to tell me what she knew about certain issues that had almost prevented me from finding a killer.

I was going over the list of possible programs to add to our May calendar, when Evelyn reappeared. I was a little nervous because Trish was scheduled to arrive within the next few minutes.

"I apologize," she said, looking shame-faced. "I must be more vigilant and find out what people are hiding so I can share it with you." She sighed. "Perhaps if I'd have done so, we could have prevented a murder last month."

I felt a chill as I put an arm around her transparent shoulders. "Let's look forward, shall we?"

Evelyn cleared her throat. "As for my niece, she's been wearing a Cheshire Cat smile all morning. You're right! She's up to something. I'll do my best to learn what it is and let you know."

"Thank you, Evelyn."

She looked at me gravely. "You certainly have grown into your job here. Of greater importance, I consider you the guardian of the library. Goodbye, Carrie. I will get back to you soon."

I smiled as Evelyn faded from view, pleased that from now on she'd be watching out for trouble and keeping me informed. I was especially touched by her compliment. I loved the Clover Ridge Library and was determined not to let anyone make mischief if I could help it.

* * *

Evelyn was true to her word and reported back to me a few times that afternoon. "Dorothy's been in a good mood. She's even smiling at patrons."

"Interesting."

Later she joined me on the stairs as I was on my way up from presenting the afternoon movie, to tell me that Sally had been rather short with Marion Marshall and with someone on the telephone.

And that the few homeless people in the reading room were quietly leafing through magazines.

"Thank you, Sherlock," I teased her. "I don't need an hourly update. But I would appreciate a report on Smoky Joe. I think someone's been giving him treats despite the signs I've posted saying that no one is to feed the library cat. The coffee shop's the most logical place to start."

She returned as soon as Trish left and before Susan arrived, as animated as I'd ever seen her. "I found the culprit!"

"It's Katie, just as I suspected," I said. "She has three cats at home, and two of them are overweight."

"Nope! Harvey's been slipping him treats—whenever he takes a break in the coffee shop."

"Really?" I was shocked.

"He and Katie talk cat talk whenever he goes there. He loves cats but never got another after his died two years ago. Katie's been trying to convince him to adopt a cat. She even offered to go with him to pick one out."

"Is that so?" I mused. "Katie and Harvey are both single. Do you think . . . ?"

"I'll see what I can find out," Evelyn said as she left, a bare three minutes before Susan came sailing into work.

* * *

Tuesday morning the library opened a few hours later than usual, because snow had fallen during the night. I made it in easily because Jack Norris, the handyman who looked after the Avery property, had plowed me out as soon as the snow had stopped at daybreak. First Dylan and then Aunt Harriet called while I was getting ready for work, to make sure I was okay.

I was surprised to see Dorothy hobbling in right behind me as I entered the library from the parking lot.

"Morning, Dorothy. Did Fred drive you to work today?"

She sniffed. "He wanted to, but I told him I was perfectly fine getting from the house to the library on my own. As soon as he cleared our driveway, off he went to work, same as me." She lifted one of her crutches. "I can manage fine with these."

"When will you stop using them, do you think?"

"The doctor said maybe next week." She zoomed off, as if to show me her superior crutch-walking skills.

I had a lot of paperwork to catch up on, so I worked until six o'clock instead of leaving at five as usual. At home, I fed Smoky Joe and made myself an omelet for dinner, then settled down in front of my computer to check my email, Facebook, and Instagram. Afterward, I crept into bed and was deep in a mystery by one of my favorite authors, when my cell phone jingled. I smiled. Since it was close to eleven, I expected to see Dylan's name appear. Instead, Lieutenant John Mathers was on the line.

"Hello, Carrie. It's John. I'm afraid I'm the bearer of bad news."

My heart lurched. "Oh no! Not Dylan! Or Uncle Bosco . . . or my dad."

"No, my dear. It's no one close to you. I know, you're thinking then why am I calling you?"

"Uh-huh." *Someone died. Who died?*

"I know it's late, but can I come over? Won't be five minutes."

"Of course."

"I'll explain everything then."

I stood on trembling legs and slipped on my robe, then walked slowly to the kitchen. Automatically, I turned on the faucet and filled the teapot to boil water for tea or coffee—whichever John preferred. I usually preferred coffee, but when it came to emergencies like this, I yearned for a hot cup of tea.

True to his word, John rang my doorbell just minutes later. He was stamping his feet, to free them of snow, when I opened the door to let him in. He looked haggard—bloodshot eyes and a five o'clock shadow—as if he'd been working since early that morning.

I took his jacket. "Would you like coffee?"

He surprised me by asking for hot chocolate, if I had any.

"I do. Come into the kitchen."

I reboiled the water, then prepared John's hot chocolate and my tea. I waited while he stirred his drink and sipped the hot liquid.

"Who died?" I asked.

John exhaled deeply. "Dorothy Hawkins. She was driving home, I imagine, after the library closed at nine thirty. A car rammed into her, and she crashed into a tree. She struck her head and was pronounced dead at the scene."

"Oh!" I covered my mouth with my hand. "That's terrible. Was it an accident?"

"Too early to say. Danny's canvassing the area. We're hoping someone caught the license plate number of the driver who hit her."

"You mean the person who drove into Dorothy ran off?"

John nodded. "A lot of that's been happening lately. People seem to take less responsibility for their actions these days."

"Unless . . ." I stared at John, who was rubbing his chin. "Unless someone ran into Dorothy on purpose."

"That's what I'm wondering." He gulped down some hot chocolate and grimaced as the hot liquid scorched his mouth.

"Like me to cool it off a bit?"

He nodded. I took the container of milk from the fridge and added some to his drink.

"But why are you here?" I asked when I was seated once more. "I haven't seen Dorothy since I left work."

For a minute he didn't answer, so I said what I was thinking. "Because I helped solve other murders?"

"No, Carrie. The police department isn't asking for your assistance."

"Oh!" Blushing, I waited for him to explain.

"Dorothy Hawkins had just dialed your number when the car struck her vehicle. Do you have any idea why she'd be calling you?"

I swallowed as thoughts whirled around in my head. *Dorothy was dead! She'd told me she'd felt threatened. I should have notified John immediately!*

"Carrie?"

"Maybe I do."

He frowned. "Care to explain?"

"I visited Dorothy in the hospital after her recent accident."

He downed the rest of his drink and smacked his lips. "You're referring to her fall outside the supermarket."

"Uh-huh. I was there when her husband paid her a visit at the hospital. Dorothy cringed when he moved to kiss her. As soon as he left the room to get a vase for the flowers he'd brought, she told me he'd knocked her down."

"She told you her fall was no accident?"

"Right. She said Fred had shoved her down. He wanted her dead, though I can't see how a fall like that would result in someone dying. Anyway, about a week later, I visited Dorothy at home. She seemed perfectly comfortable in Fred's presence. She showed no fear of him whatsoever. When I asked her about her reaction to him in the hospital, she made light of it. Said it must have been the pain meds they'd given her."

John stretched his long legs in front of him. "Interesting."

"But why are you asking me about Fred? Do you think someone set out to murder Dorothy?"

John sighed. "Judging by the extent of the damage, the vehicle rammed into hers with great force. The driver had to be going much faster than anyone ought to on a residential street with patches of black ice from the latest snowfall."

"Any witnesses?

John pursed his lips. I knew he was debating whether he ought to share this information with me, so I waited him out. "There were two. A driver called in having seen a car coming around the bend, then swerving into Dorothy's car with great force. And a man walking his dog saw the car as it sped away from the scene. Neither witness caught the make of the car, much less the license number."

"What time was this?"

"Nine forty, give or take a few minutes."

"So Dorothy stayed at the library till closing and then left for home," I mused.

"Which means there's a good chance her husband knew exactly when she'd be on her way home."

"I know you haven't asked for my opinion, but Fred strikes me as a nice guy who really cares about his wife. And—" I stopped abruptly.

"And?" John encouraged.

"And Dorothy was not well liked. She wasn't a nice person."

John groaned as he got to his feet. "Thanks for your help, Carrie, and for the hot chocolate. We'll be questioning everyone who knew Dorothy and worked with her."

Chapter Nine

The following morning, Wednesday, I left for work early. I wanted to be the one to break the news to Evelyn. But when I arrived at the library at a quarter to nine, Angela and Sally had beaten me to it. They were discussing Dorothy's death in the staff room. I didn't see Evelyn, but that didn't mean she wasn't there, listening in on their conversation.

"I wonder if one of her crutches got caught in the gas pedal," Angela was saying. "I read about that happening. Only in the news article, it wasn't a crutch, but a pole of some kind."

"She never should have come back to work so soon," Sally said. "And there certainly was no reason for her to stay till closing last night."

Angela turned to me. "Did you hear, Carrie? Dorothy died in a car accident last night."

I nodded. "The police think her death may have been intentional," I said.

"Oh no!" Angela said. "Not another murder."

"How do you know?" Sally asked. Her eyes widened with fear.

"John Mathers stopped by last night."

Sally shot me a look that bordered on hostility. "Why? Did he want to make use of your detective skills?"

I quelled my instinct to respond in kind because I knew she was worried that I'd told John about her quarrel with Dorothy.

"He came to talk to me because Dorothy was apparently dialing my number when the car crashed into hers and drove it into a tree."

"I didn't know you two were suddenly bosom buddies," Sally said.

"We weren't." I told them about Dorothy's reaction to Fred when he'd come to visit her in the hospital and her response a few days later.

Sally scoffed. "Fred Hawkins wouldn't hurt a fly. How he put up with Dorothy all these years is something I'll never understand."

"John knows that Dorothy wasn't very popular," I said.

"That's putting it mildly," Angela said.

"He called me at home to say he'll be stopping at the library to talk to everyone who worked with Dorothy," Sally said.

I suddenly realized something. "Whoever ran into Sally will have a good deal of damage to his or her car."

"Unless he or she used an old heap that's not registered," Angela said.

I left them discussing where and how such an old heap might be acquired.

Evelyn was waiting for me in my office. She'd been weeping. Though I'd known her for months and had witnessed her many moods, this was the first time I'd seen her cry.

"So it's true," she said, when she managed to get out her words. "Poor Dorothy is dead. Killed in a car wreck."

"I'm afraid so. John thinks it might have been deliberate, judging by the force of the collision. I'll let you know more when I find out. John will be questioning everyone here."

"And I'll be sure to listen in on those interviews," she said bitterly. "I know Dorothy could be infuriating, but I can't imagine someone wanting to kill her."

I thought of how upset and angry Sally had been after her argument with Dorothy, but decided to keep mum. "Dorothy was calling me when the car smashed into hers. I told Lieutenant Mathers that when I'd visited Dorothy in the hospital, she'd confided that Fred had pushed her. A week later she denied that ever happened."

Evelyn scowled. "Who knows? Maybe Fred finally reached his breaking point."

"Evelyn! You told me he adored her."

"Even a whipped dog may finally turn on his tormentor."

"I'm sure the police will do everything they can to find out who rammed into Dorothy."

"That's not good enough!" An icy chill ran along my arm as Evelyn gripped my wrist and then immediately released it. "You have to find Dorothy's murderer! Please, Carrie. For my sake. I want her killer punished to the full extent of the law."

"I'll do my best," I said, meeting her gaze, "and you have to do yours. I expect you to share with me whatever you find out when you listen in on conversations."

She nodded.

"That includes unflattering comments, Evelyn. You never know when a snippet of gossip will include an important clue. Dorothy liked secrets. We have to unravel them one by one."

"Okay."

"Between the two of us, we'll get to the bottom of this and find out the truth."

* * *

John and Danny arrived at the library in the early afternoon and questioned every member of the staff. The interviews were brief: wanting to know where we all were the previous night, asking to see our car registrations, then going outside to the parking lot to view the condition of each car. Not one vehicle had been damaged.

I breathed a sigh of relief to learn that none of my colleagues was under suspicion, at least for now. Of course the investigation would delve much deeper over the next few days to include a visit to all auto body shops and junk yards within a fifty-mile radius to examine every damaged car that had been brought in since the night Dorothy was murdered. I wasn't sure why I was holding off telling John about Sally's argument with Dorothy. Perhaps it was because I liked Sally or I was hoping Sally would tell him herself.

Trish left for the day, and I forced myself to settle down and start working on my questionnaire to be sent to every home in the district. Sally had finally agreed to let me draw one up that would ask patrons which programs and events at the library they attended, which they liked and didn't like, and what new programs and events they would like to see offered. I created a new document and typed in fifteen questions; then I stopped to call Dylan to bring him up to date after our chat late last night. Of course I left out the part about Evelyn's offer to help by listening in on conversations. One day soon I'd tell him about Evelyn and could only hope he wouldn't think I was losing my mind.

"I don't envy them their job," Dylan said. "They have to interview everyone who Dorothy spoke to in the past few weeks. And as we know, she managed to rile up everyone who knew her."

Sally stopped by my office to tell me that Fred had called, asking her to inform Dorothy's colleagues that the viewing would be held on Monday; the cremation on Tuesday morning, with only the immediate family attending; and there would be a memorial service Wednesday afternoon.

Dorothy's being cremated? "How did Fred sound?" I asked.

"Sad. Subdued. They'd been married almost thirty years," Sally said.

I decided to call Fred myself and offer my condolences.

"Fred, this is Carrie Singleton. I want to tell you how sorry I am that you've lost Dorothy." The sound of loud male voices came over the line. "I'm sorry if I caught you at a bad time."

"Hello, Carrie. The police are here and—" He stopped talking, and I thought we'd been disconnected. I heard muffled conversation, then Fred was back, sounding agitated.

"Sorry. They say they found something incriminating. It's ridiculous! I have to go down to the station and answer more questions. I have to go and sort all of this out."

I stared at my disconnected phone, wondering what on earth John and Danny could have discovered that had upset Fred. I wanted to add a closing paragraph to my questionnaire, but gave up when I realized I was too distraught to concentrate.

Susan arrived for her late afternoon–evening shift. We talked about Dorothy, and I mentioned that she, like the rest of us, would be questioned by the police.

"I left the same time she did last night. I even held the door for her when we left the building. Not that she bothered to thank me."

"When I called Fred to give him my condolences, he said the police were there, searching the house from top to bottom. It sounded as if they'd found something. Fred said they were taking him down to the station. I wish I could find out what happened after that."

"Why don't you call the precinct?" Susan asked. "Aren't you and Lieutenant Mathers great friends?"

"We are, but he'll probably tell me not to get involved in police business—even though Dorothy was calling *me* when that car rammed into her."

Susan's eyes lit up. "There's your entry. At least it's worth a try."

I stared at this girl, whom only months ago I had thought was the dullest knife in the drawer. "You're right! I'll call right now."

I dialed the police station and breathed a sigh of relief when the dispatcher, Gracie Venditto, answered the phone.

"Hi, Gracie, it's Carrie from the library."

"Hello there, Carrie. Sorry about what happened to poor Dorothy Hawkins. She wasn't the friendliest person, but she didn't deserve to die that way."

I exhaled slowly. "So they've decided it was definitely a homicide."

"Sure looks that way."

Susan was watching me. I grinned at her as I changed my plan of attack. "You know, Gracie, Dorothy was calling me when it happened."

"So I heard." Was that suspicion I heard creep into her voice? She must have covered the receiver because there was the muffled sound of people speaking though I couldn't make out any words.

"I have to go, Carrie," Gracie said.

"All right."

I was about to end the call, when Gracie told me that John wanted to talk to me from his office. I waited, a bit nervous, for what probably would be a reprimand. When his strong bass came on, he didn't sound happy.

"Carrie, I'll thank you not to question my officers about ongoing investigations."

"Sorry, John. I didn't mean to be devious, but I was on the phone with Fred Hawkins when you were searching his home. He became very upset to learn that you'd discovered something. I'm worried about him."

"And you want to know what we found."

I cleared my throat. "Yes. That too."

"You could have asked me instead of trying to worm it out of Gracie."

"I apologize. But frankly, I figured you'd tell me it was police business and clam up."

Silence. I bit my lip and forced myself to wait.

"It *is* police business and I shouldn't be sharing this information with you, but once again you've managed to involve yourself in another homicide. I know your curiosity and concern won't let you rest until you find out what happened at the Hawkins's house today."

"I guess that's true," I admitted.

"We found something that supports what Dorothy told you in the hospital."

"So Dorothy really was afraid of her husband."

"Yes."

I began to hyperventilate. "You found evidence that proves Fred killed Dorothy? What is it? Why would he kill her?"

"Not evidence exactly, but we found her journal. In it Mrs. Hawkins had written that she was afraid that Fred had tried to murder her outside the supermarket as he'd murdered her Aunt Evelyn seven years ago."

Chapter Ten

John hung up, leaving me staring at the phone with my mouth agape. How could I, who had been involved in two murder investigations, have been so wrong about everything? True, when Dorothy had returned home from the hospital she'd insisted that she wasn't afraid of Fred. Nor had she acted as though she feared him. But maybe she'd managed to delude herself that once she was back in her own house, she could control the situation. Control Fred as I suspected she'd been doing all these years.

And Fred? I couldn't believe my instincts had betrayed me, because he'd appeared so friendly and benevolent. Perhaps he'd reached the end of his patience and simply couldn't stand to live with someone like Dorothy any longer.

My thoughts returned to Dorothy. If I'd been more proactive maybe I could have prevented her murder. I should have insisted that she tell me . . .

Tell me what? That she really was afraid of Fred?

Tell me the specific reason why he wanted her gone? And if I couldn't convince her to tell me the truth, I should have told John what she'd said in the hospital.

Then it would have been John's fault that she was killed and not mine.

I sighed. As much as I had disliked Dorothy, I knew I'd do my utmost to find out who had killed her.

* * *

Thursday was my late day. I arrived at the library at one o'clock. Smoky Joe scampered off, and Trish filled me in on an incident that had taken place that morning. Doris and Henry Maris and two older women from the homeless shelter had ensconced themselves in the reading room. One of the women was obviously disturbed. She rocked back and forth, an arm across her chest, mumbling nonstop. A few patrons complained to Sally, who spoke gently to the woman and asked her to sit quietly or she would have to leave. The woman became agitated and lashed out, hitting Sally in the face. Angela called the police. Danny came and escorted the woman out of the library.

"Sally called and learned that the woman had been brought to the psych hospital in the next town," Trish said. "Meanwhile, Doris Maris and the other woman berated Sally for sending her to 'that hellhole,' as they called it."

I shook my head. "Poor Doris. Poor Sally. And what was Henry doing while this was going on?"

"Just sitting there, looking dazed."

"Unfortunately, Henry isn't receiving the attention he needs," I said. "Once the day center gets underway, I hope they'll see to it that the people they're serving are evaluated for medical and psych treatment."

Trish frowned. "So many of the homeless have psychiatric problems. Their problems are probably what drove them to living on the streets. Nobody cares and no one looks after them."

I made a mental note to stop by to chat with Doris and invite her, Henry, and the other woman to have a snack in the coffee shop with me. A small gesture, but it was all I could think of to do until Haven House was ready.

My phone rang. Fred Hawkins was on the line.

"Hello, Carrie. I'm sorry we got cut off yesterday."

"Not to worry, Fred. You were occupied with more pressing matters."

"By the time an officer drove me home last night, it was too late to call you."

"I'm so glad they didn't keep you. Are you all right?"

"I'm considerably shaken. I had to cancel all my appointments for today. I hope I don't lose my job over this."

It occurred to me that I had no idea what kind of work Fred did. "Where do you work?" I asked.

"I'm an in-home consultant for Watson's Décor Designs in town. I sell window treatments to customers in their homes."

"Oh. Good to know if I need anything." I returned to the subject uppermost on my mind. "I'm relieved that the police don't consider you a suspect."

Fred's laugh held no humor. "I wouldn't say that. Lieutenant Mathers told me to expect to be called in again for further interviews. Of course they have no evidence, no *proof* that I harmed Dorothy. For God's sake, Carrie, she was my wife! I wouldn't go and ram a car into hers with the intention of killing her!"

"When Dorothy was in the hospital, she told me that you tried to kill her the night she fell outside the supermarket."

Fred expelled a lungful of disappointment. "I know. She wrote that in her journal, the cops said, and I have no idea why."

"Were you with her the night she slipped on the ice?"

"Yes, we went shopping together, but I wasn't with her when she fell."

"Oh?"

"We'd forgotten to buy butter, and Dorothy needed it for a cake she'd planned to bake. She was very annoyed that we'd forgotten it. I ran back into the store, and meanwhile she said she'd put the two bags of groceries in the trunk and wait for me in the car. When I came out, she was lying on the ground."

"Did you tell the police this?"

"Of course I told them. Turns out the store's security camera was out. They advised me to find the sales slip for the butter, but I threw it out since I'd paid for it with cash."

"So you have no way to prove that you went back for butter," I mused.

"I don't, though the cashier might remember me."

"I still can't understand why she'd think *you* pushed her down."

"I can't figure that out, Carrie. It's all I can think of since the police told me she'd written that in her journal, but I can't come up with a reason."

"Do you think someone else might have knocked her down?"

"Sure, that's possible—but not on purpose. I mean, why would anyone want to do that to a fifty-one-year-old woman minding her own business?"

That wasn't Dorothy! She took pleasure in minding other people's business. "Maybe someone ran into her accidentally," I said, to see how he'd respond.

"She took one hell of a tumble. The doctor in the hospital said she probably blacked out for a minute or two. When she came to, I was the first person she saw."

"And for some reason, she made the assumption that you were the person who had knocked her down."

"It's the only scenario I can think of that makes sense," Fred said.

"People often can't think straight after getting a concussion."

"Thanks, Carrie. I feel much better after talking to you."

"Oh." I hadn't meant to reassure him. After learning what Dorothy had written in her journal, it was possible that Fred had killed Dorothy after failing to do so on his first attempt. But it was just as well he had no idea that I suspected him.

"The viewing will be Monday, and she'll be cremated the following day—a private affair for the family. I hope you'll attend the memorial service on Wednesday at one at Whitesides Chapel. I know Dorothy would appreciate it if you would say a few words."

Say a few words! "I—sure, that is—I'll certainly do my best to be there."

"Thanks again, Carrie, for caring."

Fred hung up before I could ask him why Dorothy had thought he'd killed her Aunt Evelyn.

* * *

As soon as Susan left the office at five o'clock to take over the hospitality desk, Evelyn made an appearance.

"Wow! The afternoons sure are difficult to get your attention," she groused.

"I do apologize," I said, rolling my eyes, "but you understand I can't go around having patrons think I'm talking to myself when I'm actually speaking to you."

"I don't know why not. Lots of people keep those gadgets in their ears so they can communicate with people electronically. *They* look like they're talking to themselves."

"True," I agreed, "but I have no intention of giving the impression that I'm talking to myself."

Evelyn calmed down and perched on the edge of Trish and Susan's desk. "What's happening with the investigation? Have the police found the person who killed my poor niece?"

"Not conclusively."

Evelyn stared at me. "What exactly does that mean?"

"They questioned Fred down at the station and managed to rattle him."

"Fred?" Evelyn cocked her head at me. "I told you he wouldn't hurt Dorothy. They're barking up the wrong tree."

I drew a breath, reluctant to bring up my ghostly friend's own demise. "When the police came to search the house, they found Dorothy's journal. In it she says she's afraid that Fred shoved her to the ground that evening at the supermarket."

"Why would he do something like that?"

"Fred and I talked about it. He'd gone back into the store for butter when someone might very well have knocked Dorothy to the ground. She must have blacked out for a moment. And Fred was the first person she saw when she opened her eyes."

"Still," Evelyn insisted, "that's no reason to think her husband would do a thing like that."

"I suppose it got her thinking." I paused.

Evelyn grew impatient. "Well. Go on."

"I suppose it reminded her of the night you—er—died. In her journal she wrote that she was afraid Fred had tried to kill her the same way he'd murdered you."

Evelyn put her hands to her head and circled my small office. Finally, she settled back against the desk. "But why would Fred want to murder *me*?"

"Money? Did Dorothy inherit money when you died?"

"Well, yes, but Fred is the last person on this earth to kill someone for a very mediocre inheritance."

I didn't know what a "mediocre" inheritance involved and was reluctant to ask her to spell it out for me. Instead, I said, "People have murdered for the smallest amount of money, which is neither here nor there. The question is, why did Dorothy think her husband killed you?"

Evelyn stared at me. "I haven't the faintest idea."

"Do you remember slipping on the ice outside in the library parking lot the night you . . . died?"

When she hesitated, I said, "Evelyn, please! You promised to be forthright and not withhold information, no matter how unflattering it might be. We need to unearth every possible clue if we hope to find out who murdered Dorothy—and perhaps you as well."

"Okay. You're right. It *is* embarrassing not to know for sure if you slipped on the ice or someone knocked you down."

"There's nothing to be embarrassed about, Evelyn. You hit your head, and as I told Fred, that affects a person's mind and memory."

"I hardly remember the day it happened. I know it was in February, a bitterly cold month that year. Robert was gone and suddenly my life held no joy. One day ran into the next. I was glad I had my job at the library. It gave me a reason to get out of bed every morning.

"The house was becoming a burden. I was thinking of selling it and renting an apartment instead. I had conversations—can't remember now with whom—about my finances. The only detail I remember is that I decided to redo my will and leave everything to Dorothy."

My pulse raced. *So, money might have been a factor in her death!* "Were you originally planning to leave a third to each of your nieces and nephew?"

"I suppose so. I had no reason to cut any of them out of my will—that I can remember. Although . . ."

I waited. After a minute, Evelyn shook her head in frustration. "It's not clear, but I do remember having words with one of the children." She grimaced. "Something about a loan. Or did one of the children want me to sell them the house for a ridiculously low price? Whatever it was, I decided to simplify things for myself and leave it all to Dorothy."

"Was Dorothy the one who needed the money?"

"I—I don't know! I can't remember."

"Did you tell anyone that you changed your will?"

"Maybe. I think so, but I don't know who I told." Evelyn's chest began to heave with anxiety. I wished I could put my arms around her.

"Evelyn, please don't excite yourself."

"But it matters! Dorothy was murdered. The same person might have killed us both!"

"Maybe not," I said as calmly as I could. "Dorothy wrote this in her journal after her fall outside the supermarket. Rightly or wrongly, she linked it to *your* fall. She offered no proof that either of your accidents was deliberate."

"Carrie, I find it hard to believe that anyone would murder me for my estate. It was pathetically small after our investment debacle with Ernie Pfeiffer."

Ernie Pfeiffer. When I'd visited Dorothy at home, her brother and Fred had wanted her to invest in another one of his schemes, but now wasn't the time to mention it to Evelyn.

"Evelyn, I intend to find out who murdered Dorothy."

"Bless you, my dear," she said as she faded from my office.

Chapter Eleven

I gazed around the auditorium at the large crowd of people that had shown up at Dorothy's memorial service despite her sour disposition and occasional acts of malice that had won her many enemies. Other than Sally, Evelyn, and Fred, I didn't know a soul who had genuinely cared for her. Though I had been the victim of Dorothy's dirty tricks, I had felt a degree of sympathy for her these past few weeks. And now someone had murdered her, which she certainly didn't deserve.

Of course the fact that she'd been murdered was the reason for the mob today. Curiosity and all that. I'm sure many were thrilled to be there, figuring that the murderer was in the room with us. And John Mathers's presence at the back of the auditorium only added to the sense of excitement.

Sally, two library board members, and I had come to represent the Clover Ridge Library where Dorothy had worked for eighteen years. When I called Fred to tell him that I planned to say a few words, he sounded very appreciative.

"Thanks so much, Carrie. My wife had a cutting tongue, and I know you suffered from it, but she also had a good heart."

Good heart? Instead of being a hypocrite and agreeing, I asked Fred if there was anything I could do for him.

"Nothing, thank you. Your presence and kind words on Wednesday are more than enough."

I stared at the large urn resting on a pedestal beside the lectern where people would be speaking. Inside it were the remains of Dorothy Hawkins, placed there, it seemed to me, so she could hear what everyone had come to say about her. The minister from her church came forward to say a few words. Dorothy had been an active member of the women's auxiliary until her work had demanded her full attention. He led us in a short prayer, and then the speakers began.

First up was Fred, looking shaken. He was short, with an unassuming stature, and wore a navy suit that could have used a good pressing. He seemed lost at first, but his confidence grew as he gave a heartfelt speech mourning his dead wife and lifelong partner. I was swayed once again into believing him incapable of having killed the woman for whom he was grieving. Unless Fred Hawkins was a star-quality actor, his words rang true in my ears.

Next, Frances walked up hand in hand with a handsome man who I assumed was her husband. Sally must have noticed me studying him because she edged closer to whisper, "That's Dorothy's sister, Francesca Benning, and her husband, Gerald. Successful lawyer."

I nodded, curious to hear Francesca talk, in between sobs, about the childhood she'd shared with Dorothy and what a loving big sister Dorothy had been. Certainly not the way Evelyn had described her niece to me. Even as a child, Dorothy had been selfish and mean, throwing her sister's new doll in the brook behind their house. Maybe Francesca had a bad memory, was overly emotional, or simply loved Dorothy despite everything she'd done.

Or Francesca was putting on an act so no one could possibly imagine that she'd killed her own sister.

Roger spoke eloquently about his memories of their childhood. Then one of the library board members got up. Leanne Walters was a large woman in her fifties, known for speaking her mind.

"Dorothy was a hard worker. She was an excellent reference librarian who knew her stuff. She helped many students find the information they needed for a report, which helped them achieve good grades. We shall sorely miss her. She will be very hard to replace."

Sally got up and talked of their friendship as if it hadn't been broken when Dorothy had tried to blackmail Sally into giving her the job I now held. She spoke haltingly, and I suspected it had something to do with the argument she and Dorothy had had the day before Dorothy died. More nice words about a person disliked by almost everyone present.

Now it was my turn. As I walked toward the front of the auditorium, a bout of public-speaking nervousness overtook me, the likes of which I hadn't experienced in months. *Why now?* I wondered as I faced a sea of faces, many of them belonging to neighbors and library patrons.

I cleared my throat, discarding the polite speech I'd prepared, and began.

"Dorothy and I started out as adversaries. That is, she was my adversary because she felt she should have been given what became my position in the library."

I acknowledged the expressions of shock and amazement before me and went on, feeling more comfortable as I treaded deeper waters. "Things settled down between us, and I believe we learned to respect each other."

I paused, realizing that what I'd just said was true. "She was an excellent reference librarian, and I am glad I got to visit her a few times while she was recovering from her fall outside the supermarket."

I swallowed. "Dorothy's death was no accident. When I saw her in the hospital, she told me she feared for her life. What's more, I was told she was in the process of calling me when a vehicle crashed into her car."

I moved my head slowly from left to right, meeting as many glances as possible. "I regret not having done more to safeguard Dorothy's life. I intend to do everything I can to help the police find her murderer."

I ignored the murmurs that chased after me as I strode up the aisle to wait for Sally in the hallway. A moment later, John burst through the doors, his face red with fury.

"What the hell did you just do up there?" he thundered.

"I only said what most everyone knows."

"I don't want you involved in this case! Dorothy's death was a homicide. The investigation is a police matter."

I let out a deep sigh. "I should have told you what she'd told me when I visited her in the hospital, even though she made light of it later on."

John's voice softened. "You're not to blame. The killer is. Even if you'd told me, there wouldn't have been much I could have done."

"Maybe we could have stopped him."

"I doubt it. The murderer was determined to kill her."

"So you think her being knocked down was no accident."

"It could have been a warning," John said. "To stop her from whatever she was doing or planned to do."

"Dorothy and Sally had a fierce argument the day before Dorothy was killed. I have no idea what it was about."

He nodded. "I'll check it out and leave out any mention of your name. I don't want to cause friction between you and Sally."

"Thank you."

John grimaced. "And let's hope you haven't pissed off the killer with your declaration just now."

Chapter Twelve

"I wish John hadn't gotten so angry. I appreciate his concern for my welfare, but I have no intention of stopping my investigation into Dorothy's death," I told Evelyn when I was back at work. Ironically, I was manning the reference desk. Sally had set up a schedule for us to take turns helping patrons with their research until she hired a new reference librarian.

"John is very fond on you," Evelyn said. "Besides, he knows your Uncle Bosco will hold him responsible if anything happens to you."

"That is ridiculous! Uncle Bosco should know by now that John can't control me. As for John, he ought to remember how helpful I've been in solving the last few murder cases in town."

Evelyn chuckled. "I suspect he remembers it all too well and wants to handle this case himself."

"Oh. The fragile male ego," I said. Something occurred to me. "Evelyn, now that Dorothy's dead, can't *you* communicate with her? Find out who rammed into her car?"

"Alas, it doesn't work that way." She waved her hand. "So many of us have shed our earthly bonds. We exist on different planes . . . much too complicated to explain."

What she meant was *she* had no intention of explaining it to me. "It was dark out when it happened," I said. "There's a chance she never saw who rammed into her anyway."

"If only they could find the car that was used," Evelyn mused. "You would think that wouldn't be so difficult."

"Dorothy irritated so many people, they probably haven't gone through half their list of possible suspects."

"Carrie, you know most of the people in Dorothy's life. I bet you can find out lots of things the police can't."

"And you can listen in on conversations here in the library and not hold *anything* back," I reminded her.

Evelyn suddenly looked guilt-stricken.

Is she holding something back? I wondered as she faded from sight.

* * *

The following day I told Angela I couldn't have lunch with her because I planned to drop off a casserole for Fred.

Angela gripped my arm. "You can't, Carrie! What if he killed Dorothy? You know what she wrote in her journal."

"I promise to be careful, but I think she only wrote that because she suddenly linked her fall with her Aunt Evelyn's fall in the library parking lot all those years ago. We don't have any proof that Evelyn was murdered."

"Still, they always say that the most obvious and logical suspect is the spouse."

"I'll remember to suspect Steve if anything happens to you," I joked.

"Promise me you won't ask any questions or say anything to Fred that might antagonize him."

"Of course I won't. And I'll mention that you know exactly where I am—as a safeguard."

Buried in the Stacks

At noon, I stopped by the gourmet market and bought their signature casserole of chicken, cauliflower, and two kinds of cheeses. It cost more than I'd planned to spend, but I figured it was a good entrée to my upcoming discussion with Fred. When I pulled up to his house, I discovered I couldn't park in the driveway because a sleek Mercedes was straddling both spaces. There went my chance of learning anything new! I couldn't speak to him confidentially if there were a bunch of other people around. But I should have realized that others would be dropping by to see how he was doing.

Fred opened the door and greeted me with a big smile. "Carrie, come on in. How sweet of you to stop by."

"Hello, Carrie."

"Hello, Frances," I greeted Dorothy's sister.

"Francesca," she corrected me as she slipped into her mink jacket. "I see we had the same idea." She sniffed. "Ah, from Gourmet Delight! I thought I recognized that delicious aroma."

She bussed Fred's cheek and patted his shoulder. "Do take care."

"I will," he promised. "And thank you for your care package."

Frances-Francesca waved his thanks away. "Don't be silly. You'll always be my brother-in-law and a dear member of our family. Gerald feels the same way."

Fred closed the door behind her. "People have been so kind. I probably have enough food here to last me a month," he said over his shoulder as he stowed the casserole in the refrigerator.

"Why don't you freeze some of it?" I suggested.

"The freezer's full. Can I get you a cup of coffee?"

I glanced at my watch. "I'm on my lunch break—"

"In which case, let me offer you a sandwich. I must have over-ordered, because I have at least a dozen of each kind left over from last night. Turkey? Ham? Tuna?"

Five minutes later I was sitting at the kitchen table, biting into a tuna sandwich on rye.

"This is delicious," I commented, when I could speak.

"And here's your coffee. Do you take milk? Sugar?"

"Milk will be fine."

When I'd devoured half my sandwich, I decided it was time to ask the question that had been weighing heavily on my mind. Reluctantly, I abandoned the other half of my lunch and faced Fred at the other end of the table.

"Fred, I believe you when you say you didn't kill Dorothy. Difficult as she was, you cared about her."

"Thank you for saying that, Carrie." He sighed. "I can tell from the way some people stare at me that they think I'd reached the end of my patience and ran her off the road, but I didn't. And I didn't push her down at the supermarket either."

"It occurred to me that Dorothy wrote what she did in her journal because someone *did* push her down that evening at the supermarket. You were the first person she saw when she came to. Seeing you there triggered the memory of her Aunt Evelyn's accident all those years ago." I paused. "I suspect the memory involves *you*. Do you have any idea why Dorothy linked you to the two incidents?"

For a minute Fred said nothing. He looked away, but not before I'd caught an expression of remorse on his usually open face.

"I think I know why Dorothy linked the two incidents but . . . it's difficult for me to talk about."

I remained silent and hoped that Fred would welcome unburdening himself to a sympathetic listener. Waiting until he was ready to share what was on his mind was my best option if I hoped to discover a possible link between Dorothy's and Evelyn's deaths.

A minute or two passed. Fred cleared his throat. "I had to tell Lieutenant Mathers where I was when Aunt Ev had her accident. He promised to keep it under wraps unless it proved relevant to the case."

I nodded.

"And I'm asking you, Carrie, not to tell anyone what I'm about to tell you. For Dorothy's sake—and the sake of someone else."

"Of course."

Fred stood and poured himself a mugful of coffee. I perched on the edge of my seat and tried to contain my impatience as he added milk and a packet of artificial sweetener. He drank deeply, then set his mug on the table.

"The night Dorothy's Aunt Evelyn died that horrible, lingering death I was with someone—a woman I had come to love."

I stared at him, totally stunned that this ordinary middle-aged man was confessing to a grand passion, then quickly chastised myself for being so ungenerous. People of all ages fell in love. It wasn't something reserved for the young and the beautiful.

Now that his secret was out, Fred turned downright chatty. "I'm not proud of myself, Carrie, but neither do I regret it. I knew what Dorothy was like when we got married, but I thought she'd grow softer with time. The truth is, her spitefulness wore me down. I never stopped loving her—don't think that I did—but her constant harping at me and everyone who crossed her path took its toll. Don't get me wrong. I wasn't looking for someone else. It just happened."

He gave a joyful little laugh. "I met my friend the way I've met dozens of women—in her home discussing window treatments. Her husband had just died, and she'd decided she didn't want to move, but that she wanted to change the look of her home to reflect her new life." Fred pursed his lips. "It hadn't been a happy marriage; still, she'd nursed him through his sickness, and now she was glad to be on her own."

He smiled at me. "The rest is very ordinary, I'm afraid. We started meeting regularly. We fell in love. We talked about spending our future together. I knew that Dorothy's meanness was wearing me down. She was toxic, and my friend made me see that I was entitled to lead the rest of my life with someone who made me happy.

"I came home close to eleven the night that Evelyn fell. I don't remember what excuse I'd made up earlier that evening, but I'd told Dorothy I'd be out late. I arrived home even later than I'd intended because my lady friend and I had spent the evening making plans for our future together. I'd finally decided to tell Dorothy I wanted a divorce.

"I found Dorothy more out of sorts than usual. She'd tried reaching Aunt Ev several times while I was out, and was growing more and more upset each time Evelyn didn't answer the phone. But we both knew that sometimes Evelyn didn't hear it when it rang—especially when she was watching TV or had fallen asleep. I advised Dorothy not to imagine the worst and to call her first thing in the morning."

"And by then it was too late," I murmured.

"Yes, Evelyn had fallen on the ice. She hit her head and was knocked unconscious. No one saw her, and so she died from exposure." He let out a deep sigh. "I felt as guilty as if I'd been the one who left her there. For once, Dorothy had taken my advice. As a result she lost her aunt, probably the person she loved the most in the world."

"And you never told Dorothy of your plans to leave?"

"No." Fred sipped his coffee. "I didn't mention it that night because I saw how upset she was. Then after we learned of Evelyn's death, I couldn't. Dorothy sank into a depression the likes of which I'd never seen. I had to practically drag her out of bed in the morning, help her dress, and see to it that she ate something before she left for the library. I told my friend I couldn't leave Evelyn in the state she was in, and we agreed it was best if we stopped meeting."

He cocked his head. "Interesting—Dorothy once asked me where I'd been that night, and I told her the same story I'd made up—that I had dinner with a friend. Afterward we went for a drink and ended up talking late into the night. She gave me this funny look but said nothing."

"Was that after Dorothy inherited Evelyn's money?" I asked.

"Actually, it was." His eyes opened wide in alarm. "You don't think Dorothy believed I'd killed her aunt for her money, do you? I mean, we always pooled our money together. Dorothy believed that was how a married couple should manage their finances."

"Were you expecting to get it all?"

"I never gave it a thought, though I was aware that Dorothy was her aunt's favorite. Actually, the subject of Evelyn's will never came up. And why should it? Evelyn was only in her sixties and in good health. Besides, we're not talking about a fortune. She and Robert had lost a lot of money in one of Ernie Pfeiffer's schemes."

"Still," I prompted, "Dorothy was one of three siblings."

"That's right. She didn't expect to be the only heir. In fact, when Evelyn died, it was Frannie—er, Francesca—who told us we'd be inheriting. She admitted that both she and Roger had hit up Aunt Ev for money more than once. Aunt Ev finally told Francesca she was sick and tired of being their cash cow and that she was leaving her money to Dorothy."

"Francesca needed money?" I asked.

"At the time, Gerald had lost a lot in an investment. He had little money for Frannie's extravagances. And Roger"—Fred burst out laughing—"he has four children and is always running short. Which is why I wanted to help him out this last time and give him enough cash to buy into Ernie's investment."

I glanced at the kitchen clock and realized I was going to be late getting back to work if I didn't leave that very moment.

"Fred, thanks for lunch and for sharing your story with me. I promise not to tell anyone."

His smile was sad when he said, "That part of my life ended years ago. Now all I want is for the cops to find Dorothy's murderer and fast."

"I want that too."

He surprised me by planting a kiss on my cheek before escorting me to the front door. "Thank you for your casserole. I plan to eat it tonight."

As I walked toward my car, I spotted Ernie Pfeiffer next door, opening his mailbox at the edge of his property. While he paused to rummage through his mail, I ambled across Fred's lawn.

"Hi, Ernie. Do you remember me?"

He squinted, then shook his head. "Sorry, I don't. Oh, right! Jim Singleton's daughter."

"Yes, Carrie."

"How's your dad? I enjoyed chatting with him when we were roommates in the hospital."

"He's good. He has a new job in Atlanta."

"Is that so? What sort of work?"

"He's working for an investigative agency."

Ernie broke into a loud guffaw that I found offensive. I was about to stalk off, when he jutted his chin toward Fred's house. "Were you paying your respects?"

"I dropped off a casserole."

"Poor bugger, losing his wife like that. But now he's free to enjoy the rest of his life."

"Ernie!" I said, pretending to be shocked.

"She was a witch." He sent me a shrewd glance. "As I remember it, you worked with Dorothy. I can't believe you didn't get a taste of her malice and mischief."

"Actually, I did," I said. "But we worked things out."

"Did you?" He shot me a look of admiration. "You must have given her a taste of her own medicine and made her back down. Her vile tongue and nasty ways brought her plenty of enemies." He snorted. "It was only a matter of time before someone decided to do us a favor and put an end to her once and for all."

Chapter Thirteen

Who murdered Dorothy? I was so engrossed in my thoughts, I almost drove past the entrance to the library parking lot. Ernie Pfeiffer had made it very clear that he hated her, and both her sister and brother had been cut out of their inheritance, small as it might have been. And although Dorothy had linked Evelyn's death with her incident at the supermarket, there was no proof that the two were related. Evelyn might have actually slipped on the ice as everyone believed. And Dorothy—any one of several people might have hated or feared her enough to have done her in.

I spent an hour making calls and answering email, then toured the building, making sure the various afternoon programs were progressing without any problems. I waved to Marion, who was reading a story to the three-year-olds. I thought about my little cousin Tacey, who was four. Next year she was off to kindergarten. I realized I'd like to have a child of my own one day. But would I be a good mother? Dylan would make a good father, I knew. I chuckled, realizing I was assuming we'd be parents together.

"Care to share the joke?"

I gave a start. Evelyn had suddenly appeared and was keeping pace beside me. "Just daydreaming."

"About Dylan?" Evelyn grinned. "And why wouldn't you? He's coming home this weekend."

"On Friday," I said, avoiding her first question. "I paid Fred a visit earlier today and dropped off a casserole."

"Learn anything helpful?"

I nodded. "I think I know why Dorothy linked her fall outside the supermarket with your fatal accident." We'd reached my office. I knew Trish was working inside, so I beckoned Evelyn to follow me to the conference room, which was usually empty in the afternoon.

I sat down in one of the plush leather chairs and told her about Fred's unhappy love affair. "He feels responsible for your death. If he hadn't told Dorothy to wait till morning to contact you again, you might still be here."

"Nonsense! Dorothy is a—*was* a grown woman! She could have called me again if she was that worried about me. Or asked Fred to go to my house and check on me. Not that I blame her for what happened. It just—happened."

I made a scoffing sound. I doubted I would have been so kindly disposed toward my so-called favorite niece in the same circumstances. I decided to take a different tack.

"Were you annoyed with Frances and Roger around that time? Fred claims they'd been badgering you for money."

"I was." Evelyn nodded. "I remember it now. At first I enjoyed their little visits. But I soon realized each visit was a prelude to being hit up for a loan. Loans that never got repaid. I grew tired of their greed. Frannie's a designer clotheshorse, and Roger is always crying poverty. My nephew's fundamentally lazy and not willing to put in the time and effort a decent job requires. I finally told Frannie that she and Roger had already gotten their shares of my estate, and the rest was going to Dorothy."

Evelyn's mouth fell open as she realized what she'd just said. "You can't possibly believe that my niece or my nephew killed me

99

because *I made Dorothy my sole heir.* But if it's true"—she pressed her hand to her heart—"then in a way it's my fault Dorothy's been murdered."

"Evelyn, please stop jumping to conclusions. This is only one possibility. We don't have any reason to believe that the person who murdered Dorothy knocked you down that night. The murderer might be someone else, someone completely unrelated to you. And your death might really have been an accident."

I tried to meet her gaze, but she was staring off into space. "Evelyn. Evelyn!"

When she turned toward me, I saw steely determination in her eyes. "I need to show you something."

"What?"

She was already striding off. "Follow me."

As we approached the research area, Evelyn pointed at the reference desk, where Angela was doing her stint. "She's your friend. Get her to leave."

"Okay," I said, headed toward Angela. "How's it going?" I asked her.

"All right, I suppose. I just helped a woman plan her next European trip, and put in requests for the library to buy three films and four e-books. I'm wondering where the research part comes in."

I laughed. "I suppose when the kids stop by after school with their projects—though they can do most of their research on their own computers at home. Times have changed, Ange, from when we did our research in a library."

"I can see that." She didn't look too happy.

"Would you like to get back to circulation? I don't have anything urgent that requires my attention. I could take over early since I'm up after you."

Angela's face brightened. "Sure, if you really don't mind."

"I don't."

Angela left. I'd no sooner sat behind the desk, when a patron came over, asking me to help her research how to test for pollutants in the home. I consulted the computer, found a few sites, and off she went to a nearby computer to check them out. Finally, I turned to Evelyn, who was fading fast.

"All right, Evelyn, what did you want to show me?"

"Open the bottom drawer as far as you can without sliding it off the rails."

"Uh-huh."

"Now run your hand under the bottom of the drawer. Feel anything?"

"I do. It feels like an envelope."

"It *is* an envelope, and it's probably taped to the bottom of the drawer."

I didn't have to be told to pull the envelope free. By the time I'd placed it on the desk, Evelyn had disappeared.

My fingers trembled with excitement. Eager as I was to discover what Dorothy had hidden, I knew it was wisest to wait until I was alone in the privacy of my cottage to examine the contents of the envelope. The fact that Evelyn had taken this long to reveal her niece's hiding place meant that whatever Dorothy had hidden could possibly contain valuable information that would help solve her murder.

* * *

The rest of the afternoon flew by. I was too busy helping patrons with their various research questions to speculate about what I might find in the envelope. I chatted with an elderly gentleman who had missed seeing a movie at the local arts movie theater, and I was happy to tell him that we'd ordered the film for our collection and it would be arriving in about a month. As we discussed various films we'd watched and enjoyed, I realized it had been some time since I'd been to the movies. Maybe this weekend Dylan and I would go and see a film.

Finally, it was time to leave work. I drove home faster than I should have, fed Smoky Joe, then sat down on the living room sofa with Dorothy's sealed envelope in my lap. Ever since it had fallen into my hands, I'd held a running dialogue in the back of my mind, debating whether to keep the envelope in my possession or hand it over to John—sealed and unopened—because it might very well contain evidence pertinent to the case.

At which point I told myself there was a good chance he wouldn't tell me what was inside the envelope, at least for a while. Besides, I reminded myself, the police had had every opportunity to search the reference desk where Dorothy had sat day in and day out. The fact that they hadn't done a thorough job was on them.

If I handed the envelope over to John, there was the problem of having to explain how it happened to have fallen into my possession. Admitting that I'd found it taped to the bottom of a drawer meant that I was still investigating, something John had specifically told me *not* to do. I didn't feel like enduring another reprimand for having done a good deed. If the information inside the envelope proved to be important to the case, I'd mail it to the police department ASAP. I didn't have to worry about their finding out that I'd sent it, since my fingerprints weren't in any database.

But what if John asked me if I'd sent the envelope to him? I thought about this for a long minute and decided I'd opt for the truth. Which was when I slit open the envelope.

There was a sheet of typewriter paper inside, folded neatly into thirds. Just one word was centered at the top: "Vases." Below were two columns. The first column consisted of two capital letters. The second column consisted of numbers rounded off to five or zero. I studied both columns until I figured out what I was seeing. The letters stood for initials; the numbers were possible sums of money.

Vases! Those beautiful vases Dorothy had on display in her home were expensive collectors' items. A tremor ran through my body as the full significance of what I was holding sank in. Angela had once told me that Dorothy liked to find out people's secrets and use them as leverage when she wanted them to do something for her. Now it would seem she had been blackmailing people for money. Money to buy her vases. Anyone on this list might have hated her enough to kill her.

All the sympathy I'd developed for Dorothy these past few weeks dissipated as I felt a wave of sympathy instead for her victims. Blackmailers were among the lowest of the low. They preyed on people's weaknesses and cashed in on their secrets. They deserved whatever misfortune befell them.

I made a copy of the page and slipped the original and the envelope inside a large volume of artwork, which I returned to a shelf where Smoky Joe couldn't get at it. That done, I reached for a pen and pad and studied the copy.

I scanned the seven sets of initials. EP was there, no doubt for Ernie Pfeiffer. I wondered what Dorothy had been holding over him that wasn't common knowledge. It must have been something appalling or illegal because, according to the number across from his initials, Ernie had shelled out five thousand dollars.

I remembered the gleam in his eyes earlier today, when he'd told me it was only a matter of time before someone decided to put an end to her for once and for all. *Ernie, did you murder Dorothy because you'd had enough of her scheming, thieving ways?*

The following four sets of initials meant nothing to me, but the next two had my heart thumping. SP and HK: Sally Prescott and Harvey Kirk.

The number next to SP was seven hundred; the one beside HK was fifteen hundred. Sally had confided to me that she'd once told Dorothy about a fiscal error she'd made when she first became director of the library. Though Sally never said so, I knew that Dorothy had tried to coerce Sally into giving her the position I now held. Sally had held her ground and offered it to me.

I liked to think that the seven hundred dollars referred to that old incident Sally had told me about. She'd shelled out money and considered her so-called debt to Dorothy paid. Then what were they arguing about the day before Dorothy was run off the road? It could have been something completely innocent. I wished I could ask Sally what it was. Perhaps I would.

I had no idea what deep dark secret Dorothy had uncovered about Harvey. And who were the other four victims? I was going to have to figure out a way to learn what I could about them all.

Chapter Fourteen

Thursday morning I wrote "FOUND IN DOROTHY HAWKIN'S REFERENCE DESK" in block letters on a sheet of paper. I placed the original list inside its envelope, slid that inside a larger envelope along with my note, and mailed it to John at the precinct on my way to the library. Lunchtime, as Angela and I walked over to the Cozy Corner Café, I told her about my visit to Fred and the list I'd discovered.

"So that's why you wanted to get at the reference desk." Angela laughed. "You're a sly one. But what made you think of it just then?"

Angela had no idea that Evelyn haunted the library. I felt bad about fibbing to my best friend, but now wasn't the time to shock her with that piece of info.

"You once told me that Dorothy loved finding out people's secrets and using what she learned to make them do things for her. I suddenly wondered if she'd ever blackmailed people for money, and I had the sudden impulse to search her desk. Looks like she was doing just that—in order to buy the gorgeous vases she collected."

"Wow!" Angela stopped walking and put her hands to her head. "That woman was worse than we ever imagined!"

"She was. I wonder—did she blackmail people so she could add to her vase collection, or did she do it to wield power over them?"

"Probably a bit of both," Angela said.

"That's what I think," I said.

As we approached the Cozy Corner Café, Angela asked, "Could you figure out any names on the list?"

"Three—Sally and Harvey are on it, and her neighbor, Ernie Pfeiffer. I don't recognize the other four sets of initials."

The café was almost full, but the hostess ushered us to a small table in the rear. As soon as we sat down and slipped off our jackets, I handed the list to Angela.

After a minute, she said, "I think two are women who used to work part time in the library. Greta Harrington died last year and LM could be Lillian Morris. She and Dorothy were friends for a while. Lillian has a wicked sense of humor, but she also has quite a temper. She blew up when Sally told her to do something she felt wasn't in her job description, and stormed out of the library never to return."

"Wow!"

"DZ might be Don Zippora, who lives down the street from Dorothy and Fred, though I believe he and his wife are spending the winter in Florida."

"I wonder who JB is," I said.

"I'll ask my mother," Angela said, jotting it down on a napkin. "She knows more people age fifty and older than I do."

"Trish or her dad might know."

Angela laughed. "Or we can leave this part of the investigation to Lieutenant Mathers."

"I'm wondering what hold Dorothy had over Sally and Harvey," I said.

"Me too," Angela said. "I sure hope neither of them decided to do Dorothy in. We're running out of librarians."

"Have you ladies decided what you'd like for lunch?" Jilly, our waitress, asked.

Angela and I each ordered a turkey-avocado sandwich on a croissant and a hot chocolate. Then our conversation turned to wedding plans.

"Just think—five and a half months from now, Steve and I will be a married couple," Angela said.

"I'm glad you guys finally decided on your wedding date and venue."

Angela grinned. "The Gilbert House is perfect for us. The back lawn will be ablaze with roses and other flowers the third week in June. We're hoping to hold the cocktail hour outdoors."

"You're not disappointed that the country club didn't work out?" I asked.

Angela shook her head. "They're too damn expensive. The Gilbert House has a wonderful new chef. Steve and I loved our dinner there the other night. Not only that, they had a Saturday night availability in June, which is exactly what we wanted."

"Good for you!" I reached across the table to pat her hand.

"And I think I know which gown I'm going with," Angela said.

I'd gone bridal gown shopping with Angela the other evening. She'd tried on several gowns, and I knew which one I thought best showed off her tall, slender figure. "Tell me."

She grinned. "You'll approve. The one with the sweetheart neckline and lacy bodice."

"Great choice! You looked stunning in it."

"Next week we'll shop for bridesmaids' dresses, okay?"

"Most definitely. I want to have a say in what I get to wear."

"As long as you remember my color scheme is yellow, silver, and cornflower blue." Angela tilted her head as she studied me. "I think you'll look terrif in blue."

"As long as it's not a dress with flounces and ruffles."

Angela opened her eyes wide. "Would I do that to you and my two cousins?"

"You wouldn't dare. Besides, Steven's sister would kill you. You know how Donna loves the tailored look. She'd wear a tuxedo if you let her."

We were still discussing bridesmaids' dresses when Jilly brought over our sandwiches and hot chocolates.

After lunch, back in the library, I found Smoky Joe waiting outside my office. He greeted me by rubbing against my legs, then flew to his kitty litter box as soon as I unlocked the door. I was spooning out a healthy amount of food in his plate when I heard a knock.

"Come in," I called.

A white-faced Doris Maris entered my office. "Carrie, please come! Henry's asleep and I can't wake him up!"

"I ran to the reading room, where another homeless woman was shaking Henry's shoulder vigorously.

"Don't do that!" I said.

The woman recoiled and began to mutter.

I apologized. "Sorry. I didn't mean to alarm you, but you shouldn't shake him like that."

She all but snarled at me. "I wanted to make sure Henry wasn't dead."

Henry blinked several times, clearly agitated by the crowd that had gathered around him. "Wha—what's happening?"

Doris slipped past me to put her arm around her husband. "You fell asleep, and I couldn't wake you."

"I was tired, so I dropped off. What's the big deal?"

The big deal is you fall asleep during the day every day and that's not normal. "Doris," I said as calmly as I could manage, "I'd like to talk to you, if I may."

Reluctantly, Doris left her husband's side. "I'm sorry I brought you here for no reason. You have work to do, and it turns out Henry's all right."

"Doris, I think you and I both know that Henry isn't all right. He needs to be seen by a doctor."

She gazed down at the floor. "We can't afford a doctor."

"You can if I call nine-one-one. They'll take Henry to South Conn Hospital, where he'll be evaluated."

She stared at me. "Evaluated for . . . ?"

"I think you know. He needs medical attention."

Doris began to weep. "They'll take him from me. I know they'll take him from me."

I put my arm around her shoulders. I could feel her bones beneath her thin jacket. "Let's not get ahead of ourselves. We need to do what's best for Henry, right?"

She nodded and returned to her husband while I made the call.

The dispatcher asked if they needed to send an ambulance. "I think I can get someone to drive him, or I'll drive him myself."

Sally was establishing order in the reading room. I told her I'd called nine-one-one, and she asked Pete, our younger custodian, if he'd be willing to drive the Marises to the hospital.

"Of course," he readily agreed.

I hugged Doris and told her I'd be calling the hospital to find out what was happening. Sally and I watched Pete shepherd them out the rear exit to his car.

"My heart goes out to them," Sally said. "Two middle-class people made homeless. And now Henry's senility requires serious attention."

"Maybe, by some miracle, there's a place that will take them both in."

"That would be wonderful," Sally agreed, but we both knew it wasn't very likely.

* * *

I hoped that Evelyn would soon make an appearance so I could discuss Dorothy's list with her. From the way she'd taken off after making sure I'd found it, I knew that, much as she loved Dorothy, she was also deeply ashamed of her niece. I was familiar with that situation. For years I'd been mortified to be associated with my father because Jim Singleton was a thief. I only hoped that he'd stick with his new job at the investigative agency and remain a permanent upstanding member of society.

Evelyn finally showed up when I was alone in my office and Susan was filling in at the reference area. She wore a rueful expression.

"I'm so sorry, Carrie. I said I'd be forthright and share whatever I knew, but I couldn't bring myself to tell you about Dorothy's list any sooner."

"I know it was difficult—letting other people know what Dorothy was up to."

Evelyn let out a mournful sigh. "My sister and her husband certainly didn't raise her to prey on people's weaknesses. I'm glad they never knew about her disgraceful behavior."

"When did Dorothy write this list?"

"About two months ago. From the way she was gloating, I figured she was up to something she had no business doing."

"Did you manage to see the list?"

Evelyn shook her head. "I only caught a glimpse of it. When I saw the word 'Vases,' the initials, and numbers, I had an idea of what she was writing. I'd overheard her on the phone with Sotheby's, making inquiries about vases that were being auctioned off."

Buried in the Stacks

So Evelyn isn't above eavesdropping when it suits her. Good to know. "I saw Dorothy's vase collection when I visited her at home," I said. "They're all beautiful and, apparently, expensive."

"Robert and I gave Dorothy an antique vase as an anniversary present the year after she and Fred were married. I suppose that's when she started her collection."

"You mustn't blame yourself," I said.

"If only I could have stopped her! I knew Dorothy loved to delve and uncover people's weaknesses. It made her feel superior. But blackmail! That is truly despicable."

I opened my pocketbook to fish out the list, and laid it flat on my desk. "Do you recognize anyone's initials besides Sally's, Harvey's and Ernie Pfeiffer's? Angela thinks the others refer to a woman named Greta, who's deceased, and that LM is another former librarian named Lillian Morris, and DZ is a neighbor of Dorothy's named Don Zippora."

Evelyn pursed her lips together. "I'd say most likely Angela's right. Dorothy once told me that Lillian occasionally took items from stores. Dorothy probably threatened to go to the police with that information if she didn't pay up. As for Don—he sometimes parked his truck in front of Dorothy and Fred's house, which irritated Dorothy no end. She called the police a few times. He retaliated by dumping a load of soil on their front lawn." She shrugged. "Who knows what Dorothy managed to dig up on him after that incident."

"And JB?" I said. "Any ideas?"

Evelyn closed her eyes. "No, thank goodness."

"I'll see what I can find out about everyone on the list," I said.

"Please be careful, Carrie. I appreciate your concern, but I don't want anything to happen to you."

"I will," I said.

Evelyn looked as though she was about to cry. "I'm so ashamed, Carrie. I should have been firmer with Dorothy when she was young, and taken her to task instead of being the comforting and understanding aunt."

I watched her disappear, thinking how sad it was that we weren't able to choose the people we love. They weren't always the most admirable, and when they hurt or disappointed us, the pain was almost unbearable.

Chapter Fifteen

At seven twenty-five I walked over to the conference room, wishing I hadn't agreed to attend the meeting about Haven House. I doubted that I'd be able to concentrate on a discussion about the day care center for the homeless. I couldn't shake Dorothy's reprehensible behavior from my mind. Much of the sympathy I'd been feeling for her had trickled away—not that I thought she deserved to be murdered. But blackmailers always ran the risk of being done in by one of their victims—at least on TV shows. Still, I continued to feel compelled to find the person who'd murdered her, for Evelyn's sake if nothing else.

In the conference room, five or six people stood chatting in the far corner of the room. As I paused in the doorway, a woman left the group and approached me with a grin and an outstretched hand.

"Hello, Carrie. I'm Reese Lavell. Thank you so much for offering us a place to meet."

"You're most welcome," I said.

"Come and meet the others."

"Carrie, dear! Thanks so much for having us!" Francesca Benning hugged me like a long-lost relative. "I don't know what we would have done otherwise."

"I imagine we'd be holding the meeting in our house," said the tall, handsome man I now knew to be her husband.

Francesca turned to him, an amused expression on her face. "Of course, dear. We're always open to a good cause. Carrie, this is my husband, Gerald Benning. Jerry, meet Carrie."

"Nice to meet you," I said, shaking his hand.

"Likewise."

His smile conveyed warmth, though he quickly turned to the man beside him. Was it "Gerry" or "Jerry" Benning? I suddenly remembered the JB on Dorothy's list who had paid a whopping five thousand dollars. *Could Dorothy have been blackmailing her own brother-in-law?*

I had no time to speculate on this because Reese was asking us to take our seats.

"Carrie!"

I turned to find out who was calling my name. Gillian Richards came dashing toward me and embraced me in an affectionate hug. I hugged her back.

"So glad to see you," I said. "I meant to call to get together, but—"

"No need to explain," Gillian said, sliding into the chair beside me. "I've been busy too."

"Are you still seeing Ryan?" I asked. I'd gotten to know Gillian when I was helping Jared Foster find out who had murdered his mother. Gillian and I had bonded when she'd been dating Jared's brother, Ryan.

"Are you kidding? It took me awhile to see past his smoldering good looks, but once I did, I was out of that relationship ASAP."

"I'm glad," I said. "Ryan's a jerk. You deserve better."

More people joined us, including Roger Camden. I counted heads. There were twenty of us. I thanked Max silently for knowing enough to add more chairs than the outside number of seventeen I'd given him. When everyone was seated, Gerald Benning called the meeting to order. I wasn't at all surprised that he was the group's leader. He was a lawyer, well-spoken, and clearly used to being in charge.

"The good news is I've worked out the kinks with the recalcitrant owner. It's a done deal! The purchase of the property that we've christened Haven House is going through."

Gerald paused for the applause and whistles that commended his achievement.

"Of course," he continued when the cheering died down, "the house was in bad shape and requires extensive carpentry, plumbing, and all new appliances. We need to raise money for those expenses."

A heavy-set man cleared his throat before speaking. "Is there any chance we can set up the upstairs rooms so people can stay there?"

Gerald made little effort to hide his exasperation. "Larry, as I've stated before, we're focusing on daytime activities. As it is, we have enough on our plate linking up with social, medical, and mental services that many of the homeless require. We need to work hand in hand with the homeless residences in the area. With this in mind, I've invited Brenda McGovern, the head administrator of the South Conn Shelter to attend a future meeting."

The comments came fast and furious. When so many homeless had addiction problems, who would monitor their behavior?

Would Haven House get enough attention from services that were in sore need of funding and sufficient personnel?

What if Haven House drew more homeless than could possibly be attended to?

And what about someone like Henry Maris? What will become of him? Of Doris? I supposed I should be concerned about all the homeless people equally, but I couldn't help caring more about what happened to the two of them.

I was impressed by the way Gerald managed to answer most of the group's questions. Some he deferred to a slender man with a beard named Theo or a white-haired woman named Martha. They appeared to be the three people in charge and most knowledgeable about the details of the project.

The questions continued. They were about to get out of hand, when Gerald brought that part of the meeting to an end.

"You've raised many important issues. Martha, Theo, and I will research as many of them as we can before our next meeting. I think we all agree that in order to establish a care center that serves the homeless properly, we must raise sufficient funds. We need to make the Clover Ridge community not only aware of our project, but willing to do their part and contribute to Haven House." He turned to Martha.

"Martha, would you please give your report on the upcoming fundraiser."

She stood. "As Gerald pointed out, we need money—and lots of it—to pay for repairs, furniture, and salaries for Haven House. Our upcoming dinner-dance fundraiser is selling well. But we still have room for more guests, and more guests means more money. With this in mind, I'd like to form a committee to promote attendance. Any volunteers?"

Francesca's hand shot up in the air. "If no one minds, I'd love to head this committee. I belong to several organizations, and I think I can urge many of the women to attend an affair for a good cause." She winked. "Especially since it's being held at the prestigious Clover Ridge Country Club, whose clubhouse is one of our oldest and most elegant manor houses."

"Yes, we're fortunate the owners of the Country Club regard our event as a benefit to all of Clover Ridge and therefore are charging us a very reasonable fee." Martha smiled. "And unless someone disagrees, Francesca, you may head the committee."

No one disagreed. Gillian and I exchanged glances. Silently we concurred there was no way either of us would join a committee headed by Francesca Benning. A few people raised their hands, eager to serve on the committee. Francesca looked triumphant as she called them to a corner to discuss future plans.

We passed on the publicity committee but decide to join the planning committee that would draw up a tentative schedule of daytime activities. With only five of us, I said we'd be able to find a quiet corner to meet the following Thursday evening in the library.

Gerald brought the meeting to an end, and everyone stood to leave.

"See you next Thursday," Gillian said.

I smiled as I nodded in agreement. Though I considered Haven House a worthwhile project, it wasn't my usual type of activity. But I'd stick with it because it offered me a connection to some of Dorothy's relatives. And I was glad I had Gillian for company.

Chapter Sixteen

Evelyn was waiting for me when I unlocked my office door on Friday morning.

"Well, that was an enthusiastic meeting in the conference room last night. I see my niece's husband put himself in charge."

"I had no idea you were there," I said.

"I decided it was time I started doing more to help you find Dorothy's killer." She gave me a searching look. "That is, if you're still determined to find him."

"I am, though I'm disgusted by the way Dorothy treated people who were her colleagues and her friends."

"My sentiments exactly, which is why I found it so difficult to share that information with you. But I was wrong. As appalling as it is, the list might be a key to finding Dorothy's killer."

"Yes, it might be," I said, thinking of the other times Evelyn had held back information for fear of incriminating her niece. "Which is why I've already mailed it to John. The police can go ahead and question anyone that might be on that list.

"Dorothy was far from my favorite person, Evelyn, but she didn't deserve to be murdered. Besides," I reached out, wishing I could squeeze her hand, "I know how much she meant to you. And I need to find out if her murder had anything to do with your death."

"Thank you, Carrie. From here on in, I promise to do everything I can to help."

"I'd like you to keep an eye on Sally and Harvey Kirk since their initials are on the list. And please continue to listen in whenever the Haven House group meets in the library. As you saw for yourself, your niece and her husband and your nephew Roger are involved in the project. Who knows if or when one of them might say something that will expose him or her as Dorothy's murderer."

"You can't be suggesting that my—" Evelyn began.

"Evelyn! Remember what you promised."

"I'll listen in," she said. "It's the least I can do."

"Good."

"Until now Clover Ridge has done little to help the homeless aside from providing a few places where they can sleep. I'm glad Frances, Gerald, and Roger are doing their part in the project, though I imagine Gerald has an ulterior motive."

"What do you mean?" I asked.

"Gerald has political aspirations. He ran for mayor two years ago and lost to Alvin Tripp. I suspect this new enterprise will win him support and votes in the next election."

"Which reminds me," I said, giving her a searching look. "Do you think the "JB" on Dorothy's list might be Jerry Benning with a J? Your niece called him Jerry last night."

"I never thought of that," Evelyn said. "I tend to think of him as Gerald, with a G, though Dorothy and Fred did call him Jerry." She scrunched up her face in a puzzled expression. "Though I can't imagine what Gerald might have done to earn him a place on Dorothy's list."

"And we may never find out," I said. "I'm going to see what I can find out about Lillian Morris and Don Zippora, but first I want to call the hospital to learn how Henry Maris is doing."

Evelyn beamed at me from her usual perch on the corner of Trish and Susan's desk. "You're a good girl, Carrie. I don't know how I managed before you came along."

Managed what? I wanted to ask, but as with so many of her other cryptic remarks, I was left in the dark.

At least now I could count on her to observe Sally and Harvey, not that I expected either of them to suddenly confess to having murdered Dorothy. Still, people revealed more of themselves when they thought they were alone.

I called South Conn Hospital and was able to connect with the charge nurse on the psych ward. She was reluctant to give me any information, but when I said I was calling on behalf of the library where Henry had been spending his days, she told me they would be keeping him for a few days for tests. I thanked her and felt a sense of relief. At least Henry was finally getting a physical and psych workup. But where would he go from there? Certainly not back to the shelter. The next step was to find a safe facility where he would be well treated, a facility that would accommodate Doris as well, hopefully.

Was there any such place? I decided to call Uncle Bosco.

Aunt Harriet answered the phone, sounding very glad to hear from me.

"Carrie, dear, we were just talking about you. How is everything? We heard about Dorothy Hawkins's dreadful car accident."

"John thinks it was no accident. Someone rammed into her car with the intention of killing her."

"Honestly, I can't say that I'm surprised. Such an unpleasant woman. I imagine she had many enemies."

"Several, and she wasn't well liked here in the library."

"I hope you're not getting involved in the investigation, Carrie. Remember what happened last time, when you chased after—"

"Don't worry, Aunt Harriet. Dylan's coming home later today. I'll be too busy to do any sleuthing," I said, to keep her from worrying.

"Well, that's a relief. You must be overjoyed."

"I sure am. Is Uncle Bosco there? I wanted to ask him something."

"He went to a breakfast meeting with the board members of the community here in Del Ray. He should be back any minute."

I laughed. "How did he get involved in the politics of the place? You guys are only renters."

"You know your uncle—always in the middle of things. Once they learned of his vast experience in Clover Ridge civic affairs, the board wanted his advice concerning a problem they're having with the local authorities."

"Which is kind of what I want to talk to him about as well." I told Aunt Harriet about the group setting up Haven House and my concern regarding Henry after he left the hospital.

"I'll have Bosco call you when he gets in. I think it's wonderful that a group is creating a day center."

We were saying our goodbyes when Aunt Harriet interrupted. "Here's Bosco now!" She called him to the phone.

Uncle Bosco listened without interruption as I told him about the homeless situation in the library, Henry's condition, and the plans to set up Haven House. When I was finished, he exhaled loudly.

"A facility like Haven House is much needed, and setting this up is a compassionate gesture, but it's a much more complicated enterprise than those people seem to realize."

"What do you mean?"

"For one thing, they seem oblivious to the fact that many of the homeless are alcoholics, drug addicts, or both. Others have mental illness. It's all well and good to provide a place that offers activities during the day, but what happens when someone turns violent? Or decides to steal the TV for drug money? Drug rehab centers in our area are understaffed. I've told the town council that more money needs to be allotted for the increase in cases."

"Well, maybe now's a good time to urge them to spend more money on the opiate epidemic affecting our community," I said.

There was pride in his voice when he said, "You might very well be onto something, Carrie, dear. Urge the leaders of this day center to contact the local mental health groups and invite them to come down to meetings."

"I will, Uncle Bosco. But what do you think can be done for Henry Maris?"

"Ah, poor Henry. Your aunt and I knew the Marises when they had their store in town. It's terrible, what happened to them. And now the poor guy has dementia. Good thing you called for emergency help. It was the only way to get him in to be evaluated."

"Can you help me find a place for Henry that's well run—one where he'll be looked after—and maybe for Doris too? She needs a permanent home. She can't spend any more time in that shelter."

"I'll make some calls, see what I can do for both of them." Uncle Bosco chuckled. "I had no idea you'd become so civic-minded. Next thing I know, you'll be running for town council."

"Are you kidding? I can hardly keep up with everything as it is. And Dylan's coming home to open his own investigative office in town. I plan to help him as much as I can."

"Your aunt and I miss you, Carrie. We thought perhaps you'd want to fly down and spend a few days with us before we come home next month."

"I'd love to, since I miss you both, but there's too much going on here for me to take off, even for a few days. I'm afraid I won't get to see you until you're back home."

"You turned out to be a true Clover Ridge citizen, through and through."

"Just as you were hoping," I said.

"Exactly. Just as I'd hoped."

I checked the morning's activities schedule for the library, then made the rounds to make sure that all programs were in progress and running without incident. That done, I walked over to the circulation desk to ask Angela if her mother knew anything about Lillian Morris or Don Zippora. I waited until she'd finished checking out movies for a patron before I posed my question.

"Mom knows Verna Zippora. She and Don are in Florida for the winter. They're staying in a community not far from where your aunt and uncle are renting," Angela said.

"So that's that," I said. "And I'm pretty sure JB is Gerald Benning. Last night Francesca called him Jerry, which means Dorothy probably did too."

"That leaves Lillian Morris. Mom hasn't heard anything recently about her, though a few months ago a friend told her that Lillian caused a ruckus at a book club meeting. The hostess had to ask her to leave. One more thing—she got herself a job at the Macy's in the mall. Women's fashions, Mom thought."

"Thanks, Angela. I'll stop by the store and tell her about Dorothy's list. See how she reacts."

"I hope she doesn't bite your head off."

"So do I."

I was about to swing by Sally's office to tell her about last night's meeting when I remembered that she was interviewing two candidates for the position of reference librarian. The sooner she found someone to her liking, the happier all of us would be. Having to take turns covering the reference section was cutting into everyone's valuable working time.

Back in my office, I made a few phone calls regarding future programs and events. Just as Trish arrived, Dylan called to tell me his plane was scheduled to land at a quarter past four. "Which means I should be arriving home anytime after five thirty. Make reservations at whichever restaurant you like for six thirty, seven."

"I thought I'd get takeout instead of going out to eat tonight. I'll place the order before I leave work and pick it up on my way home. Which would you prefer—Indian, Chinese, or Italian?"

Dylan laughed. "Any one of the three is fine. Gotta go. I still have a few ends to tie up before I leave the office."

"I hope that means you're finished with the last case you were working on."

"Well—just about. I'm looking forward to coming home and being with you."

"I changed my schedule so we'll have the entire weekend to ourselves."

"Can't wait, babe."

"Me neither."

I hung up my phone, feeling a flash of concern. After spending New Year's weekend together, Dylan had flown back to Atlanta with the bag of jewels I'd helped him recover. He'd already told his boss that he was leaving the company, when Mac had begged him to undertake one last job—tracking down an oil painting stolen from a Texas oil magnate. It sounded as if that investigation was still in progress.

Three weeks ago, Dylan had sounded excited when he told me he wanted to set up his own investigative company in town and would only take cases in the tri-state area. But maybe he'd decided he liked flying all over the country and occasionally overseas. Or perhaps he couldn't say no to Mac, who was reluctant to let go of his best operator. I didn't think that was the case. Dylan had a clear sense of how he intended to lead his life and would do exactly as he wanted.

The question was: Was he willing to limit his traveling for the sake of our relationship?

I told myself I was reading too much into a casual expression. If he was "just about" finished with the case, it probably meant he had an hour or two of paperwork to do. Then he'd be home for good.

Sally stopped by, aglow and excited because she'd been very impressed by one of the candidates. "I'll have to make some calls and talk to his present director, but I think Norman Tobin will make a great addition to our library."

"When can he start work?"

"Not for a few weeks," she said. "Sorry, but we'll have to cover reference till then."

We'll *have to cover? So far, Sally hasn't sat at the reference desk even once since Dorothy's first absence.* Sally looked at me oddly, and I wondered if she could read my mind, because she added, "I'm free now. I think I'll put in an hour or two at reference while I can."

"Well, thank you," I said. "That means I'll be able to sketch out our next newsletter today." I told her how the Haven House meeting went and about my conversation with Uncle Bosco.

"He's right. A place like Haven House needs more involvement with local health and welfare agencies. I'm surprised they didn't look into that aspect."

"I'll mention it to Reese Lavell, the woman I first spoke to. I only hope she doesn't ask me to act as liaison to those groups."

"And why shouldn't she? You're as capable as anyone involved in that project." She chuckled. "In fact, you're becoming quite the community activist. Just like your uncle."

"You think so?"

I must have sounded worried, because Sally patted my back as she got to her feet. "Don't worry. It's not some awful disease we're talking about. You care about Clover Ridge, and you're willing to work to make it a better place to live."

"Thanks, Sally. I suppose I am different from that young woman who accepted your job offer back in October."

"Thank God for that!"

I watched her leave, telling myself there was no way she murdered Dorothy.

Chapter Seventeen

I spent the next few hours blocking out the May–June edition of our newsletter. The lead article was our Adopt-a-Pet Fair, which would be held on the library's front lawn the first Saturday in May. Sally had agreed to the fair as long as I only invited three animal rescue agencies that agreed to bring a limited number of dogs and cats to the event. I'd just finished a lengthy conversation, explaining the restrictions to someone from the local animal shelter, when my library phone rang.

"Hello, Carrie. John Mathers here. I received the envelope you sent me."

My heart pinged. "What envelope are you talking about?"

"Come on, Carrie. I know it's from you. Who else skulks around the library playing detective?"

"I don't *skulk*!"

"Sorry if the word offends you. Where exactly did you find it?"

I let out a humph of exasperation. "Okay, I know you asked me to stay out of the investigation, but I was just trying to be helpful. Anyway, the envelope was taped to the bottom of a reference desk drawer."

"And you just happened to find it?" John asked, sounding skeptical.

"Everyone on staff has been filling in for Dorothy, taking turns in the reference area. I decided to check out the desk—see if she left anything that might prove of value."

"And I can only assume you looked at the paper."

"I happened to glance at it." *And made a copy of it too.*

He cleared his throat. "Can you tell me what any of it means?" *John needs my help!* I thrust my fist in the air. "Some of it."

"Oh!" The syllable expressed surprise and resentment. "In that case, I'd like you to stop by the station on your way home from work."

"Sorry, John, I can't. Dylan's on his way home and we—have plans."

"I understand. In that case, why don't I come over to the library now, and you can explain how you interpret Dorothy's code—if it really is hers."

"It's Dorothy's, all right," I answered, but he'd hung up.

Ten minutes later John was striding into my office. Susan had just arrived. She read his expression and left. He thrust a paper in front of me, which I immediately saw was a copy of the original, and said, "Okay, explain!"

"Why are you so angry?" I asked. "I can't help it if I found something you and your men missed. You should be glad I found this."

"Sorry." He sank into the chair Susan had just vacated and stretched out his long legs. "It's been a long day."

Smoky Joe chose that moment to scratch at the door. When I let him in, he flew immediately into John's lap. As John stroked him, Smoky Joe began to purr. John leaned back and closed his eyes.

"I don't know if you were aware," I began, "but Dorothy made a habit of finding out things about people, things they preferred to keep secret."

"And you know this how?" he asked, his voice relaxed. Smoky Joe was working his charm.

"Angela told me this a few months ago when Dorothy was playing tricks on me."

"You mean like smashing your car window?"

I stared at him. "I never reported it! Uncle Bosco must have told you."

"He did. Your uncle knows it's wise to keep us informed of such activities. People who commit these acts have a tendency to escalate their bad behavior."

"Or have it turned against them," I murmured.

"Case in point."

I told John about Dorothy's collection of vases and what I thought the initials and sums of money represented.

"So she extorted money from people she knew to buy those vases she had on display in her home." John shook his head. "Some piece of work, that Dorothy Hawkins."

I snorted. "I agree wholeheartedly."

"What can you tell me about the initials? Any of them look familiar?"

I hesitated.

John laughed. "You love playing detective until some of the suspects turn out to be people you know." He cocked his head. "Or work with."

"All right. Two sets of initials could be Sally Prescott and Harvey Kirk, but you probably know that. I've no idea what Dorothy might have had on either of them, but Sally and Dorothy were once friends. And they argued." I cleared my throat. "Actually, the day before Dorothy was killed." I paused. "I know I should have mentioned it to you, but . . ."

I must have looked pitiful, because John reached over to pat my arm. "But Sally's your boss and your friend. Don't worry, Carrie. I won't mention you when I talk to her and Harvey. And if it will make you feel any better, I figured out those initials and a few others besides. I'll be having a chat with the people she'd been blackmailing."

He walked to the door. "Say hello to your boyfriend for me. Tell Dylan I'll give him a call over the weekend."

* * *

I drove home, singing at the top of my voice along with the radio. I'd picked up enough Indian food for six people. Dylan had texted to say he'd be arriving home around six fifteen and wanted to shower and change his clothes before coming over. I texted back, asking him to bring a bottle of red from his wine collection.

My thoughts were positive as I drove. Soon Dylan would be coming home for good! That meant we'd be able to spend plenty of time together when we weren't working. John and I were good. I'd told him about Sally's argument with Dorothy the day before she'd been murdered, and he wasn't angry with me for snooping around his homicide case. Maybe he'd find Dorothy's murderer without any further help from me. After all, he had the authority to interview people again and again, while I could only ask the occasional question and hope I wasn't raising hackles or suspicions.

I also felt much easier about Henry and Doris's situation now that Uncle Bosco had offered to help them. Life was good and would remain so until I crashed into the next obstacle along the road.

Dylan got to the cottage a little after seven o'clock, freshly shaven and looking sexy in well-worn jeans and a rugby-style polo beneath a gray sweater. He stepped into the hall and grabbed me in a fierce hug, then we kissed for what seemed like minutes before he drew back so he could study me.

"You look wonderful, Carrie. I've missed you so much."

"Me too." I ran my hand along the side of his face.

Dylan sniffed. "Ah, Indian food! Smells delicious."

"Tandoori chicken and shrimp tikka masala and saag paneer and—" I stopped because he'd made a beeline for the kitchen.

I placed the heated dishes on the table so Dylan could choose whichever and as much as he liked. From the way he grinned at the many selections, I gathered I'd made the right choices.

"Ah! Potato and onion kulcha! My favorite." He bit into the bread and chewed. I laughed to see his delight.

We filled our plates and ate everything on them, then refilled them. Dylan asked me for an update on Dorothy's homicide investigation, and I told him about John's visit earlier that afternoon. Since he had no idea that a ghost was one of my best buds, I didn't mention that Evelyn had shown me where Dorothy had hidden her ledger. If and when we grew closer, I'd tell him about Evelyn and hope he didn't think I was delusional.

"By the way, John sends his regards. He said he'll be calling you over the weekend."

"Good," Dylan said. "I want to talk to him."

"About setting up your office in town?"

"He knows a few operators I might want to hire part time. And of a case or two that might interest me." He started to fill his plate again.

"Leave room for dessert," I advised him.

Dylan managed to polish off a serving each of rice kheer—Indian rice pudding—and ladoos—sweet balls of heaven. I couldn't eat another morsel, so I refrigerated the leftovers and started stacking the dishwasher.

We had our coffee in the living room, sitting side by side on the sofa. I brought Dylan's mug into the kitchen for a coffee refill. When I returned, he was fast asleep and gently snoring. I laughed as I covered him with an afghan. He awoke half an hour later and saw me reading in the corner lounge chair. Hand outstretched, he walked over to me and led me into the bedroom.

* * *

I awoke on Saturday morning to a furry face butting against mine and the aroma of freshly brewed coffee. Minutes later, I joined Dylan in the kitchen.

"I made a big carafe of coffee and fed the feline," he said, pouring me a mugful. "I thought I'd let you decide what we eat for breakfast."

"How do scrambled eggs and English muffins sound?" I said.

"With sausages?"

"Of course with sausages."

I set the eggs, butter, and sausages on the counter, and the two frying pans on the range, and got to work.

"Mmm, delicious," Dylan said, taking his first bite a few minutes later. This is a treat—not having to make my own breakfast or grab something in a coffee shop."

"Where did you make your own breakfast?" I asked, suddenly on the alert.

"In my apartment. In Atlanta."

"Oh. I didn't realize you had an apartment there."

Dylan shot me a quizzical look. "I never mentioned it? It's only a studio apartment the company owns."

"Yes, but I thought you were always off investigating cases."

"Sure, but the company's headquarters are in Atlanta. I often had meetings and interviews to attend to, and since I hate living out of a suitcase in a hotel room, Mac offered me an apartment."

The butterflies batted against my chest. "Do you still have it— the apartment?"

Dylan sipped his coffee. "I've been so busy with this latest case, I haven't had time to pack up all my stuff."

"But you plan to, right?"

"Of course. When I'm back in Atlanta."

"Back in Atlanta?" Had I misunderstood everything? No, I hadn't. "Dylan, I thought, except for going back to tie up loose ends of that last case Mac had you investigate, you were planning to open an office in town."

Dylan bit his lip. "Yes, that was the plan. Only . . . two days ago, Mac offered to make me a partner in the company. I thought it over till yesterday afternoon, when I gave him my decision."

The butterflies' wings beat against my ribs in their desperation to escape. "You're staying with the company?"

"I am. I'll be opening a branch in Connecticut and dealing with cases in the tri-state area and New England. Mac and I thought New Haven would be a good place to set up an office."

"And not in Clover Ridge?" I knew I sounded like a little girl being told she wasn't going to Disneyland after all, but I couldn't help it.

"Carrie, my love, New Haven's a half hour's drive from here, an easy trip into Manhattan if I need to meet a client there."

My dreams of having Dylan working in town were no more than a fantasy. "I had no idea you were considering staying with the company. When is all this supposed to happen?"

He looked shamefaced when he said, "In the next few weeks. I'm flying back to Atlanta on Monday and working seven days a week to get everything in order. I should be home for good by the middle of February. Just in time for Valentine's Day."

Who cares about Valentine's Day! "That means you won't be here next weekend."

"I'm afraid not. What's happening next weekend?"

"I told you, I joined a group that's setting up a daycare center for homeless people. They're having a fundraising dinner dance next Saturday night at the Clover Ridge Country Club."

"I'm sorry I can't make it, Carrie, but I'm happy to contribute to the cause."

I forced myself to smile. "I'll take you up on that." I got up to carry my coffee mug to the sink. He reached for my hand, stopping me.

"Carrie, I'm sorry you're upset. I should have told you about the change in plans right away, but I wanted our first evening to be about us." He smiled. "Just think—a few weeks from now I'll be living at home and working in Connecticut."

Chapter Eighteen

After breakfast, we drove to the mall because Dylan wanted me to help him pick out some new clothes, something he never seemed to have time to do. While he tried on trousers in the dressing room, I tried to figure out why I'd been so upset by his news flash. For one thing, I was disappointed that he'd be flying back to Atlanta on Monday and wouldn't be able to attend the fundraiser with me next Saturday night. For another, it was a letdown to learn that Dylan wouldn't be working in Clover Ridge as we'd discussed. No doubt his boss had influenced the decision to set up the new office in New Haven.

I told myself to be mature about it. These were work-related issues. Besides, New Haven was only a half hour's drive away. And Dylan had done the right thing—accepting the partnership in what was a successful and lucrative agency.

It dawned on me that what bothered me the most was that Dylan hadn't asked me to weigh in on his decision regarding the partnership. I was his girlfriend, and while there wasn't much I could say for or against staying with the agency, it would have been nice to have been his sounding board. I planned to tell him so, calmly and rationally. Dylan and I were both new at this relationship-type situation, and we needed to set precedents together.

"These fit you the best," I said when he came out wearing a pair of navy trousers that needed hemming.

"Good. I'll get them in brown and black."

I laughed. "So that's how men shop."

"Why not?" Dylan asked. He reached over to hug me. "When you have the right item or the right girl, you don't let either one go."

We spent the rest of the morning checking out sales in various stores. Dylan bought a leather bomber jacket and a sweater, and I found two pairs of yoga pants and a blouse, all for unbelievably low prices. By twelve thirty we were starving, so we stopped for sandwiches and coffee before driving home. A few hours later, we decided to catch a five o'clock movie we both wanted to see, then ate dinner at Due Amici, my favorite Italian restaurant in town.

That night, as we were drifting off to sleep, Dylan murmured, "This was one of the very best days I can remember."

"Me too." I kissed his cheek.

"I should have told you about Mac's offer," he said.

"That would have been nice."

"I promise to, next time something like that arises."

"Okay, but I hope you won't be looking for another job any time soon."

Dylan didn't answer. He was fast asleep.

Sunday morning we waited on line to have breakfast at a small restaurant well-known for their pancakes and waffles, then drove to New Haven, where Dylan had arranged to have a realtor take us around to various offices. We both agreed that the one in a new high rise with three good-sized rooms that offered a great view of the city was best suited. He told the realtor he'd call her during the week about his decision—and to negotiate rental terms, I knew. We ate a quick lunch, drove over to Yale to visit the Yale University Art Gallery and the Yale Center for British Art, then wended our way back to Clover Ridge.

We talked as we rode: about his methods of gathering information and tracking down the thief who had stolen his client's painting; about the investigation into Dorothy's murder and some of the people she'd been blackmailing; and the homeless situation in our area and Haven House's chance of succeeding. I loved the way Dylan listened as I expressed my thoughts, and I appreciated his attentive responses.

John called Dylan around nine o'clock, and he went into my office to speak to him privately. I told myself I had to respect his privacy when it came to work, and reminded myself that he'd asked me to help him choose new clothes and a new office. Those two were biggies and said a lot that was positive about our relationship.

Monday morning we stood holding onto each other in the hall of my cottage. Dylan's ride to the airport wouldn't be arriving for another hour, but I had to leave if I expected to get to the library on time.

"Did you have a good weekend?" Dylan whispered in my ear.

"Of course. I'm going to miss you."

"I'll be missing you more."

That made me smile. "We'll talk and text and email."

"I'll be back home for good in a few weeks."

Smoky Joe meowed loudly as he wound between my legs. We burst out laughing. I scooped him up and put him in his carrier. Dylan walked me out into the cold January air. He gave me a quick kiss and I headed for my car.

"Talk to you later," Dylan called to me.

I waved, then pushed the ignition. "Off we go," I said to Smoky Joe. He was too intent on cleaning himself to answer.

When I arrived at work, I discovered that someone had tried to break into the library earlier that morning. Whoever it was hadn't been successful because the broken window had set off the alarm.

John and Danny were on the scene, questioning members of the staff as we entered the building.

"I wonder if it was one of the homeless guys, looking for money," Harvey Kirk said as he, Gayle, and I headed to our respective areas.

"Or somebody who got angry for being tossed out of the library," Gayle said.

"Or it could be someone we know nothing about," I contributed.

They stared at me as if I had two heads.

It didn't take John long to work his way to my office. He wasted no time getting to the point. "Who knew about the list you sent me, the one you found in Dorothy's desk?"

"Why? Do you think someone on the list wanted to get hold of it?"

"Carrie!" he warned, casting a stern look.

"I mentioned it to Angela. That was it."

"No one else? Not Sally? After all, she's your boss."

I shook my head. "No. But *you* have the list."

"If someone tried to break in, he or she might not know that I have it, only that there is a list."

"I never thought of that."

"Take care, Carrie," John said, hurrying off, probably to question Angela again.

I waited fifteen minutes before I called Angela.

"Yes, John was here asking me who I told. Of course I mentioned it to Steve. He probably told a few friends and cousins."

"So, word of the blackmail list got out before John received it. But why would someone wait all this time to try to get it, thinking it was still in the library?" I wondered.

"Beats me," Angela said, "unless it was one of the homeless guys."

I groaned. "Not you too."

138

"You have to admit it's a possibility. By the way, how was your weekend with Lover Boy?"

"Great, although he had to fly back to Atlanta today." I filled Angela in on the change in Dylan's plans.

"That's not so bad," she agreed. "New Haven's not that far away. Steve and I had a pretty good weekend too. We managed to snag the best six-piece band around, and now the photographer we wanted is available. The couple he was going to shoot the day of our wedding broke up. We're signing the contract tonight."

"Things are falling into place," I said.

"Don't forget. We're shopping for bridesmaids' dresses this week. How's Wednesday night?"

"Wednesday's an early day. I can make it."

"Please put it down in your calendar so you don't forget."

I stuck my tongue out at her. "How could I forget with you reminding me all the time?"

I called Gillian at work. She was busy with a customer and called back as I was about to take my turn at the reference desk.

"Hi, Gillian. I was wondering—are you still planning to go to the fundraiser dance Saturday night?"

"I suppose so." She didn't sound happy about it. "I said I would, but the truth is, I hate going to dances by myself."

"We can be each other's 'plus one,'" I said. "My boyfriend's flying to Atlanta today and won't be back for a few weeks."

"Oh, good! I mean, I'm sorry that he can't go with you, but I'm glad we can go together."

I laughed. "I knew what you meant. We can go, stay awhile, and leave early. The purpose is to raise money for Haven House, and Dylan promised to contribute to that."

"Nice guy. I have to find myself one of those."

"Maybe you'll meet someone at the fundraiser," I said. "Someone tall, dark, and handsome."

"Of course I will. And he'll be a philanthropist with deep pockets," she kidded back.

"See you Thursday night at eight for the meeting. Or do you want to grab a quick bite before?"

"I'd love that. Anything to get out of cooking at home."

We agreed to meet at the Cozy Corner Café at six thirty.

No one required my attention at the reference desk for some time, and I managed to bring my expense sheets for January up to date. Then a patron asked me to help her find all available information about summer high school programs in Barcelona because her daughter was determined to spend the summer there. The phone rang while she was flipping through the various links online.

"Hello, reference desk. This is Carrie Singleton speaking."

"Carrie, it's John."

"Oh, hi John." I laughed. "I'm not doing any sleuthing. Just helping out patrons until Sally hires a replacement."

"We found out who broke the library window this morning."

"Really? Who did it? What were they after?"

"A bus driver overheard kids talking about the incident on his morning route. He called the principal and gave him the boys' names. The principal questioned the boys." John paused.

"And?"

"The boys gave him a name that's familiar to me. Manny Rawlson. Do you know him? He's been in trouble a few times, but never regarding something like this."

"No, I don't know him. Why? What are you getting at, John? You're scaring me."

John exhaled noisily. "Manny texted one of the boys. His plan was to break into the library and grab the library cat. When we picked him up, he was high on amphetamines."

My mind froze. I was having trouble decoding what I was hearing. "Kidnap Smoky Joe? Why would he want to do something like that? And why did he—? Oh, he thinks Smoky Joe lives in the library full time."

"I don't think the kid intended to harm the cat. He said something about keeping him for a few days, then pretending he found him wandering around, so he'd get treated like a hero. But I think it would be a good idea if you kept close tabs on him for the next week or two."

"I will," I said. "Thanks for letting me know."

"Manny's being charged with destruction of property and intent to kidnap an animal. I doubt it will result in anything more than a fine, but it puts him on notice. His parents as well."

No sooner had I disconnected from John's call than the feline himself came bounding over to the reference desk for some mommy attention. I lifted him onto my lap. "Now don't go off with anyone, Smoky Joe."

He stayed with me a few minutes, then wandered off to seek adventure. My heart was still pounding when Marion Marshall relieved me and I could return to my office. The idea that someone might try to kidnap Smoky Joe was terrifying. I'd have to check on his whereabouts more frequently and ask Angela to do the same when she could. I considered keeping him in my office for the next few days, but he'd probably meow and scratch at the door, wanting to get out. He'd never been confined to a small space, and I knew he wouldn't like it one bit.

I loved Smoky Joe. The little cat had become an essential part of my life. Until now, I hadn't worried about losing him, because he'd never shown any interest in leaving the library or the cottage. But John's visit reminded me there were twisted, malicious individuals in the world and that we were vulnerable to the loss of people and animals we loved.

Chapter Nineteen

I missed Dylan terribly. Our weekend together had brought us closer. We texted and called each other frequently, and I was pleased that he now shared more details of his daily activities with me. He'd hired a lawyer to study the agreement that Mac had drawn up, was negotiating the rental cost of the office in New Haven, and had started packing up his belongings in the small Atlanta apartment, which he planned to ship home. He told me he missed my company and counted the days till we were together again.

Since Tuesday was a late workday for me, I decided to stop by the mall in the morning for my chat with Lillian Morris. Before setting out, I called the store to make sure she was there. After a few minutes' wait, I was connected to the women's clothing section.

"Hello. I was wondering—is Lillian there today?"

"Speaking. I'm here today, all day till six. Who's this?"

I quickly made up a story, "I need to buy some clothes for a trip to Europe. A good friend said you were very helpful when she shopped the other day, so I thought . . ."

"Sure. Come in and I'll help you choose some new pieces to enhance your wardrobe. Be prepared! Your friend must have told you I'm brutally honest. I tell it like it is, and if the item doesn't flatter your figure, I'll let you know."

"I-I'll be there soon."

Fifteen minutes later I was walking into Macy's. The store wasn't very crowded, I noticed, as I rode the escalator to the women's section upstairs. Lillian turned out to be the only salesperson working in women's clothing—a short, stocky woman with short blonde hair who appeared to be in her mid-fifties. She was riffling through a batch of receipts at the register. "Need any help?" she asked.

"Lillian? I'd like to talk to you—about something important."

Clearly, she recognized my voice because she said, "Your story sounded fishy on the phone. Who are you, and what's this about?"

"My name's Carrie Singleton, and I work in the library. You must have heard that Dorothy Hawkins was murdered."

"Yeah? So? It couldn't have happened to a nicer person."

"You didn't much like her," I said.

"Are you kidding?" Lillian glared at me. "She was a snake. A sneaky, slimy snake that pretended to be your friend but—" She stopped abruptly, refusing to say more.

"The police have found a list of names of people Dorothy was blackmailing. Your name was on it."

Fear and anger flitted across her face. "Right! She hit me up for money when she found out—it doesn't matter what she found out. Like a fool, I paid it. But I told Dorothy if she tried for any more, I'd see that she regretted it. She was smart enough not to push her luck."

"Where were you—?"

"The night someone ran Dorothy off the road? I was bowling with my league." Lillian laughed. It wasn't a pleasant sound. "I'm glad she's dead, but I can't take the credit."

I thanked her for her time and exited the store. As I headed for my car, I played back my conversation with Lillian Morris. I was pretty sure she hadn't murdered Dorothy. Much as she obviously disliked Dorothy, her beef with her was old. No, Dorothy had been murdered because she'd pissed someone off more recently.

"Carrie! I didn't expect to bump into you this morning!"

I grinned when I saw Julia and Tacey waving at me. My little cousin looked to her mother. Julia nodded, probably to say it was safe for her to run to me, because she came barreling into my arms.

"Cousin Carrie, I miss you! When are you coming to visit us again?"

"Very soon." I felt a pang of guilt. I'd been meaning to call Julia, but I'd been so busy—with Dylan, work, and my investigation—that I hadn't done anything about it.

Julia and I hugged. "I just bought some clothes for the kids," she said. "They're growing so quickly."

"Mommy, you said we could have lunch out today."

"So I did. Just a quick visit to the diner. You have nursery school this afternoon, and I'm expected at a customer's house at one."

Tacey gazed up at me. "Will you come to the diner with us?"

I glanced down at my watch. It was only ten after eleven and I wasn't very hungry, but I wanted to spend time with Julia and Tacey. "Sure, I could go for a cup of coffee and a muffin."

"Wonderful!" Julia said. "The diner's only a few blocks from here. Tacey loves their French toast."

"It's yummy!" Tacey said.

Julia's car was parked close to where I'd left mine. I followed her to the exit, out to the main thoroughfare, and into the diner's parking lot. Soon we were cozily ensconced in a booth.

"I've been meaning to call you," Julia said after we gave our orders to the pretty young waitress, "but I've been so busy with work and the kids, I never found a free moment."

"Same here," I said. "And I've gotten involved in the Haven House project. A group of people have bought a house around the corner from Aunt Harriet and Uncle Bosco, where the homeless can spend their days engaging in various activities."

"So I've heard. It's a wonderful plan," Julia said. "This way they'll spend their time doing something enjoyable instead of hanging out in the library."

"I want to go to the library," Tacey said. "We never go there any more."

Julia and I exchanged glances.

"Things have quieted down considerably," I said, knowing of her concern that some homeless people had wandered into the children's section. "We try to be proactive at the first sign of trouble."

"We'll stop by the library very soon and take out a few books," Julia told Tacey.

Tacey clapped her hands. "Oh, goody!"

She grinned at me, and I knew she was looking forward to seeing her friend Miss Evelyn.

* * *

News of the attempted catnapping had spread like wildfire, infuriating staff members and patrons, many of whom offered to keep an eye on Smoky Joe. I was touched by their concern and realized how quickly my cat had become a fixture in the library. We were a caring community and looked after one another.

Despite the fact that not much progress had been made regarding the investigation into Dorothy's murder, the atmosphere in the library had calmed down somewhat. Susan and I had a fun time decorating the walls and bookshelves with hearts and cupids—most of which she'd made herself—for Valentine's Day. We needed Max's help to hang her fantastic mobile of hearts, flowers, and "LOVE" signs in the reading room. I found myself grinning whenever I overheard patrons telling Susan how much they loved her artwork. Her self-image was much improved, and I figured it was time to suggest that she start making her wonderful craft items to sell on Etsy or at craft fairs.

At a Wednesday morning meeting, Sally announced that she'd received fewer complaints from patrons in the past week. Even the situation with the homeless had died down. The few who continued to spend time in the library sat quietly reading books and magazines.

A major reason for this change was due to the fact that Dorothy was no longer with us. I felt a pang when I realized days had passed since I'd last thought about her or done anything to help solve her murder. Evelyn showed up and asked for an update. She was disappointed to hear that I had no way of finding out what John had learned from questioning the people on Dorothy's blackmail list, and even more so when I added that I hadn't the slightest idea how to proceed with my own investigation.

At five o'clock that evening—after asking Marion, who was working till nine thirty, to keep an eye on Smoky Joe until I returned—Angela and I hopped in her car and drove to the mall to choose the bridesmaids' dress for her wedding.

"My cousin Vicki is matron of honor," Angela reminded me as she pulled into a parking spot near the bridal gown store, "so she gets to pick what she'll wear. That leaves the four of you."

I laughed. "Which won't be easy. We're four different shapes and sizes."

"Short, fat, tall, and you," Angela said, never one to mince words.

"Something to keep in mind," I agreed.

I tried on long dresses, short dresses, midi-length dresses. Dresses with strapless tops, tops with spaghetti straps, off-the-shoulder tops. Climbing in and out of these complicated garments proved exhausting. My energy level was flagging when we agreed we loved a knee-length dress with a sweetheart neckline and short petal sleeves that would suit all four of us. Yay! No strapless bra for Angela's bridesmaids!

Selecting the color was almost as difficult a decision. Should we go for silver or cornflower blue? Both were available. Silver was classy. Blue was a good color for most people, which was why we opted for it in the end. Besides, we were ravenously hungry. I ordered my dress, then we made a beeline for a restaurant a few doors away, known for its delicious soups, salads, and sandwiches.

A cheerful hostess led us to a table in the middle of the room, which was half-empty. Not surprising since it was after seven o'clock. I shrugged out of my parka and raced to the bathroom for a much-needed visit. I washed my hands, combed my hair, and returned to our table. I gave the large menu a quick look and decided on a cup of tomato soup and half a tuna salad sandwich on multi-grain bread.

Angela leaned back in her chair, looking very pleased with herself. "Now the bridesmaids' dresses are taken care of. You can buy navy shoes or fabric ones and have them dyed to match."

"I think I'll get a pair of strappy navy heels that I can wear again," I said.

"Good idea. Did you tell Dylan the day we're getting married?"

I rolled my eyes. "Haven't mentioned it. We're still in January, and your wedding's not until June."

Angela grinned. "Who knows? Maybe you two will be talking weddings by then."

"Here comes our waitress. What are you having?"

Angela ordered a chopped salad, I ordered my soup and sandwich, and our waitress hurried away to fill our requests. As soon as she left, Angela began talking about her honeymoon.

"We've pretty much nixed the idea of the Caribbean now that we're definitely getting married in June." Her eyes sparkled with excitement. "Now we're thinking of Napa Valley in California or a fabulous resort in Arizona."

"Don't you have to make reservations really soon?" I asked.

"Steve's cousin Stella is a travel agent. She said as long as we decide in the next two weeks, she can book us on a flight and hotel wherever we want."

"Now all you have to do is make up your mind," I said.

My own mind began to wander as Angela elaborated on the reasons for choosing one spot over the other.

"Of course we're not ruling out Hawaii. Not by any means."

"Of course. Not by any means," I echoed. "Ah, here comes our food."

We were hungry and ate quickly. Our waitress cleared our dishes, and we ordered coffee and a piece of carrot cake to share. I checked my phone and smiled as I read Dylan's message.

"The lease for the New Haven office is being faxed over to him tomorrow," I told Angela.

"Great. Too bad he couldn't make the dinner dance Saturday night. The mansion at the country club is to die for. Steve and I would have loved to have our wedding there, but it was way out of our price range."

"Marion texted me. Smoky Joe is fine. She let him into my office so he could use the litter box."

Our coffee and dessert arrived. I took a sip of my coffee and looked around. The place had pretty much emptied out while we'd been eating. A couple sitting at a table for two against the far wall caught my eye. The man had his back to me, but something about his posture looked familiar.

"What are you looking at?" Angela asked. "Oh, isn't that Fred, Dorothy's husband?"

"It is!" I agreed.

"Who's that woman with him? Look! She just wiped something from his face with her napkin."

I stood. "I'm going to find out. Right now."

Fred and his companion were too engrossed in each other to notice me approach. When I tapped his shoulder, they both gave a start.

"Hello, Fred! I thought it was you. I was out shopping with my friend Angela for her wedding—you know Angela Vecchio who works at circulation in the library?—and we stopped here afterward for a quick dinner."

Fred's smile was forced. "Hello, Carrie. Nice to see you. Thank you again for your casserole. It was delicious."

"How are you doing? I'm glad to see that you're getting out."

He glanced at his female friend. "Leila's making sure that I do. Carrie Singleton, Leila Bevins. Leila, Carrie works in the library."

And you're the woman he's been in love with all these years. And now you're back in the picture.

Leila was an attractive diminutive woman in her mid-fifties. As we shook hands, she assessed me with intelligent brown eyes.

"Nice to meet you," we said at the same time.

"I'm glad you're looking after Fred," I said.

She smiled, suddenly accepting me. "He needs looking after," she said.

We exchanged a few more pleasantries, and I returned to my table.

"Who is she?" Angela demanded before I sat down.

"A lovely lady Fred's known for years." I told Angela about their history. "He was about to tell Dorothy he wanted a divorce, when her aunt died suddenly."

"Yes. Poor Evelyn," Angela said. "Sad to think she fell in the library parking lot, and no one found her until it was too late."

"So I've heard. Dorothy was devastated, and Fred couldn't bring himself to leave her. When someone knocked Dorothy down outside the supermarket, she remembered that Fred had been out late the night her aunt had died, and mistakenly thought the same person must have knocked them both down."

"That person being Fred," Angela said.

"Only Fred was with Leila the evening Evelyn died. Of course he couldn't tell Dorothy."

"Of course not," Angela agreed. "She would have killed him had she known."

We both snickered, then polished off the rest of our dessert.

The subject of Dorothy's murder was still on our minds as we drove back to the library.

"The fact that Fred fell in love with another woman is proof that he wanted to be free of Dorothy," Angela said. "Maybe something set him off recently, and he decided he couldn't bear to live with her any longer."

"I hate to admit it, but the same thought was running through my mind," I said. "We know how awful Dorothy could be. Poor Fred had to live with her day in and day out."

"Who could blame him if he decided to murder her?" Angela said. "If you found evidence that he'd done it, would you bring it to John?"

"Good question," I said. "I'd be tempted not to, but I'd end up telling John. Even though I just about lost all sympathy for Dorothy when I found that list of people she'd blackmailed."

"They all must be glad she's dead."

"And Fred looks relaxed and happy. He clearly cares about Leila, and she cares about him."

"I'm glad they reconnected," Angela said.

"Me too."

Back in the library, I went looking for Smoky Joe. I was tired and ready to plop into bed to veg out and watch an hour of television. I stopped in the coffee shop, where patrons often fed him tidbits of food despite my posters telling them *not* to feed the library cat. Only Katie was there, wiping down the tables for the night.

When she saw me, she said, "He was here half an hour ago, begging for treats."

For once I wasn't concerned about his eating habits. "Did you happen to see where he went?"

"Sorry, no." Katie grinned. "But you know Smoky Joe. He could be anywhere in the library."

True, I thought. But I was starting to worry. He had a good sense of time and usually came looking for me when the library was ready to close for the night.

I called to him softly as I headed for the children's section. A few patrons started looking for him. When I asked, none of them had seen him recently.

My heart began to pound. Had someone walked off with Smoky Joe? He was the friendliest of cats, and while patrons rarely tried to pick him up, I suspected he wouldn't react in fear. *Don't think the worst,* I told myself. *He's probably in the children's section with Marion. She's one of his favorite people.*

But Marion hadn't seen him since she'd let him into my office so he could use the kitty litter. "I do apologize for not keeping an eye on him after that, especially after the break-in, but all the third-grade teachers have arranged a read-a-thon for their students. The kids have to read a book, write a report, and draw a picture. Parents kept stopping by to ask me for book recommendations."

Max appeared, broom in hand, ready to start cleaning the children's section. But when he heard that I couldn't find Smoky Joe, he leaped into action.

"Don't you worry, Carrie. We'll search every nook and corner. That cat has to be someplace."

"What if somebody took him?" I asked, blinking back tears. "Maybe that high school boy decided to grab him while the library was open."

Max leaned on his broom and shook his head. "I think Smoky Joe's too smart to go off with anyone, much less some kid he doesn't know."

I sniffed. "I hope you're right."

Max and I each took half of the library. I peered around stacks, in offices—even in the ladies' room. Smoky Joe was nowhere in sight. It was nine twenty-five. Five minutes to closing time. I felt a moment of panic.

"Maybe he went downstairs," Max said.

"He never goes downstairs," I said.

Max laughed. "There's always a first time for everything."

I trembled as I walked down the stairs behind Max. I dreaded driving back to the cottage without my furry feline friend. Maybe he'd followed one of the patrons outside. He didn't know how to deal with streets and cars.

I wandered into the storage room. No sign of Smoky Joe.

"Carrie, come here!" I followed Max's voice to the closet where we kept supplies. There in the corner, Smoky Joe was stretching out his front paws as he awoke from a very deep sleep.

I scooped him into my arms and squeezed him so tightly, he meowed a complaint. "Too bad! You scared me half to death."

"Told you he wouldn't leave with anyone but you," Max said.

"Thanks, Max." I stood on tiptoe to kiss his cheek. Then I nuzzled my face against Smoky Joe's warm furry chest. "And I'm taking you home right now."

I drove slowly, savoring my relief that Smoky Joe was safe in his carrier beside me. I loved him so, I didn't know what I'd do if someone had taken him. My mind drifted, and I found myself thinking about Fred, Leila, and Dorothy. Though I was glad that Fred and Leila had rekindled their romance and were enjoying happiness, I'd never give him a free pass if he'd murdered Dorothy. Or anyone else, for that matter. If Fred had been so unhappy, he should have gotten a divorce. Homicide was no solution. Once a person committed murder, what was to stop him from murdering again? I had no idea if Evelyn's death was a homicide or connected in any way to Dorothy's murder. But I was back on the case and determined to find out.

Back home in my cottage, I fed Smoky Joe some treats, then called Dylan. I told him of my scare in the library after going with Angela to choose my bridesmaid's dress for her wedding.

"What's the date?"

"The third Saturday night in June."

"I'll put it on my calendar."

I grinned, happy that Dylan was in my life and sharing my special events. "We ran into Fred Hawkins having dinner with his girlfriend."

"His girlfriend, eh? That was fast."

"Not really. They fell in love years ago."

"Interesting. Anything new regarding his wife's murder?"

"Not that I know of," I said. "John hasn't said a word to me about the list of blackmail victims I sent him."

Dylan laughed. "That's good. Babe, I think you should stay out of this one."

We spoke a few minutes more, then said goodnight. I went into my office and turned on the computer. After checking my email, I typed in Leila Bevins's name. Sure enough she had a Facebook page filled with entries and photos. Lots of photos. I read her bio. She'd grown up in Virginia and attended college in Connecticut, where she'd married her husband. They had three children—two girls and a boy. She'd taught school for several years. More recently, she was working in a women's boutique in town called Trendy Elegance.

I glanced over at Leila's many photos. Most were of her grown children in the midst of outdoorsy activities like waterskiing and skiing. There were a few of a wedding of one of her daughters and many of a baby in pink. No mention of her husband, who'd either died or they'd divorced. But there was one of her and Fred in glamorous clothes. Interesting. I wondered when that had been taken.

Could Fred and Leila have planned the murder together? Perhaps Fred *had* knocked Dorothy down outside the supermarket. Then, when that failed, Leila ran her off the road.

I wondered if John was aware that Fred and Leila were seeing each other again. John had never mentioned finding the car that had sent Dorothy to her death. Would he know to check out Leila's car for damage or to ask her for an alibi the night that Dorothy was murdered?

Hmm. John had told me to stay out of the investigation. Was it my obligation to tell him what I knew?

Chapter Twenty

T hursday morning I asked Sally if our Haven House activities
planning group could meet in the conference room that evening since it was free. She agreed. I thanked her and left word at the
hospitality desk for whoever was attending the meeting. Later on,
I'd ask Susan to set up coffee and hot water for tea shortly before
our meeting time of eight o'clock. That taken care of, I went to my
office to start my day's work.

I spent twenty minutes chatting with a chef about the program
he'd be presenting at our library. Though he wouldn't be coming
until May, I felt a surge of excitement. Charles worked in one of the
most famous restaurants in the area and was a frequent guest on
TV cooking shows. Our first food program was scheduled to take
place the first week in February. Patrons had rushed to sign up for
it as soon as registration opened. Fifteen minutes later every slot
had filled, with twelve standbys in case of dropouts.

Evelyn appeared shortly before Trish was scheduled to show up
for work. I told her I'd run into Fred and his lady friend in the restaurant the previous evening.

"I still don't think Fred has it in him to kill Dorothy," she said
when I finished.

"Any thoughts about Leila Bevins?" I asked.

Evelyn's mouth fell open. "That's who he's seeing—*Leila Bevins?*"

"Yes. Why? Do you know her?"

She snorted. "I've known Leila for years. She sold me some of my favorite outfits. Fred and Leila Bevins! I wouldn't think she'd give Fred a tumble, let alone kill someone for him."

"We're back to square one," I said, "but I'm not giving up. I'll be meeting with a few Haven House people in the conference room tonight. I hope you'll be there. There will only be five or six of us, but you might pick up a comment or bit of information that I miss."

"I'll be there, though I hate to think that any relative of Dorothy's—and mine, for that matter—might have murdered her."

"I can imagine how awful that must be for you." I gave her a searching look. "But we have to consider that Dorothy was on to something when she said that the person who killed you also was trying to kill her."

"I thought you'd discarded that idea," Evelyn said.

"Perhaps I shouldn't have. Just think—who might have had it in for Dorothy? A relative, a colleague from the library, and Ernie Pfeiffer. Except for a few of her blackmail victims, you had relationships with the very same people."

I gave her a minute to think this over. "That's true," she conceded.

"Your niece or nephew might have been angry that you left all your money to Dorothy. You and Dorothy both had run-ins with Ernie Pfeiffer." I cocked my head, trying to be tactful about what I was going to say next.

"Then there's Sally and Harvey Kirk."

'Yes? What about them?" Evelyn asked.

"Were you on good terms with them both?"

Evelyn shrugged. "Good enough, I suppose."

"What's that supposed to mean?" I asked. "I wish you'd explain."

Evelyn let out a whoosh of an exhalation—as though she found my questions exasperating when, in fact, the shoe was on the other

Buried in the Stacks

foot. "Let me put it this way. Sally and I didn't always see eye to eye. She's mellowed quite a bit this past year—actually in these past few months since you've become head of P and E—but when she came to work here, she was rather overbearing.

"True, I was only an aide, but the previous director had recognized my bookkeeping skills. I filled out purchasing forms and helped keep financial records *for years* before Sally became director."

I laughed long and loud.

"What's so funny?" Evelyn demanded.

"So that's why you encouraged me to take the position. You thought I'd be a thorn in Sally's paw."

"Kind of," she admitted. "And then the two of you became good friends."

"Did you ever have a serious argument with Sally?"

"A few times. The worst was the day I . . . became deceased."

"You never said."

"You never asked."

Wow! "I never knew to ask," I said. "Tell me what happened."

"The situation had escalated to the point that we could barely hold a civilized conversation. I no longer had anything to do with purchasing forms or financial records. Sally was doing all that herself and making a right mess of things. So I learned when I stopped by her office to tell her something. She was out, but the accounts were spread across her desk. I was surprised at how our expenses had suddenly skyrocketed in the past few months. At that rate, we'd be spending way beyond the budget allotted for the year. Then it occurred to me—Sally was making gross errors, overspending, or out-and-out stealing.

"She walked in and started yelling at me when she saw me looking over the accounts. I told her if she was thinking of making fraudulent claims, I'd inform the board that she was embezzling library funds."

157

"That was the day of your accident?"

Evelyn nodded. "I think I managed to put enough fear into her to stop her from doing anything foolish. At least when I looked at the records months later—from this side—everything seemed in order."

"What were Dorothy and Sally fighting about the day before Dorothy was run off the road?"

Evelyn shook her head. "I don't know. For a while they were good friends, until Dorothy used a confidence that Sally had shared with her and held it over her head. Silly girl. Not a good way to keep friends."

Something to look into. "What about Harvey Kirk?" I asked.

"What about him? Do I like the man? No, I do not."

"Why not?"

"I had a problem with my laptop. Harvey was kind enough to fix it. But when the same problem cropped up again, he turned cranky. He said he was glad to help me with my problem once, but he didn't have the time to fix it again and again. He offered to recommend a techie who was reliable. When I alluded to the fact that money was tight, he laughed and said a fool and his money are soon parted."

"And you did—what?"

"Added a touch of salt to the mug of coffee he's always holding in his hand."

"And he found out," I finished for her.

"He did."

"I can't believe you'd do that."

"It's not something I'm proud of." Her eyes pleaded with me not to be turned off by what she'd just admitted. "I only get that way when someone pushes my buttons."

"Evelyn." I shook my head. "I'd say that's more Dorothy's style than yours."

"Please, Carrie! You know I'm nothing like Dorothy." Evelyn looked like she was about to cry.

We stared at each other for a long minute.

"I promise to listen in on all Haven House conversations and continue to listen in on conversations in the library," Evelyn said. "And to report what I hear."

"Good!" I said heartily, but my faith had been shaken by two people I'd looked up to until now. I'd just discovered that Sally might have embezzled money from the library, and Evelyn, whom I was counting on to help me solve two homicides, could be less than kind.

* * *

I left Smoky Joe in the library while I went to meet Gillian for dinner at the Cozy Corner Café. Angela was working late and promised to check on him occasionally. So did Susan. The Café was crowded, and Gillian and I had to wait for a table. We chatted as we stood near the cash register.

"What got you involved in Haven House?" I asked.

"I was kind of floundering after Ryan and I broke up. I thought it would be nice to do something that benefited our community."

"I kind of felt the same way," I said. "Once the cold weather set in, the homeless started coming to our library, and some were wreaking havoc. When I heard about Haven House, I thought it was great that a group of residents was generous enough to want to set up a daycare center for people in need."

Gillian shot me a knowing look. "Of course the word is out that these very same residents will be making a bundle of money under the guise of their act of charity."

The hostess beckoned to us and led us to a table near the kitchen.

"What do you mean?" I asked when we were seated.

"To start with, they wrangled it so that a state agency supplied a handful of cash to help pay for the place. And the fundraiser at the Clover Ridge Country Club will bring in lots of money—more than the cost of the renovations. So will the extravagant fundraisers in the works." Gillian raised her eyebrows. "Then there's talk of Haven House being used for other activities."

"What other activities?" I asked, suddenly alarmed.

Gillian waved her hand. "High-stakes card games, for one."

"Really? I had no idea."

Gillian laughed. "Carrie, you look like I just told you there is no Santa Claus. Why do you care how Haven House is used at night? Those big money card games take place all over. What does it matter if a few take place at Haven House? As for their glamorous fundraisers—lots of rich people are happy to attend. They get a nice tax write-off and an evening of entertainment. Nothing in this world is free, and if that's what it takes so the homeless in this town can have a daytime place of their own, then we can do our part and look the other way."

Chapter Twenty-One

I was glad that Evelyn had promised to observe the activities planning committee meeting, because I had difficulty keeping my mind on track. I sank back in one of the conference room's well-padded leather chairs and considered what a terrible judge of character I'd turned out to be. I was fool enough to take people at their face value when their true natures were more devious. Sally and Evelyn had murky secrets, and now Gillian couldn't care less what illegal activities went on in Haven House when the homeless people were gone for the day.

Maybe everyone had murky secrets, and I was naïve to assume that the people I cared about were as upright and honest as I believed them to be. Maybe everyone had a dark side but put on a fake front for the public. After all, my father, who had been a thief for most of his life, was charismatic and loving, despite his thieving ways.

"What do you think, Carrie? You haven't said much this evening."

I jerked to attention. Reese Lavell was smiling at me from the other end of the table. "I'm sorry," I said. "Could you please repeat the question."

"It's not a question, exactly. We were discussing what electronics to buy for the Haven House people. We've agreed to put a TV in at least three of the rooms and a computer or two in another."

"And they'll be well secured so no one can walk off with them," said one of the two men present.

"The library will be happy to contribute books and magazines," I said, "as well as some older CDs and DVDs—as long as DVD players and stereo systems are provided."

"We'll have to get a few of those too," Reese said.

"I think it would be nice if we brought in cookies from time to time—to serve with coffee and tea," Francesca said.

"Which brings up an important question: Who will be overseeing the activities?" Gillian said as she glanced at me. "The library's had their problems with some of these people."

"I suppose we'll have to raise money to pay people to run the place and supervise," the other man said.

"We hope to get a counselor here part time from the health department," Francesca said. "And some of us can volunteer to spend a few hours a week helping out."

"That will be difficult for those of us who work during the day," Gillian said.

Having made my offer, I tuned out. The more I thought about Haven House, the more I agreed with Uncle Bosco. Haven House, by its very nature, was bound to have problems. And if Gillian was right about the evening activities, it would only be a matter of time before they were discovered. And when they were, the entire project might go down the drain.

Reese finally brought the meeting to a close. "Thank you all for coming. You've brought up wonderful suggestions and raised very important questions that I'll be sure to bring to the attention of the board."

The six of us got to our feet and began bidding one another good night. Francesca made a big show of hugging us all as we were leaving.

"She thinks she's our hostess," Gillian murmured.

I laughed and started gathering up coffee cups for Susan, who would be coming by to clear the room of debris as soon as she realized the meeting had ended.

Gillian and I hugged good night.

"I'll call you Saturday when I'm leaving for the country club," I said. "This way we'll arrive close to the same time."

"Good idea," Gillian agreed. "I'd feel like an idiot, standing around with no one to talk to."

I slipped on my parka and reached for my pocketbook. I had to skirt around Francesca because she was hugging her husband, who had just made an appearance, in the most theatrical manner. *Oh no! What's he doing here?* Next to Gerald stood Ernie Pfeiffer.

"Well, hello, Carrie Singleton!" Ernie greeted me. "So nice of the library to open its arms to help our Haven House project."

Our Haven House project? "Of course," I said, relieved that my voice didn't betray my agitation. "It's a wonderful venture for the benefit of the community." *I hope.* "I had no idea you were involved."

He smiled dismissively. "Only in a small way."

Gerald, who had released himself from his wife's embrace, patted Ernie's shoulder. "Let's give credit where credit's due. Ernie here is one of our biggest contributors."

"How nice." I smiled at them both and wished them a good evening.

"We hope to see you at the next meeting," Gerald called to me. "Next week. Here, if it's all right with your boss."

I drove to my cottage, my nerves jangling like a loose bicycle chain. Gerald Benning and Ernie Pfeiffer were both involved in the

Haven House project! Gillian had said there were rumors that the project was a front for criminal activities. Now that I knew Ernie Pfeiffer was a contributor, I was certain of it. Which meant Gerald was crooked. I shook my head in disbelief. Was the whole world on the take?

At home, I fed Smoky Joe a late dinner and made myself a mug of hot chocolate, something I only drank when I needed comfort. My world, which I'd believed to be warm and caring, was looking pretty bleak and corrupt. I was surrounded by every kind of deceit. Even Evelyn was capable of spite. I wondered what sinister secret Harvey Kirk was hiding. I'd always thought he was a nice person, but how well did I know him? The fact that he was on Dorothy's list meant he'd done something reprehensible or illegal.

I changed into my nightgown and slipped into bed with the book I'd been reading. My cell phone jingled. I reached for it eagerly, hoping it was Dylan. The meeting he'd had to attend that night must have finally ended.

"Hello, Caro, honey. I hope I'm not calling too late."

"Oh, hi, Dad."

"You don't sound very happy to hear from me."

"I am! Really. It's just that I thought you were Dylan."

"I just left him."

"You were at his meeting?"

"I was. I told Dylan I'd be calling you tonight since we haven't talked in a while."

"How's the job? You still like catching thieves instead of being on the other side of the fence?"

My father laughed. "The truth? I love it! I helped Dylan out on his last case. Ask him—I figured out every one of the perp's moves."

Perp? My father's beginning to sound like a cop. "I'm glad you're no longer in your old business."

"Naw. That's all in the past. I'm glad to be on the right side of things, for a change."

"I wish I were," I said.

"Why? What's going on, Caro?"

I sighed. "Nothing. Everything. I'm finding that people aren't who they claim to be. They all have bad sides. Secret sides. Even this project I've gotten involved with—Haven House. It's supposed to be a place where homeless people can spend the day, but the people funding it are planning to use it to make lots of money for themselves."

"Does John Mathers know this? Let him do the investigating."

"Good idea, Dad. I'll call John and tell him what I know, but it's more than that."

I told my father about finding Dorothy's list of people she'd been blackmailing. "Some of the people on the list work in the library. Which means they must have done something dishonest."

"So?"

"So?" I was shocked. "Maybe they stole—or worse. Who knows what they've been up to? It makes me realize I've been naïve to think that people are basically good."

"Caro, honey. People *are* basically good. I know it sounds strange coming from me—but most of them are basically honest. Everyone's done something they're ashamed of at one point in their lives. Don't give up on a person because of one or two mistakes."

"I don't know," I said.

"Hey, kiddo. You didn't give up on me."

"That's true," I said.

I heard a woman's voice in the background.

"Good-night honey. We'll talk soon," my father said.

"Who's there with you?" I asked.

Too late. He'd disconnected.

I found myself smiling and shaking my head at the same time. My father had managed to calm me down and improve my outlook on everything. I fell asleep shortly after our conversation. I woke up at my usual time to see snow falling. Sally called to tell me that, because of the weather, the library would be opening at eleven instead of nine o'clock.

Great! I jumped out of bed, fed Smoky Joe, then made myself a batch of blueberry pancakes with real Vermont maple syrup. Highly energized, I hummed as I put the kitchen back in order and went outside to clear off my car. Jack Norris was plowing the private road that coursed through the Avery property. I waved to him as he drew closer to the cottage.

"Thanks for clearing the road so I can get to work," I said.

"Are you kidding!" He shot me a grin. "The boss called me last night. Said to make sure I was out plowing as soon as the snow stopped so you could be at work on time."

I went inside and called Dylan. He picked up immediately.

"Hiya, babe. I was just about to call to see how you're faring with the snow."

"It stopped and Jack did a great job of clearing the road. I don't have to leave for work for another hour. Because of the snow, we're having a late start."

"Good. I would have called last night to ask about your meeting, but I was beat. Fell asleep as soon as I got into bed. Speak to your dad?"

"Yep. Sounds like he loves his new job."

"That he does. Jim knows all the angles thieves use to pull heists and some of the places where they fence their goods."

"He should," I said wryly. "Does he have a lady friend?"

Dylan laughed. "He won't say, but I suspect he does. I tried to get in touch with him a few times in the evening, and he didn't pick up."

"Really? Well, I hope she's nice," I said.

"So says the possessive daughter."

"I'm not—" I stopped. "I just don't want him to get mixed up with the wrong sort of woman."

Dylan laughed. "Do you hear yourself?" When I didn't answer, he said, "How was your meeting last night?"

I told him what Gillian had heard about the project and my assumptions after seeing Ernie Pfeiffer there with Gerald Benning.

"Now don't go playing detective. Tell John what you heard and suspect. Let him handle things."

"I will." *After the dinner dance.*

"Sorry I'm missing the gala," he said as if he'd heard my thoughts. "I've mailed the check. You should receive it today or tomorrow."

The new snowfall gave the streets and lawns a crisp, clean look, and the reflection of the shining sun made the morning look especially bright. The library's late opening had created a festive holiday air. When I freed Smoky Joe from his carrier, he made a mad dash for the children's room. Marion must have been giving him special treats.

Sally was sitting at the hospitality desk. She waved me over. "How did the meeting go last night?"

"All right."

"You don't sound very happy about it."

Are my emotions that easy to read? "We'll talk about it later—in private."

"Well, okay." She seemed perplexed as she turned to a patron who was waiting to be helped.

Trish came in a few minutes after I'd settled down to check my email. We talked about the snow and the day's programs. Evelyn wouldn't make an appearance until she found me alone.

I walked around to check the ongoing programs. Despite the weather, every teacher and programmer had shown up, along with close to the usual number of participating patrons. I stopped by Sally's office and told her of my suspicions regarding Haven House.

"I thought it was too good to be true when a group of residents decided to create a day center for our homeless," she said. "And to think the state provided funds to help renovate the place."

"Maybe things will turn out all right after all," I said.

Sally smiled. "I'm glad you haven't lost your optimistic outlook. I've come to depend on it."

"Really? Lately I've been having some dark and gloomy thoughts."

"Maybe the snowfall washed them away, and you're thinking positively again."

I wanted to run to the other side of the desk and hug Sally, but she'd think I was going bonkers. Sally was my friend, and I hated suspecting her of having done something illegal or of killing Dorothy. I was going to have to ask her some tough questions, but now wasn't the time.

Instead of going out for lunch, Angela and I ordered in sandwiches from the Cozy Corner Café, which we ate in our small staff room. Gayle and Sally joined us. Sally was elated because all of Norman Tobin's references had given him glowing reports. And his present director was willing to release him, which meant that our new reference librarian would be able to start work right away, on Monday morning.

We chatted for a while—about the new librarian, the snow, and our plans for the weekend—until Gayle noticed the time, and the three of them took off in a flurry of activity. I checked the email on my phone and was about to leave too, when Harvey Kirk entered the staff room.

"Hi, Harvey," I said.

"Hi, yourself," he said and poured himself a cup of coffee.

He reached inside our small refrigerator for a brown bag that held his lunch and set it on the table. My pulse raced as I tried to figure out the most effective yet tactful way to question him about Dorothy.

"Did you have trouble driving in this morning?" I asked.

'Nope." Harvey unwrapped his sandwich and took a huge bite.

"I didn't either," I said. "They cleared the roads quickly. Besides, I don't think this snow will last long. They expect warmer weather the next few days. I bet it starts to melt soon."

"Mmm."

Harvey wasn't one for small talk, which made things more difficult. I smiled as I suddenly got a brainstorm.

"Did you hear the news? Sally's hired a reference librarian to take Dorothy's place. His name's Norman Tobin, and he starts on Monday."

"About time. Now we can stop filling in for reference."

"I hope Norman's a nice person. Not like Dorothy."

A scowl darkened Harvey's face. "What a bitch she was. I'm glad someone decided to take her out." He chomped another bite out of his sandwich.

"I heard she was blackmailing people," I said, hoping for more from Harvey, but his mouth was too full of food to answer. "I wonder how she managed to learn all that stuff about her victims."

"Figure it out. She was a reference librarian. Research was her specialty."

"Yeah, I guess you're right," I agreed. *Time to leave.* "Well, see you. Have a good weekend."

Harvey looked up from his sandwich and shot me a wicked grin. "Carrie, I hope you're not trying to find the person who killed Dorothy. Some murders are best left unsolved—for everyone's sake."

My hand shook as I opened the door. I stood outside the staff room, too dazed to move.

"What's wrong?" Evelyn demanded. "You look like you've seen a—something scary."

"It's Harvey. When I brought up the subject of Dorothy blackmailing people, he advised me to stop investigating her murder. I think he meant it as a threat."

"Nasty man," Evelyn mumbled under her breath. "I'll keep an eye on him."

"I wish I knew what Dorothy had on him," I said.

I took in a few deep breaths and headed downstairs to the supply room so I could speak to Evelyn in private. When I was safely inside, I turned to face her.

"Did you get to the meeting last night? I didn't see you there."

"I decided not to make my presence known," she said, smoothing down her black pencil skirt. "I wasn't happy to see my niece's husband show up with Ernie Pfeiffer—the two of them acting like BFFs."

I burst out laughing, then quickly apologized when I caught her scowl. "Sorry, but hearing you use that expression is kind of bizarre."

"I must have picked it up from the teens who hang out in the young adult section," Evelyn said.

"I wonder if Haven House was the project your nephew Roger wanted to get in on when Dorothy refused to lend him the money."

"Sounds like it could be. And since Ernie Pfeiffer's involved, you can bet he's making a bundle on it. He never does anything out of the goodness of his heart. He doesn't have one."

"Gillian said it's rumored that Haven House will be used at nights for high-stakes card games."

"And parties," Evelyn said darkly. "That could mean drugs. Prostitutes."

"What bothers me most is that once word gets out, the place will be shut down," I said. "So much for helping the homeless in Clover Ridge."

"And they're so looking forward to having a place to go to during the day," Evelyn said. "I hear them talking among themselves in the reading room. For the first time, they sound excited about having activities and games to play and TVs to watch."

I sighed. "Maybe I shouldn't tell John about the rumors. I hate to see the plans for Haven House fall through for the people who need it the most."

"John Mathers is nobody's fool. If he doesn't already know, he's sure to find out about the other uses intended for Haven House, whether you tell him or not."

Evelyn faded away, and I climbed the stairs to the main level. I hadn't taken more than five steps when I heard, "Cousin Carrie! Cousin Carrie!"

Tacey came bounding toward me. I swept her up in my arms and swung her around.

"Mommy said I could go to Miss Marion's read-aloud today!"

Julia approached, several books in her arms. "I decided to let Tacey attend this afternoon's program. I came early to pick up a few books I'd reserved."

"Were you planning to stay for the program?" I asked.

A look of indecision crossed Julia's face. "I suppose I should, though I have several errands to run for the new decorating job I've taken on."

"Tacey can stay with me until the program starts. I'll walk her over and pick her up at the end of the hour. She'll be in my office until you come for her. That way you can run your errands without feeling pressured."

"Are you sure? You have your own work to do without keeping an eye on Tacey."

I waved away her concern. "I'd love to spend time with her." I turned to my little cousin. "When Miss Marion finishes reading her stories, would you like to stay with me in my office? You can draw while I work."

Tacey's eyes filled with delight. "Can we stop at the coffee shop and get a brownie?"

"I don't see why not," I said. "You can always call me on my cell," I told Julia. "Or text me."

The last of her doubts disappeared. "I'll do that. And let you know if I'm running late." Impulsively, she hugged me. "Thanks so much, Carrie. Sometimes I feel there aren't enough hours in the day to get everything done."

Tacey skipped beside me as I headed for my office. Trish was getting ready to leave for the day.

"Well, hello, Miss Tacey!"

Tacey giggled.

"You got three phone calls," Trish said to me as she slipped on her parka. "I took care of two of them, but the third is a woman who wants to give a talk on snakes and insisted on talking to you. Her number's on your desk."

"Interesting," I said. "Was she planning to bring in snakes as part of the program?"

"I think so. See you tomorrow."

"Where's Miss Evelyn?" Tacey asked when we were alone.

"Good question, honey. She comes and goes. I never know when she'll show up."

"I'm right here," Evelyn said, manifesting before our eyes.

"Oh, goody!" Tacey said. "I've missed you, Miss Evelyn. I wish I could hug you."

"So do I, Tacey. What have you been up to?"

"I'm learning to write my letters. I can write my name!"

"Good for you," Evelyn said.

I sat down in front of my computer and ran through the email I'd been sent during the past few hours, trying to give my two guests some privacy. As they whispered and laughed, I marveled at their fondness for each other and how Tacey had learned not to talk about Evelyn, who Julia used to worry was her daughter's imaginary friend.

I glanced at my watch. It was five minutes to the hour, which meant I'd better start walking Tacey over to the children's section. I put my arm around her. "Tacey, honey, it's time to head over to Miss Marion's. We don't want to be late and miss part of the story."

Tacey pursed her lips. "Not yet."

"Go with Cousin Carrie," Evelyn urged her. "We'll talk again real soon."

"Well, all right." Tacey reached for my hand, and we walked over to the children's section. "I wish Miss Evelyn could come to my house."

"I bet she'd love to come, but we can't always have exactly what we want."

"I know. Mommy tells me that." Tacey brightened as she had a thought. "But at least I can visit her here in the library."

"Of course," I agreed.

Tacey let go of my hand and skipped the rest of the way to story time.

Chapter Twenty-Two

Since I was off on Saturday, I got up to feed Smoky Joe and then went back to sleep for another hour. After breakfast, I straightened up the cottage and answered some long overdue email. I slipped into a pair of yoga pants and a T-shirt and checked through my list of errands. I needed a few items at the supermarket and had to stop at the bank for some cash, fill the car with gas, and look for a dress for tonight's gala.

I had a dressy outfit I could wear, but this was the perfect opportunity to shop in Trendy Elegance, the boutique where Fred's girlfriend worked. I wanted to talk to Leila Bevins. She'd impressed me as a nice, caring person, which didn't mean she was off my list of possible suspects. And perhaps she might tell me something about Fred and Dorothy's relationship. Or share a comment Dorothy might have made to Fred about a person she disliked or feared that he'd passed on to her. I sighed. The problem with investigating Dorothy's murder was that there were just too many suspects.

Trendy Elegance was located on a street of shops and galleries facing the Green. Our village center was abuzz with activity as neighbors stopped to chat with one another between errands on this sunny Saturday morning. I managed to find a parking spot a few doors down from the store. I pulled open the ornate wood and copper-trimmed door and spotted Leila assisting a middle-aged woman scrutinizing herself in the three-part mirror in the rear section of the shop.

"May I help you?" an attractive young woman in a sleek black dress asked.

I gestured at Leila. "I need a dress. I'll wait till Leila's free."

"Certainly," she said, though she didn't look pleased as she flounced off.

I stopped to admire a pile of sweaters, then walked through the shop to the back. Party dresses and gowns hung on both sides of the room. The customer Leila had been helping must have gone into a dressing room because she was nowhere in sight.

"Carrie!" Leila said, sounding both surprised and happy to see me. "What brings you to Trendy Elegance?"

"I need a party dress for tonight. I'm hoping you'll find something I can wear."

She studied me quickly and professionally. "That should be easy enough with your lovely figure. Why don't you look through the sixes and eights over here?" Her arm swept to the left side of the shop. "I shouldn't be too long. My customer is deciding between two outfits."

As though Leila had summoned her, the woman appeared in a navy suit. "This is exactly what I wanted, but it seems so boring after the dress."

"I agree. The dress is lively. Sexy." Leila smiled, her eyes twinkling with mischief. "Your husband will love it. So will your daughter."

When the woman sent her a worried glance, Leila added. "And if she doesn't, you can always bring it back and exchange it for the suit, which is certainly more sedate."

The woman wrinkled her nose. "Sedate! I'll take the dress."

"Wonderful! Would you like to try it on again, or shall I ring it up for you?"

"Ring it up, please."

I skimmed through the rack of party dresses, shocked by their cost. The least expensive was over five hundred dollars. Leila, her customer's dress draped over her arm, must have read my expression, because she burst out laughing.

"Why don't you check out the dresses on sale? The smaller sizes don't go as quickly as the larger ones." Her grin grew larger. "And today we've increased the discount to fifty percent off."

She left to complete her customer's purchase, and I turned to the sales rack. Three dresses immediately caught my eye. One was a slinky black number; another, a mauve and purple print with gold metallic highlights; and the third was a deep violet with a sweetheart neck and a lovely draping skirt.

"Good choices," Leila said when she returned and saw what I'd selected. "Why don't you try them on, and we'll see which suits you the best."

In the dressing room, I hummed as I stripped to my bra and panties, then reached for the black party dress. I wasn't crazy about clothes shopping, but today I was enjoying myself. This was, I realized, largely due to Leila's warm and breezy assistance. I slipped on the black high-heeled slingbacks left in the room for exactly this purpose and stepped in front of the three-part mirror.

Leila scrutinized me from head to toe and had me turn around. "Elegant, and it fits you like a glove."

"But?" I said.

"Too formal. Too sophisticated. No fun is what I mean," she added quickly when she saw that I'd taken her comment as a criticism. "Let's see how the mauve print looks. By the way, what's the occasion for the new dress?"

"I'm going to a dinner dance at the country club," I told her from the dressing room. "It's a fundraiser for Haven House. A house is being renovated and turned into a center where the homeless can spend their days."

"Fred and I are going too."

"You are?" I poked my head out.

"Yes. His sister-in-law asked us to come. We thought it was a good cause, so Fred told her we would be there."

I exited the fitting room in the second dress.

"Stunning!" was Leila's reaction after I'd spun around and she'd finished scrutinizing me.

"You don't think it's a little—drab?" I asked.

"You can carry it off, especially after you've put on makeup."

"I don't use much makeup," I said, frowning. "Maybe I'll wear the outfit I have, after all."

"Isn't that what you were planning all along?" Leila asked.

"What do you mean?" I felt my cheeks grow warm.

"I think you came here to ask me questions about Fred—and Dorothy."

"Maybe I did," I admitted. "But how did you guess?"

"Carrie, dear, Clover Ridge is a small town. Everyone knows you've helped solve mysteries and murders, and Dorothy was a colleague of yours. You're our own Nancy Drew."

I gaped at her. "Is that what people are calling me?"

Leila shrugged. "One or two. Don't be offended. It's not an insult, you know."

"I would like to ask you something, now that you mention it," I said.

Leila gestured to the loveseat in the corner. "Fire away. Of course, I don't know how much I can help you. Fred and I were out of touch for years. We only reconnected after Dorothy's death."

When we were both seated, I said, "Dorothy offended people left and right. And the police have a list of people she was blackmailing, so there's no shortage of suspects."

"Including Fred and me," Leila said, suddenly solemn. "The sooner the mystery of her death is cleared up, the sooner we can marry."

So that's why you're so willing to talk to me. "I was wondering if Dorothy ever told Fred that she was afraid of someone."

"You mean aside from insisting that Fred attacked her?" Leila said sarcastically. "Let me think."

"Was she afraid of Ernie Pfeiffer? Did she think he would retaliate because she tried to sue him more than once?" *As well as blackmailing him.*

"I don't think so. According to Fred, Dorothy didn't spend much time worrying about what people thought of her. Except for her Aunt Evelyn, of course, but Evelyn's dead."

"Yes, she loved her aunt and respected her opinion."

After a minute, Leila said, "Believe it or not, she seemed very upset after an argument with her sister, Frances—Francesca, I suppose I should say. Fred's not even sure what the argument was about. Money, he thought, but Dorothy refused to go into details. She did say her sister was as sneaky and treacherous as they come. She had this flighty, airy manner that masked a manipulative, scheming mind. Even when they were children, she managed to make Dorothy look like the bad one and got her way with their parents."

"Very interesting," I said. "Did Fred say when this argument took place?"

"A week or so before Dorothy's accident at the supermarket. And they argued another time when Dorothy was home from work. It was after that fight that she decided she'd had enough of staying home and was going back to work the following morning."

"Really?" I said. "Did Fred mention this to the police?"

"I doubt it," Leila said. "It's all conjecture, as they put it, isn't it? Fred had no idea what they were arguing about. And it's difficult to imagine that Frances—er, Francesca—was capable of killing her sister, and in such a brutal way."

"Still," I began.

"Why don't you try on the violet dress? Maybe that will suit you best of all."

I changed into dress number three and zipped it up. The moment I saw myself in the mirror, I knew this was it! My first thought was that it was a shame Dylan wouldn't see me in it when I wore it tonight. With that in mind, I took a selfie and sent it off to him, then left the dressing room to get Leila's opinion.

"This is it!" she exclaimed. "Perfect fit, perfect length."

I peered at the flattering neckline, the slenderizing bodice and flouncy, feminine skirt that suited me in every way. "And I already have the perfect shoes!" I exclaimed. "And jewelry."

Even with the discount, the dress cost three hundred and fifty dollars. But it was worth it, I thought as I put on my yoga pants and T-shirt. I walked behind Leila as she carried my dress to the cash register at the front of the store, as she had for the previous customer.

"We thank you for shopping at Trendy Elegance," she said when I handed over my charge card. With a wink, she added, "Fred and I look forward to seeing you tonight."

Chapter Twenty-Three

I hummed as I drove to the Clover Ridge Country Club. In my new party dress and favorite black strappy spiked heels, I looked pretty darn good, if I had to say so myself. For once, I'd fussed with my hair, brushed on some blush and eye shadow, and mascara'd my eyelashes. I wished Dylan were there at my side. Still, I found myself looking forward to the evening.

One of the young valets drove my car off to the parking lot while another held open the clubhouse door. I entered the elegant lobby, glittering under the blaze of its two chandeliers. As soon as Gillian spotted me, she leaped up from the sofa where she'd been waiting to join me. I handed my jacket to the woman working the coat room and slipped the ticket into my tiny pocketbook that held nothing more than Dylan's check, a lipstick, my cell phone, my license, and a twenty-dollar bill for emergencies.

"You look great!" Gillian said.

"So do you," I said, admiring her one-shouldered silky black dress that showed off her shapely figure.

We paused in the doorway to have our names checked off and to hand over our hefty entrance fees—mine kindly paid for by Dylan—then strode into the room where waiters were circling with trays of cocktails and hors d'oeuvres. In the far corner, a harpist strummed a gentle tune that served as the perfect background music for the animated conversations around us.

"I've been to two weddings here at the country club, and this is my favorite room," Gillian exclaimed.

"It is beautiful," I agreed, admiring the décor that managed to be both elegant and glitzy at the same time.

Gillian pointed across the room. "Behind that wall of drapes are floor-to-ceiling windows that open onto a terrace with a fantastic view of the mountains."

"What a great place for a summer wedding! No wonder the country club was my friend Angela's first choice—except for the cost, of course."

"I'd love to get married here," Gillian said. "Wouldn't you?"

I was saved from having to respond by a waitress offering us flutes of champagne from her tray. We raised our glasses to each other and sipped.

"Mmm, this is the good stuff," Gillian said.

"Whatever it is, I love it."

"Well, hello, Carrie and Gillian! Don't you both look stunning!"

I turned to see Frances bearing down on us. She wore a gold-colored satin cocktail dress with stiffened pieces of the same fabric jutting out from her shoulders. Was this supposed to be the latest in fashion? To emphasize her importance, she'd placed a sparkling tiara atop her head of fair hair.

"Hello, Frances—er, Francesca." *Did you kill Dorothy?* I wondered, remembering my earlier conversation with Leila.

A good-looking man joined us. "I agree, sister, dear. These are two of the loveliest women in the room—aside from you, of course."

"Roger, hello," I said, suddenly recognizing Dorothy's brother. Standing side by side, the family resemblance was obvious. Francesca was certainly pretty, but Roger's good looks were dazzlingly to the eye. In a photograph with her siblings, poor Dorothy must have looked as plain as one of Cinderella's stepsisters.

"Have we met?" Roger eyed me, a puzzled expression on his face. At last, his eyes lit up in recognition, and he laughed. "I remember now. Carrie from the library. You were at Dorothy's house when we were having one of our rip-roaring fights."

I nodded, but his attention was already on Gillian. "And you are?"

"Gillian Richards."

"Pleased to meet you, Gillian. I'm Roger Camden. Fran-ces-ca's brother." He grinned at his sister to take away the sting of his mocking pronunciation of her self-styled name.

She merely rolled her eyes and murmured, "Stop acting like an ass."

"I'm so sorry for your loss," I said, to see how Dorothy's siblings would react.

Gillian's face turned grave. "I was so sorry to hear about what happened to Dorothy."

"Yes, we're all very sad," Roger said.

"And hoping the police will soon find her murderer," Francesca said. "So far they've come up with zilch."

I couldn't think of an appropriate response, so I said nothing. So did Gillian.

Francesca, who'd been surveying the room, suddenly declared, "Ah, there's Reese! I must talk to her. Catch up with you later." With a wave of her hand, she took off.

"I too will catch up with you later," Roger echoed, fixing his gaze on Gillian.

"God, he's so handsome!" Gillian said, watching him stride off.

"You think? He's also married and has four kids," I said.

"Oh, well. I was just admiring the scenery."

At that moment a waiter appeared before us, bearing baby lamb chops, and our pre-dinner feasting began.

Gillian and I ate and chatted the hour away. The doors to the dining room opened, and we found our seats at a table for eight. Our dining companions were two couples our age and a congenial older couple. Mick and Maureen must have taken dancing lessons, because as soon as they finished their salads, they were up on the dance floor. The other two couples soon followed. Then Roger approached our table and invited Gillian to dance.

Where's his wife? Why isn't she here? I wondered. Finding myself alone, I went to the ladies' room to fill the time. As I was returning to my seat, Fred and Leila called me over to their table. Leila was stunning in a gray chiffon dress, and Fred looked rather handsome in his navy suit.

"Here on your own?" Fred asked.

I explained that Dylan couldn't make the gala, and Gillian was dancing up a storm with his brother-in-law, Roger.

"Ah, Roger," Fred said, shaking his head.

"Where's his wife?" I asked.

"Home, I suppose. They're separated."

"Oh? Was this sudden?"

Fred grimaced. "For years we saw it coming."

"That's too bad."

"It is—for the children. Carrie, would you like to dance?" Fred asked.

I drew in breath. "Sure. Of course."

"Go on," Leila urged. "After all, this is a dinner dance."

"Well, if you don't mind," I said.

Fred and I walked onto the dance floor. The band was playing a fox trot. We fell into step. He led me easily—and smoothly, I soon realized.

"You're a good dancer!" I exclaimed.

"Surprised you, didn't I?" he said with a wink. We danced close to Francesca and Gerald and exchanged smiles with them.

"It's amazing she doesn't stab someone with those weapons," Fred murmured, referring to her shoulder ornamentation as he whirled me around.

A good dancer *and* a sense of humor. I was beginning to realize there was more to Fred Hawkins than I'd first thought.

The beat picked up, and we started bopping up and down with the rest of the crowd. When it slowed down again, Fred said, "Leila told me you came to the shop this morning."

"Yes, I bought this dress."

"Lovely," he said.

"Leila's lovely," I said.

"Yes," Fred said, "we're lucky to have found each other." After a minute, he said, "She told me you asked if Dorothy was afraid of anyone." His eyes peered into mine. All traces of frivolity were gone. "Dorothy was afraid of her siblings. She claimed they hated her."

"Really? Leila said Dorothy and Francesca argued around the time of her death."

"They were always arguing," Fred said, twirling me around. "Growing up, her sister and brother often ganged up on her."

I thought about that. "Wasn't she the oldest?"

"That didn't matter," Fred said. "From the time they were small, Frannie and Roger worked as a team. They quickly learned how to play their parents and get what they wanted. They got the most fun from tormenting Dorothy. They were so sneaky, their parents never caught on. Dorothy acted out and got labeled the troublemaker."

Why didn't Evelyn tell me the truth about Dorothy and her siblings? Was it possible she simply hadn't seen it?

"Do you think they killed Dorothy?" I asked.

"I wouldn't be surprised. I mentioned it to Lieutenant Mathers, but he didn't seem impressed by my theory."

The music stopped and someone announced that our main course was being served. Fred escorted me to my seat.

184

Somehow Roger had managed to wrangle a seat at our table. He sat on the other side of Gillian and regaled her with story after story, sending her into fits of laughter. His hand often came to rest on her arm. When our plates were removed, they were back on the dance floor. *Uh-oh,* I thought. *Gillian's playing with fire.*

After some dancing, the speeches began, and coffee and dessert were served. I decided now would be a good time to leave. I walked over to the dance floor, where Gillian and Roger were swaying to a bittersweet Cole Porter song, and said I was leaving.

"You're going?" Gillian asked, sounding surprised.

"Uh-huh. Good night."

Roger peered down at me and gave me a big smile. "Good night, Carrie. Great seeing you again."

I left the ballroom and headed for the coat room. It was after eleven. I'd done my duty by staying through dinner. I'd even danced. Time to go home. Tomorrow was a workday for me.

As I was putting on my jacket, I saw Francesca and Gerald turn down a hallway. He had his arm around her and seemed to be comforting her. *What could be the matter?* Curious, I waited a moment, then followed them. There were two rooms on either side of the hall, and the door of one of them had just closed.

I put my ear to the door. Francesca was sobbing.

Chapter Twenty-Four

"Relax, Frannie. You're working yourself up into a state," Gerald said, a trace of exasperation in his tone. "And fix your mascara. It's running down your cheek. There's an hour left to this shindig before we can leave."

"Jerry, how can I relax when I just found out what you've gotten involved in?" Francesca asked between gulps. "You said there was nothing to worry about."

"There *is* nothing to worry about. Pat Spalding doesn't know what she's talking about."

"Their lawyer told the Spaldings to pull out of the project. They only came tonight because they'd paid for the tickets, and to warn people. And you can be sure others will follow suit, once they hear it from Pat."

Gerald tried for a laugh. "Everyone knows Pat's a nutcase, Frannie. They'll remember the last time she carried on, claiming the tennis club's treasurer was stealing money. She had to apologize to Nick."

Francesca sniffed. "Maybe, but she says it's because Ernie Pfeiffer's involved."

"Ernie put up his share of the money, just like the rest of us," Gerald said.

"Only it was his idea to start with. I told you not to get involved."

"Frannie, he swore to me this is on the up and up. How do you think we got the money from the state?"

Francesca let out a sound of disbelief. "The man's a crook, Jerry. Did you forget the stunt he pulled on my aunt and uncle? They never recovered all their money they invested in his bogus scheme."

"I promise you, I went over every aspect involving the purchase of Haven House. Didn't the state send us a hefty start-up present?" He laughed. "In fact, I'm hoping to get more from them in the near future."

"Whatever you do, I don't want you to get disbarred. And then where would we be?"

"Shh, Frannie. I know what I'm doing. And in due time I'll run again for mayor, like we planned."

She let out a deep sigh. "I just wish that Ernie Pfeiffer wasn't involved."

"Forget about Ernie. Now give me your hankie, and let me dry your eyes."

"Yes, dear."

I made a beeline out of there and was exiting the front door when the Bennings stepped into the large entrance hall. Arm in arm, they headed for the ballroom. I drove home, deep in thought. Gerald *had* to be lying to Francesca. And how could she not have known about Ernie's plans? But what exactly were his plans? So far I'd heard whispers and rumors. Nothing for certain.

I *had* to find out what Haven House was going to be used for when the homeless people left for the day.

* * *

Sunday was always a busy day at the library because it was a day off for most working people. It was the day many patrons dropped by to pick up or return a book, DVD, or CD. Most Sunday afternoons we presented a program of live music in the meeting room. Today it was a concert of popular music. I knew the room was sure to fill to capacity.

When Evelyn showed up mid-morning, she was eager to hear all about the dinner dance. I began with my visit to the boutique where Leila worked. I took my time because neither Trish nor Susan worked on Sundays, and I was determined to find out what I could about Dorothy's relationship with her siblings. As usual, Evelyn had left out important information about her family that she felt uncomfortable discussing. But everything had to be factored in when solving a murder, especially motives and emotions. It was time she came clean.

"You never mentioned that Dorothy felt threatened by her brother and sister," I said.

Evelyn laughed. "Where did you get that notion?"

"From Fred."

"Oh."

"Did Dorothy hide it from you, or did you decide not to tell me?"

When she didn't respond, I said, "I have to know everything, Evelyn, if I'm going to find out who killed Dorothy."

"Frannie and Roger are younger than Dorothy," Evelyn said, as if she were speaking about young children instead of forty-something adults.

"And you're still trying to protect them."

She looked away from my glare. When she turned back, she wore a shamefaced expression. "I suppose I hoped you'd search in other directions."

"I will, but let's get back to Francesca and Roger, who are now almost middle-aged adults. If they hated Dorothy—have hated her since they were children, in fact—we have to consider that they might have killed her."

Evelyn released a deep sigh. "The truth is, Dorothy reacted badly to the births of her siblings. She didn't like sharing her parents and Robert and me with her brother and sister. I had to scold her when she covered baby Roger's head with a blanket, and the time I caught her pinching five-month-old Frannie. Roger and Frannie joined forces to get back at Dorothy. Once they lured her into the garden shed by telling her that my sister needed her there. They locked her inside for hours. Of course, Dorothy retaliated by destroying some of their favorite toys. Roger and Frannie reacted by ruining some of Dorothy's favorite books. And so it went.

"My sister and brother-in-law tried everything, including therapy, to get the three of them to stop their aggressive behavior, but nothing worked. I think their malicious treatment of one another turned all three kids into selfish individuals. Dorothy grew more secretive and mean. Frannie went after money and prestige. She broke up with the boy she'd loved in high school as soon as Gerald Benning asked her out over Christmas vacation, when he was home from college."

"And Roger?"

"Still as handsome as a movie star?" Evelyn asked.

"Absolutely. He made a big play for Gillian Richards, who came to the dinner dance without a date. I told her he was married with children, but she didn't seem to care. She's smitten."

Evelyn sighed again. "Roger's incorrigible! Women throw themselves at him, and he's not one to say no."

"I suppose that's why he and his wife are separated. Fred told me."

"I'm not surprised. Who could blame Trudy for finally getting fed up enough to throw him out?"

"Roger was at Dorothy and Fred's house the one time I went to see her there. He wanted to borrow money from them so he could join in on one of Ernie Pfeiffer's ventures. Fred was thinking of going in on it too, until Dorothy put her foot down."

Evelyn scowled. "Idiots! Did they forget what that man did to Robert and me?"

189

"It seems Ernie convinced them that this investment was on the up and up. Which I very much doubt if the investment turns out to be Haven House. Though last night Gerald was doing his darnedest to convince Francesca that the Haven House project was A-OK and that he wasn't doing anything illegal."

Evelyn shook her head in disgust. "I wouldn't trust that Gerald one bit. He'll do anything for money. And he's a social climber. So ashamed that his father owned a shoe repair shop."

"He's a lawyer and the person spearheading this project. Whatever illegal plans they have for Haven House, I bet Gerald Benning's in as deep as Ernie Pfeiffer."

Evelyn tsk-tsked. "My sister and I were brought up to be forthright and honest. How did her children turn out this way?

"How does Roger earn his money?" I asked. "I suppose most of what he makes goes to support his four children."

Evelyn let out a snort. "Roger is a brilliant mathematician, but he got it into his head that he needn't work hard to get somewhere in life. He never keeps a job for long—poor attendance will do that. Another reason Trudy must have called it quits. Good thing she has her job. It's what puts food on the table."

Evelyn was silent for a moment; then she giggled. "The only thing he was good at was being an escort. Of course that was before he and Trudy married."

"An escort? You mean—?" I burst out laughing. "Are you telling me that before he married Trudy, Roger was a gigolo?"

"Well, he escorted rich older women around, and they provided him with funds," Evelyn said stiffly now that I was in on the joke.

"A gigolo! Roger was a gigolo?" I said between gales of laughter. "I suppose."

"A gigolo," I repeated as tears streamed down my cheeks.

"It isn't very funny when the person's a member of your family," Evelyn said reprovingly.

She evaporated in a flurry of irritation. I shouldn't have laughed so much at her latest revelation, but Evelyn was at fault too. She'd agreed to pool everything we knew that might help solve Dorothy's murder. Yet once again she'd withheld important information, this time for the sake of protecting her niece and nephew.

Were all families—when viewed objectively—dysfunctional in their own unique way? After helping to solve a few murders in the recent past, I was beginning to think this was the case. For many years, I'd felt that my brother and I were the only kids in the neighborhood who were growing up in a family so very different from the norm. Our father was a thief. Jim spent most of his time away from home, which was probably why our mother finally divorced him. Not that she was warm, cuddly, or maternal. A few years ago she'd married Tom Farrell, an actor years younger than her, and changed both her first *and* last name. I supposed she thought Brianna was more exotic than Linda.

Though Tom wasn't a well-known actor, they'd gone to live in Hollywood, where he got bit parts in movies. Last year, when I was at my lowest and had asked if I could stay with them awhile, my mother had claimed they didn't have room for me. Which was how I had come to stay with Great-Aunt Harriet and Great-Uncle Bosco in the town where my father's family had owned a farm for generations.

Enough! I told myself. I was in a good place in more ways than one. I had a job I loved, a man I adored, and people who cared about me. I was grounded, and my father was now gainfully employed. As for my mother . . . I'd send her an email one of these days. My brother, Jordan, whom I'd adored—the one person I could count on growing up—had died in a car accident when he was twenty-three and I was nineteen. I still missed him terribly.

I turned my thoughts back to what Evelyn had just shared with me. Her niece and nephews—I included Gerald and Fred—were not model citizens, but that didn't mean they were murderers. And Evelyn had a point. I couldn't limit my research to just Dorothy's relations. There were other people who had wanted to see her dead.

Chapter Twenty-Five

I got some busy work done, ate a quick lunch alone at the Cozy Corner Café (since Angela was off today), then walked back to the library, intent on finally talking to Sally about Dorothy. I found her in her office. She was in a good mood and quick to sing Norman Tobin's praises.

"I think he'll be a big asset to our library, Carrie. He has all sorts of innovative ideas—like Kanopy, which can provide another source of electronic downloads to our patrons."

"I suppose he'll have to work with Harvey Kirk on that," I said.

Sally waved her hand dismissively. "No problem. Norman told me he enjoys working with colleagues. And while I don't mean to be sexist or genderist, if there's such a word, I like the idea of there being another male librarian in the building."

"Do you think Harvey will agree?"

Sally shot me a questioning glance. "Why should Harvey have a problem with someone wanting to update our system?"

"Because up until now he's been in charge of everything electronic."

She thought a moment before saying, "Harvey sometimes comes across as a bit gruff, but I've always found him to be reasonable. I'm sure he and Norman will get along just fine."

"I'm sure you're right. Sally, I'd like to talk to you—about something else."

Sally sank back in her chair. "You mean Dorothy."

I nodded. "Yes, Dorothy. I was the person who found the sheet of paper with the list of people she'd been blackmailing."

Sally frowned. "I figured it was you. Who else would go sniffing around her desk after the police were done searching for clues?"

"I suspected it long before. I'd heard rumors, and I got the feeling that she was pressuring you to give her my job when Barbara left and it became available."

"Only I gave it to you, didn't I?" she said.

"Not willingly," I reminded her.

Sally let out a bark of a laugh. "You're like a dog with a bone, Carrie. So tenacious. So determined. I suppose that's what makes you good at what you do."

"You mean being head of programs and events or helping the police solve murders?"

This time her laughter was genuine. "Both, I suppose."

"I wish you'd tell me what she tried to hold over you. I won't tell anyone," I said softly.

"I know. But every time I think of it I feel stupid—and ashamed."

I waited for Sally to gather her thoughts.

"I was new at the time—when she got her claws into me," Sally continued. "I'd had experience being a librarian, even overseeing the staff, but I hadn't had much experience with the financial side of things. I'd no sooner become director of the Clover Ridge Library than I had to present the yearly budget to the board. The previous director had left things in a mess. Her notes were a jumble. One of the aides said she used to help the director finalize the annual budget and even managed some of the other accounts. She offered to do the same for me. In return, she wanted a raise in salary. I thought she was being high-handed and presumptuous. I was insulted that she assumed she could handle me because I was young and new at the job, so I told her I could do very well without her."

Oh, Evelyn! You got off on the wrong foot with Sally. Was this after Ernie Pfeiffer had managed to lose your savings, and you were desperate for money?

Sally drew a deep breath. "I should have taken her up on her offer or asked one of the librarians to help me, because I made my own mess of things. I left out expenses I should have included, then added in more expenses than I should have." She sighed. "I made the mistake of telling this to Dorothy. We'd become friends, and I thought I could trust her because she acted friendly and concerned. Until one day she wanted to change her schedule and take a day off. I couldn't do it easily and told her so. That's when she asked if I wanted her to tell the board what I'd done to pocket some money for myself. I caved and gave her the day off. Shortly after that, she asked for money. I gave her that too."

"But you offered me the position of head of P and E, even though you knew she wanted it."

Sally smiled. "So I did. For one thing, your Uncle Bosco's on the library board. When he asked me to consider you for the job, I knew I had to. And since *you* had the right qualifications, I offered the job to you and not to Dorothy"

"So Uncle Bosco didn't *make* you give me the position."

"Of course not. How could he?"

"But you seemed so—unhappy when you offered me the job."

"I was. I resented his having asked me to consider you when I had serious doubts about Goth Girl."

I laughed, remembering how I used to look when I temped as an aide in the library—purple hair, Doc Martens, dressed all in black.

"I gave you the job and finally told Dorothy off. I'd decided I wasn't going to go on as director of this library living under the fear of her threats. I figured that if she went ahead and told them I'd embezzled funds, which wasn't true, the board knew me well enough to hear my side of the story. And by then I had a written account of every penny spent in the library since I'd started as director."

"So she had nothing more to hold over you," I said. "Then what were you arguing about the day before she was murdered?"

Sally grimaced. "I don't know why it took me so long, but after I shook myself free of her threats, I realized that Dorothy must have done the same to other people, probably people I know. And sure enough, after her first accident—falling down or being pushed down outside the supermarket—I ran into Lillian Morris, who used to work here and had been a friend of Dorothy's. When I told her Dorothy was laid up after a fall, the woman said, 'It couldn't have happened to a nicer person.' I asked her what she meant, and she told me that she had once told Dorothy about a petty crime she'd committed. Dorothy had demanded money from her and threatened to tell the head of the library at the time. Lillian said she'd paid up but warned Dorothy she wouldn't again, and Dorothy never bothered her again.

"When Dorothy came back to work, I told her I knew what she'd been doing. She merely laughed and asked how I planned to stop her. I said I'd go to the police. She stormed out of my office. That was the last time I ever saw her."

I nodded, trying to take it all in. "Did you tell this to John Mathers?"

"I did. John asked me if I recognized certain initials, and I was able to help him with a few—with people who once worked here and former friends of Dorothy's."

"Harvey Kirk was one of Dorothy's victims," I said. "What on earth did Harvey do? Play computer games when he should have been helping patrons?"

"Harvey's a compulsive gambler. Sports are his downfall, especially football. He's lost a lot of money over the years. He's gone into debt. His wife left him."

"I had no idea," I said. "Do you know what Dorothy was holding over him?"

"I'd rather not say, Carrie. It's not my secret to share."

I nodded. "Fair enough."

I headed back to my office, wondering if anything Sally had told me shed new light on Dorothy's murder. Or murderer.

"Harvey often gambles online when he should be working," Evelyn said, suddenly manifesting at my side. "Dorothy found out and started looking up online gambling sites. When his name appeared as a big winner, she decided to add him to her list."

"Thank you," I murmured as someone called out my name.

I looked up. Doris Maris was waving to me from a chair in the reading room. I hurried over to her, feeling a bit guilty. I'd been so busy, I hadn't had a chance to speak to her in the past few days.

"I wanted to thank you for asking your uncle to look into a facility for Henry. He's settled in nicely, and they're taking good care of him."

I squeezed her hand. "I'm so glad."

"It's such a relief not to be worrying about him."

"And what about you? How are you doing?"

Doris sighed. "I'm managing. The good thing is, the shelter has hired a counselor to place us in permanent homes." She gestured to the woman sitting across from her. "Now that Henry's being cared for in his residence, Shondra and I are hoping to share an apartment in the spring."

I smiled at the woman, who glowered back at me. I hoped Doris wasn't making a mistake, planning to room with someone so angry.

"We'll have to share a bedroom, but I suppose we're not in a position to ask for more," Shondra said.

Doris touched Shondra's arm. "Not to worry. We'll work it out."
Shondra seemed to soften before my eyes. "I know."

"And they want us to work at least fifteen hours a week," Doris
said. "As long as it's not in a factory, I look forward to having a job."

Shondra sent her a cocky smile. "You'll do fine, Doris, wherever
they place us. And we'll have plenty of time to watch our TV shows."

"Or we can spend time in Haven House when we're free," Doris
said. "This is the best thing that's happened to us. It's the reason
why we now have Mary, our counselor. She'll also be working in
Haven House, once the renovations are completed.

I chatted with them a few minutes longer, then wished them
well and left. I was happy that Henry was being cared for and that
Doris would soon be leaving the shelter. Haven House was such a
marvelous venture. I wished that providing the homeless a place to
spend their days were its only purpose. With all the rumors and
innuendoes about the place, it was time I did some actual digging
to see what facts I could unearth about the project.

Chapter Twenty-Six

Ken Talbot sounded happy to hear from me when I called him Monday morning.

"I'm glad I found you in the office," I told him. "Are you free for lunch today? My treat."

"Turns out I'm free at noon for an hour or so. To what do I owe this honor and pleasure?"

"I want to pick your brain, but I can't afford your lawyerly rates."

Ken laughed. "Carrie, dear, you're always free to pick my brain. Tell you what—I'll come by the library for you at noon and whisk you away to one of my favorite restaurants, but only if you agree to be my guest."

"How can I refuse the best offer I've gotten all day?"

Hours later I stepped into Ken's low-slung Porsche and clicked on my seat belt. "Where are we off to?"

"A cozy Asian restaurant that serves everything from Thai to sashimi. Adam and I go there at least once a week."

"Sounds good to me."

We chatted about the people we knew in common—the Foster family and Ken's college roommate, George—until he turned into the parking area of a strip mall of shops. I spotted the restaurant immediately.

"Asian Fusion! I've heard about it. My friend Angela loves this place."

"Well, if you love it, you can ask Dylan to bring you back here for dinner." He cocked his head. "If you guys are still dating."

"We sure are," I said, climbing out of the car. "Dylan's still involved in a case for his old boss. He's opening up an office in New Haven in the near future—as a partner in the agency."

"Good for him and good to know," Ken said as we walked toward the restaurant's entrance. "Sometimes I need an investigator to check out a few places or people."

The host, a smiling Chinese gentleman in his sixties, led us to the only empty booth in the place, which was off by itself in a corner. All the tables were occupied as well.

"I asked for this booth so we can talk about whatever you like," Ken said.

I slid onto the cushioned seat and stripped open the paper covering on the wooden chopsticks. "I like it here," I said, admiring the red and gold Asian décor and figures set on black walls.

"You'll like the menu even more," Ken said.

The menu was so extensive and appealing, it took me awhile to choose what to eat. I finally settled on an avocado salad and negimaki—strips of marinated beef rolled around scallions. Ken ordered soup and an order of sashimi. The young waitress, who spoke little English, brought us tea. I sipped, feeling both energized and relaxed.

"So," Ken said, "what's on your mind? Does it have anything to do with Dorothy Hawkins's murder?"

I smiled at his keen observation. "I couldn't say—though, oddly enough, some of the people I want to talk to you about are related to Dorothy."

I told Ken about Haven House and how I'd gotten involved in the project.

"I heard that a few people in town planned to turn that run-down house around the corner from your aunt and uncle's place into a center for the homeless."

"That's right. They bought the house at a rock-bottom price and got some start-up funds from the state. They're raising money through fundraisers, like the dinner dance I went to this past weekend."

"Interesting," Ken said, munching on a few dried noodles our waiter had placed on the table.

"Remember Gillian Richards, who used to date Ryan Foster? She's working as a volunteer for the project—same as me."

"Gillian Richards," Ken echoed. "Nice girl. The best thing that happened to Ryan in years. I'm not surprised she broke up with him. Ryan has yet to learn to control his temper and to keep a job. Right now he's in Florida, working in a restaurant."

"I'm fond of Gillian," I said, "but she has no sense when it comes to men. Ryan was bad enough, but this past Saturday night she spent the evening dancing and making goo-goo eyes at Roger Camden. She couldn't have cared less when I told her he has four kids and was just separated from his wife."

"Roger Camden," Ken said slowly. "Why do I know that name?"

"Did you ever represent him?"

"No, I don't think so."

"He's Dorothy Hawkins's brother. Lives in the area."

"Of course! Jerry Benning's brother-in-law. A good looking guy. Smooth talker. Isn't he kind of old for Gillian?"

"I'd say. So you know Gerald."

"I know every lawyer in and around Clover Ridge. Benning and I run into each other in court and other places."

The waitress brought my salad and Ken's appetizer. We picked up our chopsticks and started eating.

"Gerald Benning's one of the main proponents of Haven House. So is Ernie Pfeiffer," I said between bites.

Ken laughed. "I'd never have figured on those two working together. Pfeiffer's as crooked as they come. Hard to believe he'd shell out money to help the homeless unless he has an ulterior motive."

"The homeless will only be at Haven House during daytime hours. I heard Ernie and his crew intend to use the building for high-stakes card games and parties."

"That doesn't sound like Benning," Ken said. "For all his faults, I've never known him to do something illegal. Basically, he follows the straight and narrow—from the way he dresses to his politics."

"Tell me about his faults," I said.

"I don't like the man, so whatever I say is tainted by my sentiments," Ken said.

"Maybe you don't like him because of what you know about him."

"He's a snob and a social climber, and he's driven to make his mark. Any controversy in Clover Ridge, he makes his voice heard at every town hall meeting. I don't think he really cares what he's promoting as long as people notice and ask him to represent them. Benning's out to make a name for himself. He ran for mayor a few years back but never got anywhere."

I chewed on a mouthful of avocado and lettuce as I thought. "I'd like to know how Ernie Pfeiffer plans to use Haven House once the homeless leave for the day."

Ken sent me one of his stern lawyerly looks. "Carrie, I know what a curious mind you have, but I'm advising you—don't get involved. Tell John Mathers what you've heard, and let him handle it. For all you know, he's aware of Pfeiffer's plans. But plans mean nothing. Keep in mind, John can't do anything until these shenanigans actually take place. It will be months before the renovations are complete and Haven House opens for business. Right now it's in pretty bad shape."

"Okay," I said, trying to sound meek.

Ken didn't fall for it. "I'm serious, Carrie. It's fine to talk to me about this, but don't go around questioning people involved in Haven House. Ernie has his spies. You don't want to make the man your enemy."

I shuddered. "What do you mean?"

Ken's expression grew more solemn. "A few people who complained about losing money via one of his get-rich schemes were sorry they did. One man's car was damaged; someone else's garden shed was set on fire. They soon got the message."

"I had no idea he'd go that far," I said.

Ken smiled. "There's nothing for you to worry about as long as you don't go around asking questions about Pfeiffer or Haven House. I'm not saying be an ostrich and bury your head and your concerns in the sand, but tell John what you suspect and leave the detecting to the police. Ah, here comes our waitress with our main course."

Ken's warning had frightened me, as he'd meant it to, but I was too hungry not to pay my lunch the attention it deserved. My beef dish was delicious. I offered a piece to Ken, and he gave me a piece of salmon sashimi, which was excellent too. When Dylan came home for good, this was one of the first restaurants I wanted us to visit.

Ken asked me if any progress had been made regarding Dorothy's murder investigation.

"Nothing, really, though they found a list of people she'd been blackmailing for money. Ernie Pfeiffer may very well have been on that list," I said.

"Really?" Ken chuckled. "There were many things you could say about Dorothy, but she sure had plenty of nerve."

"She used the money she'd extorted to add to her vase collection. I happened to see them when I visited her after her fall."

"A vase collection, eh? We all have our weaknesses."

"What's yours?" I asked.

"Buying good wine," he answered quickly. "I find I spend hours perusing wine reviews before I order a case."

We finished our meal and drove back to the library. I thanked Ken profusely for the lovely lunch.

He reached over to kiss my cheek. "My pleasure, Carrie. I'll do a little checking and let you know what I can find out about Haven House."

"Thank you. Give Adam and George my best," I said, referring to Ken's partner and his former college roommate. I'd gotten to know George Ruskin when I helped his nephew, Jared Foster, solve his mother's murder.

"Will do." He drove off, and I entered the library.

I had difficulty concentrating on work that afternoon because Ernie Pfeiffer kept intruding on my thoughts. If he'd destroyed a car and a garden shed in retaliation, who was to say he hadn't gone further and murdered Evelyn and Dorothy? I'd been naive to think I could go up against a lowlife like him. I appreciated Ken's advice to keep out of it. Still, it irked me that Ernie Pfeiffer could use a worthwhile project like Haven House for his own moneymaking scheme that could very well close the day program before it even got off the ground.

I wanted to speak to someone who might know what was actually going on before I called John to tell him what I'd heard. I couldn't very well call Francesca, her husband, or her brother, but perhaps Fred would give me an honest answer.

I called Trendy Elegance and asked to speak to Leila.

"Hello, Carrie. What a pleasant surprise to hear from you."

"Hi, Leila. Could you please give me Fred's cell number? I figured he's at work, and I was hoping to reach him between customers."

"Of course, dear." She rattled off the number. "Did you have a good time Saturday night? Fred and I danced until midnight, when the party ended."

"I would have had a better time if my boyfriend, Dylan, had been there. But I'm glad I got to dance with Fred. He's quite a good dancer."

"You looked stunning in your new dress. I hope you'll keep Trendy Elegance in mind when you want to buy another cocktail dress."

"Of course. As long as you promise to take care of me."

After hanging up with Leila, I called Fred. To my relief, he answered.

"Hi, Fred, it's Carrie."

"Hello, Carrie. Anything the matter?"

"Well—actually, there might be." I decided to play the innocent, concerned volunteer. "I'm kind of upset about something, and I'm hoping you can give me some information and advice."

"I'll try. What's troubling you?"

"You know I'm a volunteer for the Haven House project. I'm sort of the liaison for the library. We're especially interested in this going through because some of the homeless stay in the library day after day, and there are occasional incidents and disruptions."

"Uh-huh. So I've heard."

I cleared my throat. "There are rumors that Haven House is only a front for some people to make money on the fundraisers, and there are plans to use the place for high-stakes card games and parties at night."

"I've heard the same stories, Carrie."

Was it my imagination, or had his tone turned cold?

"Are they true?"

"I've no idea. Why are you asking me?"

"Isn't your brother-in-law one of the people who spearheaded the project?"

"He is, and I advise you to ask Gerald your questions. I have to go now."

He disconnected. I stared at the phone, shocked by his reaction to my questions. I'd always found Fred to be friendly and easygoing. Was that all an act, or was he now wishing he'd never gotten involved with the likes of Ernie Pfeiffer and was now as frightened as I was beginning to be?

One thing was certain: I never should have called him. I remembered how eager he'd been, telling Dorothy he wanted to be part of Ernie's latest venture, which Dorothy had shot down as soon as he'd mentioned it. That venture had to be Haven House. What a fool I'd been! Of course that was why he and Leila had been at the dinner dance on Saturday night! They were part of the group that had invested in Haven House and expected to benefit from whatever Ernie was planning.

Chapter Twenty-Seven

Sally asked Marion, Harvey, Gayle, and me to join her in the conference room at three o'clock to meet Norman Tobin. He was a nice-looking, slender man, about five eight, with a winning smile and a good sense of humor—both positives in my book. Sally told us about his work background, then introduced each of us with a sentence or two. I beamed when she called me spunky and enterprising. Norman shook my hand and said he looked forward to working with me. Everyone seemed to like him. I was especially glad to see him having an animated conversation with Harvey—until Harvey happened to look my way, and his pleasant demeanor changed to a glower.

As we sipped coffee or tea and noshed on the petit fours Sally had brought in for the occasion, I mused that lately my detecting skills were failing me. Instead of learning anything helpful regarding Dorothy's murder and Haven House from the people I'd spoken to, I'd only managed to offend each and every one of them.

It was snowing lightly when I started for home. I'd been berating myself all afternoon for having alerted Fred Hawkins regarding my concerns about Haven House. How could I have forgotten he was a suspect in Dorothy's murder? That he'd been eager to put up money to join one of Ernie Pfeiffer's schemes? I promised myself I'd call John that evening and tell him everything I'd been up to.

The roads were slippery and turning icy. I drove slowly, hoping I wouldn't slide into a skid. The weather was affecting Smoky Joe. He couldn't settle down inside his carrier. He kept changing positions and meowing his discomfort.

"We'll be home soon," I told him, "and I'll feed you the minute we walk through the door."

He finally grew calm and closed his eyes.

The cottage felt cold when I walked inside. That was odd because I knew I'd left the heat on. I switched on lights and felt a rush of air as I walked past the kitchen. I gasped. The side door was wide open. Snow was blowing into the house because the heavy glass vase I kept on the living room table had been jammed against the open door to prevent it from slamming shut.

Someone had broken into my cottage!

I picked up the vase, slammed the door shut and locked it. I looked around. Nothing seemed out of place.

I have to change the locks!

I have to call John!

I shivered. *What if whoever broke in is still in the cottage?*

I retched and rushed to the bathroom but didn't throw up. I gulped down mouthfuls of water from the faucet. Smoky Joe came over to find out why I wasn't feeding him his dinner. I picked him up and held him close. I must have squeezed him too tightly, because he began to struggle free.

Who did this? Someone that knows how to open locked doors. Or someone who knows someone that knows how to open locked doors. There were too many possibilities. Fred could have done it. Or he might have told his sister-in-law, who told her husband, who told Ernie Pfeiffer. Ernie would know someone. Or was it Leila? Maybe Harvey Kirk? I remembered how he'd glared at me that afternoon.

My hands trembled as I fed Smoky Joe. While he was chowing down, I checked out the rest of the rooms. I gasped when I entered my office. A note had been placed on my computer. I approached it slowly, dreading what I was about to read.

"STAY AWAY OR . . ."

Beneath it was a crude drawing of a cat lying on its side with a noose around its neck.

I called John and left a message on his cell phone. He called back minutes later when I was nursing a cup of hot tea.

"Are you all right, Carrie?"

"Yes—I don't know. Someone broke into my house and propped open the side door with a heavy vase. They left a note warning me to stay away or—" I began to hyperventilate. Between breaths I said, "they would kill Smoky Joe."

"I'm coming right over. Don't let anyone in."

As if I would. Minutes later, I heard the doorbell and went to let John in.

"Is anything missing? Damaged?" he asked.

I shook my head. "No."

"Where's the note?"

"I left it on top of my computer. I didn't touch it."

John followed me into my office. "Good thinking. In case the perp left fingerprints."

He pulled on a pair of rubber gloves and placed the note in a plastic bag. Then he walked through the cottage, examining windows, opening closets.

"And you didn't leave the side door unlocked?" he asked.

"Of course not" I scoffed. "Why would I?"

John opened the front door and then the side door, using his flashlight to scrutinize the locks and the hinges. "No sign of any damage, though some thieves know how to open a locked door with the simplest of tools," he mumbled as he worked.

"Not very reassuring," I grumbled.

"Still, I think you should tell Dylan to put in a security system."

"We've talked about it," I said, remembering that the last person who had broken into the cottage had been my father.

Finally, John sank into a kitchen chair and stretched out his long legs. "The way I see it, you've been given a warning. You pissed someone off. That person wants you to know he can get to you in your home anytime he likes and do away with your cat—or worse. He or she, I should say. Equal opportunity."

I shivered. "I will definitely have a security system installed."

"Good idea," John said. "Are you all right, Carrie?"

"No, but I feel better now that you're here."

"Are you up to staying here, or do you want to spend the night at a friend's?"

"I'll be okay here."

"I think the person who broke in made his point. So, who did you piss off recently?"

"I guess a few people." I drew a deep breath and told him about my conversations with Lillian Morris, Sally, and Harvey regarding Dorothy's murder and with Gillian, Ken, and Fred regarding Haven House. I also told him about the conversation I'd overheard between the Bennings.

By the time I'd finished, he looked even sterner than Ken had earlier. "You've been a busy gal. It's remarkable you've found time to squeeze in your work-related responsibilities."

I felt my cheeks grow warm.

"Ken's right. You're in over your head regarding the homicide investigation and Pfeiffer's alternate agenda for Haven House. I'm well aware of what he's planning, but as Ken said, there's not much I can do at this point."

"What can I do to help? I want the homeless who camp out at the library to have a sanctuary like Haven House."

"Continue to go to meetings for the project. Just don't ask the type of questions you asked Fred Hawkins today. And for God's sake, don't interrogate your colleagues about their motives for wanting Dorothy dead. You're too smart to put yourself in harm's way like that."

"I won't."

John put an arm around me. "Your Uncle Bosco would have my head if anything were to happen to you. Not to mention your boyfriend and your father."

I gave him a bittersweet smile. "They would know better than to blame you for anything dumb that I do."

John took off, leaving me considerably calmer. I heated up a can of tomato soup and ate it along with a grilled cheese sandwich. Comfort food. I called Dylan and told him about my day, all of it. I dreaded another tongue-lashing, but I needed to share every important aspect of my life with the man I loved.

When I'd finished, he said, "Carrie, you're important to too many people for you to be so careless with your life."

That got to me more than anything John and Ken had said. "I'll be careful," I promised.

"Good, because I love you. I'll call Jack tomorrow to hire someone to install a security system ASAP."

* * *

Despite the break-in and the threatening note, I couldn't stop thinking about Dorothy, Evelyn, the homeless people in town, and Haven House. They were all part of my life. They impacted my life. I felt a responsibility to do what I could to identify Dorothy and possibly Evelyn's killer. I felt obliged to learn what I could about Haven House. Part of that was finding out who was in on Ernie Pfeiffer's crooked plans. And I had to move cautiously and surreptitiously. John and Dylan were right. No more asking questions.

Whoever had broken into my cottage had to believe I was heeding his or her warning.

Tuesday was a late day for me. I appreciated having a schedule that gave me a few free mornings to do my food shopping and run errands instead of doing these on weekends, when the stores were crowded.

It also gave me an opportunity to make one official check-up to satisfy my curiosity. I wanted to know who besides Gerald Benning and Ernie Pfeiffer were listed as owners or buyers of Haven House. Would I find Fred's name on the list? Roger's? I was almost certain that Haven House was the project Ernie had tried to get them to invest in, the project that Dorothy had so vehemently opposed.

Could her refusal to support the project have been the reason she'd been murdered?

Town Hall was located around the corner from the library, a block and a half past the Cozy Corner Café. I parked in the lot behind the two-story building. Though it wasn't situated on the Green—our unofficial town center—and wasn't centuries old like the library and other buildings surrounding it, Town Hall had been built in the same white, wooden-framed, simple New England style. I remained vigilant, making sure that no one was watching me as I exited my car and climbed the few steps to the back entrance of the building. I followed the narrow corridor to the front of Town Hall and approached the high counter. A woman sat at a desk, speaking on a phone. When she finished her conversation, she asked how she could help me.

"I'd like to look up something in the records room—the documents regarding the sale of a house that was recently sold here in Clover Ridge. I understand sales become public record for anyone to see."

"As long as the sale has been completed, you're free to check it out."

"It has been."

She spun around in her chair to face the inner offices. "Bridey, would you please come out here?" she called. "There's a visitor who needs your assistance."

A petite, hunched-over woman who looked to be well in her eighties appeared.

"She'd like to view documents for the recent sale of a house here in Clover Ridge."

"Certainly. Follow me. After you sign the book, I'll direct you to the documents you want to see."

Sign the book! I hadn't thought of that. I considered leaving, then decided to use a fake name. After the cottage break-in, I couldn't risk the chance that someone involved in Haven House might see I'd been checking out home sales in Town Hall.

I scribbled a made-up name and address as quickly as I could, glad that there was only space for one other name beneath mine before the page would be turned.

"Thank you!" Bridey said, lifting the large ledger and putting it away. "And sign this too, saying you won't take any papers with you when you leave this room."

"Of course."

I took the form she handed me and signed it.

"Come with me. Do you know the address of the residence? The date the sale went through?"

"I'm not sure of the date—some time in the past month, I believe—but I have the address: 27 Garrett Street."

"That should be enough."

I followed Bridey into the adjoining room. Tall filing cabinets that almost skimmed the ceiling lined all four walls. There was a table and chair in the center of the room. Bridey stood before one of the cabinets and pulled open a drawer. "Garrett Street. Garrett Street," she mumbled. "Here it is."

She lifted out a folder and glanced through it. "I don't know what you're after, but there's not much here." She set it on the table and left.

I opened the folder. There was the contract for the purchase of the single-family dwelling at 27 Garrett Street for the sum of two hundred and fifty thousand dollars. Not a lot of money for a house only blocks from the Green. But I'd driven by and had seen the terrible run-down condition it was in. I didn't recognize the seller's name. And the buyer's name—oh no! All it said was Lennox Incorporated. I almost tore the document in my eagerness to check out the signatures on the last page.

The name scrawled beside Lennox Incorporated was indecipherable, and there was no printed name beneath it.

"That proves it!" I said, slamming down the contract. A bogus corporation. An indecipherable signature. Whoever bought Haven House had chosen to remain anonymous. The intent was clear from the get-go. Haven House was no more than a front. Its purpose: to make money for a few people.

But was any of this proof of wrongdoing? And how to ID Lennox Incorporated remained the problem.

The subject never left my mind as I shopped and ran errands, then headed back to my cottage. I was stymied and getting nowhere. Now that questioning the people involved was *verboten*, I couldn't think of a way to find out more about Haven House. I had no choice but to follow John's advice and stop investigating. At least for now.

My cell phone jingled. It was Gillian. I frowned as I answered. I wasn't in the mood to hear about her love life. But she'd stayed at the dinner dance longer than I had. Maybe she had fresh info about the Haven House group.

"Hi, Carrie. How are you?" If a voice could glow, hers was on fire.

"I'm fine. And you?"

"Couldn't be happier."

Uh-oh! "Does your good mood have anything to do with the dinner dance and Roger Camden?"

"Absolutely!"

Silence fell as I struggled to think of something to say. I'd already told Gillian that Roger was recently separated from his wife. Repeating it would make me sound like her mother.

"I know what you're thinking," she said, "and ordinarily I'd agree with you, but Roger is a sweet and caring man. He happens to be in a sticky situation right now—he's between jobs and about to divorce his wife."

"What kind of work does he do?"

She laughed, pleased by my question. "Roger's something of a math whiz. He's held various math-related positions as a college professor, and he's written software programs. Now he's looking to try something completely different. Maybe robotics or becoming a financial planner."

"Interesting. Those two fields are about as far apart from each other as we are from Jupiter."

"I'm well aware of that," she said coldly. "Once Rog decides which he intends to pursue, he'll go back to school. The trouble is, money's tight, especially now that he's moved out of his house."

"I suppose he's rented an apartment somewhere close by so he can see his kids."

"I think he's staying with his sister and brother-in-law for the time being. Francesca and Gerald have plenty of room because their kids are grown."

I couldn't help it—the words tumbled out of my mouth. "Just be careful, Gillian. Getting involved with a guy who has lots of responsibilities and no job might not be the best situation for you."

"Thanks a lot, Carrie! You were fun before you turned into a know-it-all authority on relationships. As if you have better taste in men—picking a boyfriend who's never around."

Chapter Twenty-Eight

I arranged to meet Angela for lunch at twelve fifteen. I told her I'd pick her up at the library since I planned to drop off Smoky Joe before we went to our favorite Indian restaurant. Trish would keep an eye on him until I returned.

"Uh-huh," she said in a tone I recognized. She knew I wanted to discuss something important but didn't want to get into it on the phone.

She talked about recent wedding plans as I drove. I nodded or shook my head to let her know I was listening. The smiling owner seated us, and we went up to the buffet. After we'd filled our plates and sat down to eat, I asked Angela, "Do you think I'm a know-it-all?"

I didn't like how long it took her to answer. "I wouldn't label you a know-it-all, but you sure stick to your guns once you've made up your mind."

I can live with that, I decided. I cut into my chicken tandoori and looked up. "Do you think I deliberately chose to get involved with Dylan because he's away so much and we don't get to see each other all the time like you and Steve do?"

Angela snickered. "Are you kidding? Dylan Avery's a catch for anyone. Besides, he's moving home soon, isn't he?"

"In a few weeks," I said.

Angela shot me a searching glance. "Hey, girl, what's this all about?"

"Gillian Richards. This morning she called to tell me how happy she is with her new love—Dorothy's baby brother, Roger. He's good-looking, has no job, and his wife just threw him out of the house."

Angela laughed. "She sure knows how to pick 'em. And you told her so, which is why she called you a know-it-all."

"Kind of," I admitted. "Then she said I'm no authority on men since I chose someone who's hardly ever here."

"But who will soon be around all the time."

"I guess so, since Dylan signed the papers that make him a partner in the company, and the new office is being painted next week."

"See!" Angela was triumphant. "She's dead wrong. Your boyfriend *will* be around. You shouldn't let her rattle you."

"You're right. I feel bad because she got angry when I warned her for the second time that Roger Camden is bad news."

"Gillian's an idiot. You were trying to look out for her, and she insulted you for your trouble."

"I suppose." I sighed. "I'm disappointed in myself for thinking she could have been a good friend. Instead, she takes up with good-looking creeps and couldn't care less if Haven House is used for high-stakes card games and parties after hours."

"Don't beat yourself up over this," Angela said. "It takes awhile to get to know someone. Hey, I'm still getting to know some of Steve's sides, and I'm not crazy about them all."

"You guys are great together. The important thing is you love each other and care enough to make your relationship work," I said.

Angela reached out to cover my hand with hers. "I know, and I appreciate hearing you say it."

"And I appreciate your getting my head straight right now."

"That's what best friends are for," Angela said.

* * *

As soon as we entered the library, I sensed agitation in the air. Something had happened. Trish explained that Jimmy Belco and another young man from the shelter had gotten into an argument. Sally had asked them to leave, but they ignored her and started punching each other. Max and Pete came on the scene to break up the fight. Pete ended up getting punched in the eye just as Danny Brower arrived—Sally had called him—and took Jimmy and his pal to the station.

"Wow!" I said. "I thought Jimmy was barred from the library."

Trish shrugged. "No one's been stopping him lately, so he comes on in. They can't finish that Haven House fast enough."

"They'll have people there who can handle all sorts of situations," I said. *A major reason why I hope it doesn't get closed down.*

After I checked on the various programs in progress, I stopped by the reference desk to ask Norman Tobin how he was adjusting to working in a new library. He greeted me with a wide grin.

"I'm doing just fine, Carrie. Thank you for asking. Everyone's been nice and friendly. The patrons I've been in contact with have been very appreciative of my help."

I bet! They're glad to see a smile instead of a scowl.

"Sounds like you have everything under control. Text me if there's anything you'd care to discuss."

"That's very kind of you, Carrie. Let me say, it makes a difference when an old hand like you takes the time to make a new staff member feel welcome."

I walked away, smiling for the first time that day. *Old hand.* Interesting to be called that when it was only this past October that I had become head of P and E. Just three months ago, but it seemed more like three years.

"Anything new to report?" Evelyn asked as she fell into step beside me.

"Not a thing. Haven House was bought by the Lennox Corporation. There are no names listed at all. One signature, but I can't for the life of me make it out."

"Of course you can't! That Ernie Pfeiffer's no fool. And neither is Gerald. Besides, a corporation is regarded as an individual."

"So I've learned. And I was warned off snooping. Yesterday someone broke into the cottage and left me a threatening note. John made me promise to stop questioning people—about Dorothy's murder and the illegal plans concerning Haven House."

"Of course, Carrie. I don't want you to get hurt."

"Though he doesn't see a problem with my attending Haven House meetings—as long as I don't stir things up."

Evelyn looked sad as she faded from view. I wished I could offer her more.

I was answering a slew of email when my library phone rang.

"Hello, Carrie Singleton."

"Carrie, it's Uncle Bosco."

"Hi, Uncle Bosco. Is everything all right?"

"No, everything is not all right!"

My heart began to thump. "Is Aunt Harriet—? Is she . . . ?"

"No, she's fine. Why?—oh, sorry, we're both okay. Didn't mean to scare you. I'm calling about that Haven House project you got yourself involved in."

"What about it?"

"Al Tripp is fuming about it. So are members of the town council. Everyone seems to know Pfeiffer's behind it and is planning to use it as a front for gambling and so-called 'social events.'"

"I know. I've heard the rumors."

"There's nothing Al can do about it—yet. Pfeiffer's wily. There's no paper trail, but he'll trip up eventually. He even got the state to give him a *grant*. I spoke to the other members of the library board, and we've agreed: we want nothing to do with Haven House."

"Oh."

"That means we don't want them meeting in the library."

"A meeting's been scheduled for Thursday."

"Sorry, Carrie. You have to cancel it."

My hand was shaking as I put down the phone. I'd never heard Uncle Bosco so disturbed over a library issue. I couldn't blame him either. But I wanted Haven House to become a reality, and not just because it would remove the homeless and their disruptions from the library. The promise of the center had already brought a counselor to the shelter. Once Haven House was up and running, more counselors would be employed to help the homeless find homes and jobs. This was a project very much needed by our community, but already its future was unraveling.

I called Sally. She agreed—I had to let the group know ASAP that they could no longer meet in the library. I punched in Reese Lavell's number, hoping she wasn't home and I could leave the message on her phone. She picked up on the third ring.

"Hello, Carrie." She sounded breathless. "I just walked through the door."

Lucky me.

"Everything all set with our meeting Thursday night?"

I drew a deep breath. "No, actually, that's why I'm calling. I'm afraid it's been decided that the group may no longer meet in the library."

"Really? Why?"

"There's been talk that the Haven House organizers plan to use the house for other purposes during evening hours."

"That's ridiculous! I've heard those lies. We all have. There's no truth to them at all."

"I'm sorry, Reese. I'm only following orders."

"And I'm sorry the library has taken to believing rumors and gossip. Don't worry. We'll find someplace else to meet."

"Reese!" I shouted before she disconnected.

"What is it?"

"I still believe in Haven House. Please let me know where your next meeting is scheduled. I'd like to attend."

"Okay," she said abruptly and hung up.

* * *

Reese called back an hour later to say that the Bennings had graciously offered their home for the meeting on Thursday night. She gave me the time and address, sounding considerably calmer.

"I'll be there," I said.

"I'm glad you aren't leaving us," Reese said. "Perhaps you can convince your board that we're only out to do good."

"I'll try," I said, wondering if she truly believed what she was saying or was part of the group making money off the project.

Thursday evening, I put the Bennings' address in my GPS and started out for the meeting. Francesca and Gerald lived on the other side of town, in a development of homes that cost in the low seven figures. I'd always wanted to see the interior of one of those homes, and at last I was getting my chance.

Francesca came to the door wearing a beige cashmere sweater set and brown leather trousers. Her diamond pendant sparkled like a miniature copy of the chandelier shining above me in the three-story hall.

"Carrie! So nice you could make it!" No hug. No kiss.

I followed her to the den at the back of the house, gawking at the elegant décor of the living and dining rooms on either side of the hall. *Concentrate! You're here to find out what you can about Haven House.*

"Pour yourself a cup of coffee or tea and join us," Francesca said. "I'll take your jacket."

More gawking as I entered the kitchen, which was four times the size of mine. The shiny appliances all had what appeared to be miniature dashboards that managed their various tasks. I set down my pocketbook and filled a mug of coffee from the old-fashioned coffee maker.

I was trying to decide which dessert to choose—a brownie or a miniature fruit tart and had opted for both—when a male voice said, "Carrie Singleton. Fancy meeting you here."

I turned swiftly, startled to see Harvey Kirk.

"Harvey! I didn't realize you were interested in Haven House."

"Why not? It's a great project, especially where our library's concerned. It gets those shelter people out of our hair. Not very wise of the board to oppose it, don't you think?"

I shrugged. Harvey was the last person with whom I'd share my thoughts. "I'm here as a private citizen, same as you."

Gerald came into the kitchen and headed for the coffee maker to refill his mug. He greeted me with a smile. "Hello, Carrie. I'm so glad you decided to come."

"Of course. I wanted to. I'm sorry the library can no longer offer the group a place to meet."

"No problem there. The construction work is going faster than expected. Haven House will be ready to open in a month or so." He glanced at Harvey, then back at me. "I hope we can count on you both to convince the library board to reconsider their attitude. The library benefits from our noble project, and we in turn would benefit from whatever help and materials you can offer."

I was saved from responding when Francesca bustled in. "Jerry, dear, everyone's waiting for you."

"Coming, dear."

"Good." She lowered her voice. "The natives are getting restless."

Are they asking uncomfortable questions? I wondered.

The den had a pitched ceiling, exposed beams, and a fireplace set in a wall of stone. About fourteen people sat chatting with one another in a large circle within easy reach of a marble-topped coffee table covered with bowls of snacks. I spotted Reese, who grinned at me, and headed for the empty Eames-style chair next to her. Too late, I realized I'd also be sitting next to the loveseat that Gillian and Roger occupied. Roger greeted me with a big smile. Gillian turned away and actually stuck her nose in the air. I felt my ears grow warm. Although I accepted that Gillian and I would never be friends as I'd once thought, I didn't want her to view me as her enemy.

Francesca and Harvey sat down. Gerald followed them into the room and stood against the wall. Two men joined him. One of them was Theo, the man with the beard. They conversed in low tones. Gerald nodded and took out his cell phone. He disappeared inside the kitchen to speak in privacy. Minutes later, he appeared to be stressed when he called the meeting to order.

"Sorry about the delay," he said, "but we had a minor problem at the work site. I just spoke to our contractor and resolved the issue."

"That's the second or third problem this week," a red-faced man I didn't recognize commented. "Want to tell us about it?"

"It something to do with the heating system, Doug. Nothing to worry about."

The other man who had been whispering with Gerald said, "Problems always arise. More so when you keep on top of things."

Gerald smiled at him. "Thanks, Ben. Why don't we get started? I'm glad to see you all could make it tonight. Ben will tell you about the progress we've made building-wise." He gestured to Theo. "Then Theo will give the treasurer's report."

I looked around at the various guests as I listened to Ben and Theo speak. Most of them had been at the meeting in the library. I was glad to see that neither Fred nor Ernie Pfeiffer was present.

Ben gave a detailed report on what had and had not been done in Haven House. The new interior walls were up; there was a problem with the flooring in one of the rooms, but things were moving along well. Theo gave the financial report. When it came to the fundraiser, he nodded to Martha, the gray-haired woman who had answered questions at the last meeting.

"I'm happy to announce that, after expenses, we cleared eighteen thousand dollars," she said.

Everyone clapped. Doug, who had raised a question earlier, asked Theo if he thought the project could get more aid from the state.

"I think we'd better hold off on that," Theo answered. "My friend said it will serve us better if we wait until Haven House is functioning."

So Theo was the one with connections to the department that provided funds to a project like Haven House.

A minute later, Reese was standing and being applauded for having helped chair the successful dinner dance. From the corner of my eye, I watched Gillian and Roger elbow each other and exchange knowing glances. *You idiot!* I thought, feeling twenty years older than Gillian instead of the actual three years separating us.

After the committee heads' reports, Gerald threw open the discussion to new business. He asked for location suggestions for future fundraisers. Several ideas were offered, among them a winery and a nearby museum. Martha and Reese offered to look into them.

"Why do we need to raise more money?" Doug asked. "It seems to me that we already have enough to cover construction costs. Local residents have offered furniture and older TVs and computers. We're getting books and magazines from the library." He turned to me. "Unless the library has changed its mind about giving us what they'd normally discard or sell in a book sale."

I felt my ears grow warm with embarrassment, and was relieved to see that most of the others were staring at Doug and not at me. Gerald, Ben, and Theo glowered at him.

"Yes, Doug," Gerald said, "we are fortunate to receive many basics from the community, but we expect Haven House will be an ongoing enterprise. We'll always have expenses and upkeep. And don't forget the personnel we'll be hiring." He gave a little laugh. "Some of the population we're expecting will need looking after. And we're hoping to have a drug counselor and a social worker to help with housing and job hunting. We may have to pay for these services."

Almost everyone present stood to applaud Gerald. When it died down, a gray-haired woman who appeared to be in her seventies said, "It sounds wonderful and I'm doing my part to help it become a reality, but what about the rumors we've been hearing—that Haven House will be turned into a bordello at night? How do we know they're not true?"

"And what makes you think they are true?" Gerald asked her.

She shrugged her shoulders. "People say . . ."

"Shirley, you can check for yourself that none of the upstairs rooms are done up in red velvet and mirrors."

The room burst into laughter as Gerald had meant it to. His beaming smile indicated that he knew it too. "And that's it for tonight. We will be holding another meeting next week, the location to be decided. We'll notify you all via email, text, and phone calls."

The meeting ended. People stood and got ready to leave. I turned to Reese to wish her good night.

"Thanks so much for coming, Carrie. I hope you can convince your uncle and other members of the library board to change their mind about us. As you can see, our goals are pure and altruistic."

I smiled. "Unfortunately, it isn't up to me, but I plan to come to the next meeting and do what I can to help the cause."

I thanked Francesca and retrieved my parka. I started for the door, eager to head for home, when the elderly woman who had raised the bordello question came over to me.

"Carrie Singleton! I've been wanting to have a word with you for some time now."

"Really? Perhaps we can—"

"Yes, indeed! My name is Shirley Klauss. I love to make handicrafts. I took every class the library offered when Barbara was in charge. From knitted toys to painted wine glasses." She gave a little laugh. "I enjoyed them all! And now there aren't any more."

"I'm glad you had the chance to enjoy them when you did, Shirley, but I'm sorry to say the classes weren't well attended. We had to make room for more popular programs."

Shirley pressed her lips together and appeared to be deep in thought. I was longing to leave but hesitated to remove her hand from my arm. Suddenly, she offered me a brilliant smile. "I know! Why don't you set up a club for knitters and crocheters? We could meet once a week. I bet that would be very popular."

I looked around. Except for Harvey, who was chatting with Ben and Theo, the few remaining people were saying goodbye to Francesca and Gerald. "That's an excellent suggestion. Of course it depends on available space. Knowing our busy schedule, I doubt a weekly meeting would be possible."

Her grip on my arm grew tighter. "That's too bad."

"Let me think about it." I shook my arm free. "Why don't you call me at the library next week, and we'll talk about it."

"I will! You can count on me to follow through!"

I stepped toward the door. Shirley kept pace beside me. "My friends Mary Wallace and Jeannette Robbins will be so happy when I tell them we'll soon be meeting in the library. Mornings work best for us."

"I didn't say—" I began, but she'd spun around and was walking toward another woman who had been waiting for her.

I thanked Gerald for his hospitality, apologized because the library offer had fallen through, and followed Shirley and her friend outside.

I breathed in the cold winter air, glad to be homeward bound. I tried to decide if coming to tonight's meeting had been a waste of my time. True, I had been surprised to see Harvey Kirk there, and I'd be sure to mention it to John. But what had I actually learned that was of any value?

I started driving to my cottage. It was only when I slowed down as I approached the town's center that I realized I was being followed.

Chapter Twenty-Nine

A chill ran down my spine. Had the car been following me since I left the Bennings's house? I drove along the Green, hoping to see someone—anyone—but it was cold, and the shops were closed for the night. Still, the area was well lit. As the car behind me passed under a streetlight, I was able to see it was large and black. I slowed down and circled the entire Green, whose four sides were each three or four blocks long. I clicked on my phone and called 911. I was surprised when Danny Brower picked up immediately.

"Danny, it's Carrie. A car is following me. I'm driving around the Green."

"I'm in a squad car a block away. Be there ASAP."

What is he doing answering 911 calls in a squad car? I didn't have time to wonder further because a police siren sounded, splitting the silence. The car tailing me swerved around my car and took off at top speed. A minute later Danny pulled up beside me.

"Are you okay, Carrie?"

"I think so," I said. "It was a black Mercedes sedan. I think it followed me from the Haven House meeting at the Bennings' tonight."

"Catch the license number?"

"Sorry. I didn't."

Danny insisted on following me home and seeing me into the cottage.

"I'll drive by a few times tonight to make sure you're safe. Call if you hear or see anything suspicious."

"I will," I said, locking the door behind him.

I sank down on the living room sofa, holding my head in my hands. I shouldn't have gone to the meeting. No matter that I hadn't asked a question or made a comment regarding the subject on everyone's mind. Ernie Pfeiffer and his little group didn't want me around. They saw me as a snoop who meant to bring the law down on them. For once, the fact that I'd helped solve previous crimes was a detriment.

I had no idea who'd been tailing me. Gerald Benning had a Mercedes. Maybe some of the others did too. Something for the police to follow up on.

I went into the kitchen and poured myself a glass of chardonnay. I drank deeply, welcoming the warm feeling that pervaded my body and helped calm me down. Smoky Joe appeared, yawning from his nap, and I gave him some treats.

I returned to the sofa and found myself analyzing what I'd learned that night. As far as I could tell, Gerald, Ben, Theo, and Ernie Pfeiffer were the ones in charge. Were Fred Hawkins and Roger Camden involved as well? If this was the project Ernie Pfeiffer wanted them to invest in, they were. Fred hadn't been at the meeting, but he certainly had resented my questions about the group. And Roger was too busy romancing Gillian to pay attention to what anyone was saying.

Ernie Pfeiffer wasn't the only one to be reckoned with. Gerald was one cool character. I'd seen how quickly he'd made a joke out of Shirley's legitimate question. He, Ben, and Theo all did their part to make Haven House the perfect front for their moneymaking scheme. Any one of them could have broken into the cottage and left that note. I shivered. If the mayor and John and other leaders of the community couldn't stop them, how could I?

*   *   *

I spent a restless night tossing and turning, suddenly aware of sounds both outside and inside the cottage. I left my bed two or three times to see if anyone was trying to break in. Thank goodness, Jack Norris had told me the new alarm system would be installed tomorrow, or I never would have shut my eyes.

I called John as soon as I arrived at the library the next morning.

"I was just about to call you. Danny told me what happened last night. No more meetings for you," was his gruff response.

"Any news regarding the black Mercedes? I wish I'd seen the license plate."

"Gerald Benning and Ben Stockton each have a black Mercedes. I'll question them both, but we know how that will go."

I let out a sigh. "So we've nothing to go on."

"Don't get discouraged. I'd like to stop by the library so you can give me a rundown of the meeting while it's still fresh in your mind."

"Sure, John, and you might want to talk to Harvey Kirk while you're here. He was there last night."

"Is that so? Interesting."

"Why do you say that?" I asked.

"I shouldn't be telling you this, so be sure to keep it under your hat. His ex-wife came in asking for a restraining order. She complained he got physical when she confronted him for not sending her her monthly check."

"Harvey? Physical?" I asked. "He can be sarcastic, but I wouldn't have thought him the physical type."

"Carrie, dear, anyone can be physical when they're desperate."

"High gambling debts," I said.

"You didn't hear it from me. See you in an hour or so."

So that's why Harvey was there last night! He must have heard about the scam and wanted to get in on it. But didn't he realize he had to put money up front to get involved? Or maybe he simply wanted to find out about the high-stakes card games. I shrugged, realizing I had no answers.

My cell phone played its jingle. It was Dylan, sounding jubilant.

"The case is over! I'm flying home tomorrow for the weekend, and then I'm back here for a few days to tie up loose ends. After that, I'm coming home for good."

I let out a deep sigh. "I'm so glad. I'll feel safer with you here."

"Are you feeling nervous about the break-in? I spoke to Jack. The security system's being installed right now."

"Thank you! Last night I went to a Haven House meeting at Dorothy Hawkins's sister's house. Someone followed me partway home until Danny Brower came to my rescue."

Dylan let loose a deep whoosh of air. "Carrie, please! Promise me—no more meetings. No more investigating."

"I promise. John and Uncle Bosco and the mayor are up in arms against this group, but no one can touch them. They need proof that the house is being used for other activities."

"They'll get it once they start holding parties and expensive fundraisers."

"But then Haven House will be closed. I don't want that to happen either."

We chatted a few minutes more, then I settled down to work. John came by, and I told him who had attended the meeting and what had been discussed.

"Ben Stockton and Theodore Pruitt," he mused. "Two shrewd characters and wheeler-dealers who stay just on the right side of the law. That's quite a group Pfeiffer's organized."

"Ernie wasn't there last night."

John's laugh held no humor. "He didn't have to be. The meeting was just a cover—for the sake of the general public and to convince their volunteers that nothing untoward is going on. Even so, they don't want you there."

"Did you find fingerprints on the note left at the cottage?"

John grimaced as he shook his head. "The few prints were too smudged to be of any use."

I let out a deep sigh. "Bad luck all around. It's occurred to me that so many of the people involved in Haven House were connected to Dorothy. Maybe the person who broke into my cottage and followed me last night is her murderer and was warning me off her case."

"Honestly, Carrie, I have no idea if there's a connection. We don't have any new leads, I'm sorry to say."

"Nothing on the car that smashed into hers?"

"The paint's been analyzed. It's a color that was used on an old Buick almost twenty years ago. It was probably someone's old clunker that hasn't been registered in years. Now I imagine it's been compacted or broken down for parts. We've checked MVB registrations, garages. Nothing."

"That's disappointing."

"We're still working the case. New information often pops up when you least expect it. Someone who saw something that night might still come forward."

"Dylan's coming home for the weekend. He expects to be home for good very soon."

"Glad to hear it." John stood. "Forget about solving the homicide and the evils of Haven House. You're young. Enjoy your life."

He surprised me by wrapping me in a bear hug. "Give Dylan my best. Tell him I have a few leads for investigative jobs when he's ready to start work."

"Will do."

I hummed as I opened my email folder. Dylan was coming home, and I was taking a break from detective work.

Chapter Thirty

Dylan was waiting for me at the cottage when I arrived home Friday evening. We hugged and talked, then went out for dinner. After breakfast Saturday morning, I put Smoky Joe in his carrier and drove to the library. While I was at work, Dylan would be in New Haven, organizing his new office.

I studied the February calendar to see what, if any, requests the upcoming presenters might have made for the day of their programs. In honor of St. Valentine's Day, a local romance writer would be speaking about romance in literature and reading from one of her novels. And Alfred Valdes, the chef of a well-loved restaurant a few towns away, was giving our very first cooking program the first Wednesday evening of the month. His menu: butternut squash soup, chicken medallions, and a surprise Valentine's Day dessert. Alfred would use the demo table that Sally and I had bought some months earlier to demonstrate how each course was prepared and then serve samples of the food, which he'd make beforehand, to the thirty patrons in attendance. I hoped all would go well. Alfred said not to worry—as long as we provided the electricity to heat up the various dishes, and paper plates, plastic utensils, and napkins for the patrons.

Shirley Klauss called to find out when the first meeting of the Knitters and Crocheters would take place.

I laughed. "Shirley, I love your enthusiasm, but as I told you, our schedule's very tight. There are no available meeting rooms next month."

"Really? But you said we could meet once a week. I told Mary and Jeannette you agreed. They're all excited about having our own group in the library."

I bit back my impatience. "I'm afraid you misunderstood me. A knitting and crocheting group is a wonderful idea. I'm hoping we'll have the space available after the library is renovated, but that won't be for another two years. Meanwhile, I'll try to find a morning when the group can start meeting in the spring once or twice a month."

"Mary and Jeannette will be so disappointed," Shirley said. "Why don't you meet in one another's homes in the meantime?"

"We could do that, I suppose, though Mary's husband smokes, and Jeannette's dogs are a terrible nuisance."

"And your home?" I suggested.

"Much too small," she said quickly.

"I'll let you know when a time slot becomes available for a knitting-crocheting group."

"Thank you so much, Carrie," Shirley gushed. "I knew you'd come through. And if it's at all possible, try not to make it on Tuesdays. That's when I go to the supermarket."

I sighed. "I'll do my best. Goodbye, Shirley."

"Shirley Klauss?" Evelyn said. She'd appeared as soon as I'd disconnected the call, and perched on the corner of Trish and Susan's desk.

"That's right. She wants to have a knitters and crocheters group meet in the library when and how often it suits her."

Evelyn laughed. "Shirley's one of the reasons Barbara stopped offering crafts programs at the library. Once she broke three wine glasses during a wine glass painting class. Another time she spilled paint all over another woman's project."

"I don't think she can do too much harm at a gathering of knitters and crocheters," I said. "She proposed the idea last night at the end of the Haven House meeting."

"Did you learn anything new?" Evelyn asked.

"Not really, but I gather that two men—Ben Stockton and Theo Pruitt—are involved with Gerald and Ernie."

Evelyn clutched her throat. "Gerald, what on earth have you gotten yourself into?"

I stared at her.

"There have always been rumors that Ben has ties to organized crime."

"That is worrisome," I said. "Your nephew Roger and Gillian were at the meeting, behaving like two lovebirds."

"The idiots."

We both laughed. "And Harvey Kirk was there too."

"Really? The other day he was pecking away on his computer," Evelyn said. "He sure got annoyed when a patron interrupted to ask for help."

"What was he busy doing?" I asked.

"Gambling. What else? He looked unhappy most of the day but was beaming by the evening. I think it was Tuesday night."

"Ah," I said. "He must have raised enough money to buy his way into the group," I said. "I wonder how he knew about it."

"He's invested with Ernie before," Evelyn said.

"I'm afraid my investigating days are over. I got a second warning last night. Someone from the meeting was following me home until Danny scared them off."

"Oh no! We can't have that."

Evelyn disappeared as my cell phone rang. It was Ken.

"Hi, Ken. Find out anything about the Haven House group?"

"I did a little poking around. A pal of mine knew the old man who used to live in the house on Garrett Street they're now calling Haven House. He left it to a nephew who lives in California and couldn't wait to unload the property. When two Clover Ridge residents made an offer, he took it and agreed to sell it to the Lennox Corporation."

"Thanks, Ken. Just as we thought. You'll be happy to know I'm off the case. I've been warned off, and I'm not taking any risks."

"Good idea, Carrie. Let the officials handle this."

I chuckled as I disconnected our call. For someone who was off the case, I'd spent the entire morning gathering information.

*   *   *

Saturday night, Dylan and I enjoyed a leisurely romantic dinner at a restaurant on Long Island Sound. He told me about the case he'd just completed, and I brought him up to date on everything I'd learned about the investigation into Dorothy's murder and Haven House.

"Interesting how the people closest to Dorothy are involved in this Haven House investment," Dylan said when I'd finished.

"I thought so."

He reached over to run his fingers along my cheek. "But I'm glad you're out of the picture. I don't know what I'd do if anything were to happen to you."

Sunday morning we got up early and drove to Dylan's new office in New Haven.

"I love the feel of the place," I said, admiring the newly painted walls and gray carpet, the modern wooden desk, and two tall cabinets waiting to be filled. "So bright and sunny."

"I need a bookcase and a desk for my secretary. I thought I'd get your input on choosing them."

"Have you hired a secretary?"

"Not yet. My advertisement goes online and in the local paper next weekend."

I turned to beam at him. "It's really happening! You're starting out in your new office next week."

Dylan grinned. "And I get to spend my free time with you. Until you get bored having me around."

I slipped my arm through his. "Hah! Fat chance of that happening."

We stopped in a few office furniture stores until Dylan found exactly what he wanted. He ordered office supplies to be delivered the following week. I liked shopping with him, discussing the pros and cons of various items. It felt comfortable, as though we'd been doing it forever. *This must be what it's like when couples furnish their first home together.*

We ate a late lunch and headed back to Clover Ridge. I tried not to think about tomorrow, when Dylan would be flying off to Atlanta. At least we had the rest of the day to enjoy each other's company.

We were halfway home when Dylan put his hand to his head. "I almost forgot!" he said, interrupting my reverie. "John called when you were in the ladies' room, and then Mac called . . . anyway, I hope you don't mind spending an hour or two at John and Sylvia's."

"John and Sylvia *Mathers*?"

He laughed. "Do you know any other couples named John and Sylvia?"

"No. I just—I mean, I seem to talk to John a lot and I'm fond of Sylvia, but I've never been to their home."

"You do remember that he and I work in related professions."

"Of course! And John mentioned he'd get in touch with you when you were home."

"He did, and he knows of a few cases I might be interested in. We figured we'd discuss them while you and Sylvia chat, then go out for a light dinner."

"Sounds lovely."

Sylvia and John lived in an old Victorian house that was as modern on the inside as it was old on the outside. As John and Dylan settled down for a chat in the wood-paneled den, Sylvia gave me a tour of the other downstairs rooms and the four bedrooms above. Each room was tastefully decorated in various color schemes.

"Your home is lovely," I said as we headed downstairs again. "Did you hire an interior decorator?"

Sylvia laughed. "That's all my handiwork. I love choosing colors and furnishings."

We sat down at the kitchen table and sipped chardonnay, never at a loss for words. Sylvia regaled me with stories about my Great-Aunt Harriet, whom she'd known since she was a little girl.

"I can't imagine Aunt Harriet getting up and dancing in front of all those people!" I exclaimed when Sylvia finished one of her anecdotes.

"Oh yes! Harriet was a lively firecracker in her younger days."

"Her forties, you mean," I said. And we both laughed.

Sylvia refilled my glass and fixed her gaze on me. "Are things getting serious with you and Dylan?"

I shrugged. "I don't know. It's too soon to say."

"Of course it is," Sylvia said. "Besides, it's none of my business. It's just that the two of you make such a wonderful couple."

I covered her hand with mine. "Thank you. And thank you for caring."

We talked a bit more, and then Dylan and John joined us. Eventually, we set out for a Chinese restaurant that John and Sylvia frequented. The conversation turned to Dylan's new office and

Clover Ridge politics. I ate my fill of hot and sour soup and shrimp with broccoli and almost fell asleep in the backseat of John's car as we rode back to their house to get Dylan's car.

"Remember, no investigating," John murmured in my ear as he hugged me good night.

"Of course not," I answered. "I'll leave that to you."

Chapter Thirty-One

I kissed Dylan goodbye Monday morning and drove to work. I knew he'd return by the end of the week, but by mid-morning I was already missing him terribly. In only a few days, I'd gotten used to having him close by. He'd become an integral part of my life. The person I loved and needed the most in the whole, wide world. The realization frightened me. What if something were to happen to him? Or if he decided he didn't love me anymore?

I told myself not to be silly. People endured separations, sometimes for months on end. Dylan would be home on Friday. Saturday at the latest. It wasn't as though I had nothing to fill my days in the meantime. I had a full-time job. I had friends. And there was Smoky Joe to look after too.

But Dylan's absence wasn't the only hole in my life. For weeks I'd been trying to find out who had killed Dorothy, and perhaps Evelyn. My investigation and my concern for the homeless who had been spending their days in the library had led me to the founders of Haven House, the very people who were planning to use it for their own selfish ends. I'd been warned to stop nosing around. The people who cared for me wanted me to do just that, but it felt wrong to simply abandon my investigations. Doing nothing left me feeling useless and disloyal.

If only I weren't feeling so restless! Angela had agreed to go out for dinner after work, as long as we went shopping afterward—this time for furnishings for her new condo. Though she and Steve had already ordered most of their furniture, they still needed several small tables and decorative pieces.

Dylan called twice—once to tell me he'd landed safely, and the second time just to say hi and that he missed me. We chatted for a few minutes, and I mentioned my evening plans.

It made sense for Angela and me to leave right from work, so I fed Smoky Joe and decided to leave him in the library. Gayle and Fran agreed to look out for him until I returned from my evening out.

Angela drove us to the mall, where we ordered burgers and salads in one of the popular restaurant chains.

"Sounds like you guys had a busy weekend," she said when I'd finished telling her all that Dylan and I had done.

"We sure did, and now I miss him."

"Of course you do. But soon he'll be based here in Clover Ridge and working in New Haven."

"Except work could still take him all over the country. Though, if business is good, Dylan said he'll hire an investigator to do most of the traveling."

We'd finished eating and were waiting for our check when Angela's cell phone rang.

"Uh-huh. We can stop there." After listening for a few seconds, she said, "Give me a minute." Angela fished a pen and notepad from her pocketbook and started scribbling. "Yes, I wrote down the measurements. I'll jot down the SKU numbers of the ones I like."

Angela smiled. "Me too. Talk to you later."

She was still smiling when she disconnected the call. "Steve wants us to stop by the electronics store and check out the television consoles. He finally agreed that a console would be of more use than mounting the TV on the wall."

I laughed. "I find it hard to believe that Steve is showing an interest in how your family room is going to look."

"Me too. He came with me the other evening to look at wallpaper for the kitchen. He chose a paper with bright red and orange flowers. I thought it would be garish until I brought it over to the condo and stuck it up on the kitchen wall. It looked great."

"I suppose getting married changes some men," I mused. "They become more domestic."

Angela winked. "You'll see."

We stopped at various stores and checked out tables, lamps, and TV consoles. Angela took notes, indicating the pieces she liked best. "I'll come back with Steve and let him negotiate prices. He's better at that than I am."

I was weary by the time Angela dropped me off at the library fifteen minutes before closing time. I found Smoky Joe curled up in a chair in the children's section, fast asleep. "You've had a big day, and now we're going home," I crooned. I took him in my arms and thanked Gayle and Fran for keeping an eye on him.

He was still half-asleep when I put him in his carrier and lugged him out to the car. "And we're off." I started the motor and exited the parking lot. But suddenly I was wide awake and eager to do something, go somewhere. My restlessness had returned with a vengeance. Haven House and Dorothy—two subjects I'd avoided thinking about all day—were back in the forefront of my mind.

I found myself heading for Dorothy and Fred's neighborhood. I slowed down as I passed their house. A shiny red SUV, which I assumed belonged to Leila Bevins, was parked in the driveway. Light was shining through the sheer curtains covering the living room and dining room windows. It emanated from the kitchen at the rear of the house, where I imagined Fred and Leila were enjoying their after-dinner coffee. I squelched the impulse to walk around to the back of the house to try to hear what they were discussing.

I glanced at Ernie Pfeiffer's house next door. No lights were on, no car stood in the driveway. He didn't appear to be home.

"It's a good thing I'm officially off the case because I'm coming up with zilch," I told Smoky Joe. "This time we're really homeward bound."

* * *

Tuesday turned out to be a long working day. I was supposed to start at one in the afternoon and work until closing time, but Sally called and woke me at seven to ask if I could come in at nine.

"The *Clover Ridge Gazette* is sending over a reporter and a photographer for that feature article about our library." She sounded frantic. "They'll be here at ten."

"Really? I thought that wasn't scheduled for another two weeks."

"It was, but one of their lead stories for Sunday fell through so the editor-in-chief begged me to let them do it today instead. And he wants you and Smoky Joe to be a big part of the article, so you need to come in early. You can leave at five if you like."

"But Susan can't come in tonight—"

"Don't worry about that! Just get here by nine."

I showered and dressed, taking time to blow-dry my hair and put on eye makeup, something I rarely wore to work.

"Smoky Joe, we're going to be in the paper again," I told him as I set the alarm, then locked the front door behind us.

The furry feline blinked, not very impressed by my news.

There was an air of excitement in the library, with everyone buzzing about the upcoming article. Somehow residents had gotten wind that the Gazette was coming, because the library soon filled up with twice the usual number of patrons.

At ten o'clock they arrived—a tall, slender, blonde woman no more than twenty-five and an equally young and slender male photographer dressed all in black. Sally greeted them, then went around the library introducing Peggy and Rico to each of us heads.

"Nice to meet you, Carrie. Where's Smoky Joe?" Peggy asked when she met me.

"He's around here somewhere. Should I go find him?"

Peggy laughed. "Nope. If he's around, I'm sure we'll see him. We're going to start in the children's section."

Half an hour later, she and Rico were back in my office.

"We got some great shots of Smoky Joe with the little kids," Rico said.

"He loves spending time in the children's section," I said. "Actually, he loves spending time in every section of the library. He's become the most accomplished little beggar. Librarians and patrons alike know better than to feed him—I've posted signs to that effect—but they don't always listen."

"I suppose it's tempting to feed him treats," Peggy said, looking guilty.

I heard scratching at the door and went to let Smoky Joe in. He didn't want to eat or use the kitty litter, but had come to be a part of the action.

Peggy pulled out a small tape recorder. "Do you mind?"

"Of course not."

"How did Smoky Joe become a library cat?" she asked.

"He showed up one fall morning outside my cottage. I was getting ready to drive to work. He jumped in my car, and I found myself bringing him here." I laughed, remembering how Smoky Joe had run into the children's section and let them make a fuss over him as Marion and Sally were leaving Marion's office. "I announced he was our new library cat. Sally and Marion saw how friendly he was and how much the children adored him, and so Sally went along with the idea."

"But Smoky Joe is really *your* cat," Peggy said. "I mean, you take care of him and bring him home with you every night."

"I do, and I'm responsible for him, but whenever I'm here in the library, Smoky Joe is here as well. The patrons love him because he spends time with them and soaks up their attention. He only comes in here when he needs something or requires a break."

As if he'd understood what I'd just said, Smoky Joe leaped into my lap and closed his eyes.

Rico shot photos of him snoozing and then shot some of my office. I was glad I'd straightened up my desk.

"Smoky Joe's a hero, isn't he?" Peggy said. "He helped solve a mystery right here in the library."

"Oh yes. One of your colleagues wrote a story in the paper about that."

Rico took a few photos of me, and they left shortly afterward. I heaved a deep sigh of relief.

Dylan called to say he'd be coming home Friday after all. I whooped with delight, then told him about being interviewed for the library article.

"You and Smoky Joe are becoming Clover Ridge celebrities," he teased.

I decided to work until the library closed. For one thing, Susan couldn't come in to work her usual evening hours, and despite the morning's interview and the good news that Dylan was coming home on Friday, I was still feeling restless.

Evelyn made an appearance after Trish left for the day, and asked me if there was any news to report.

"Sorry, no," I said. "I drove by Fred's house last night. His girl-friend was over."

She perched on the corner of Trish and Susan's desk. "Could you hear what they were saying?"

I shook my head. "I didn't get out of the car. What about you? Has Harvey done anything suspicious?"

"Difficult to say. He made a few calls on his cell phone, but he didn't mention any names, and I couldn't make any sense of what he was saying except 'I'll be there.'"

I felt a stirring of excitement. "I wonder if he was talking about a secret meeting of the investors. The regular meeting isn't until next week."

Evelyn sent me a sharp look. "Carrie, you're not thinking of attending."

"Don't worry. Not after those two warnings."

She faded, leaving me feeling totally useless.

At six o'clock I fed Smoky Joe his dinner and ate the bowl of chili I'd ordered from the Cozy Corner Café. At seven twenty-five I went downstairs to the meeting room to introduce a young writer who was giving a talk about her two novels. Jodi Li was a few years younger than me and lived outside of town, just a few miles from my cottage. Thirty patrons had signed up for the program. I knew from our three phone conversations that she was upbeat and had a great sense of humor. We both were hoping this program would help stir interest in the eight-session class on fiction writing she'd be teaching in the late spring.

I touched on Jodi's childhood in Taiwan, her move to the United States at the age of eleven, and why she'd decided to become a novelist while studying finance in college.

"Her books are chock-full of insight into the immigrant experience and a pure reading delight," I said. I called Jodi up to the front of the room to start her presentation.

Her voice sounded shaky as she began a tentative introduction of her own. I was surprised. Talking to her, she'd always come across as confident and witty. But I'd come to realize that some people freeze in front of an audience.

When she paused, I said, "Why don't you tell us about your first day in seventh grade?"

Jodi covered her mouth. "That was *sooo* embarrassing."

"I know," I said, sending her a huge smile. "People love to hear about embarrassing situations that didn't happen to them."

The audience broke up laughing. That did it! Jodi returned my wink and started off with a joke, probably the one she'd planned to tell as soon as I'd called her to the front of the room, but hadn't managed to get out.

I stayed awhile, enjoying her anecdotes about her childhood and her family. I finally left, knowing that Jodi would be a big hit tonight and that we'd get the required sixteen people to make the writing course a go.

Which reminded me that I had to make a decision about the knitters and crocheters group that Shirley Klauss wanted me to arrange. I sat down at my computer and went to our Facebook page and posted:

Please message me if you're interested in joining a knitters-crocheters group that meets one morning a month.

At closing time, I carried Smoky Joe's carrier out to my car. The temperature was in the twenties. I was still shivering as I heated my seat and turned on the windshield wipers to clear off the dusting of snow that had fallen earlier. I pulled out of my parking spot, surprised that despite my long day I wasn't tired. Once again, I was energized and raring to go.

Go where? I wondered. I couldn't very well go peeking into people's houses. Besides, hoping to overhear something incriminating was like looking for a needle in a haystack.

Also, I wasn't sure that anything I might hear while eavesdropping would hold up in court.

And finally, it was too damn cold.

As I exited the parking lot, I decided to water Aunt Harriet's plants one last time before she and Uncle Bosco returned from

Florida. I drove around the Green, past stores closed or closing for the night, and onto the street of residences on the far side of the Green, across from the library.

My chore accomplished, I returned to my car and found myself turning the corner onto Garrett Street. Haven House, though built in the same white wooden-frame style as the rest of the neighborhood, was considerably more modest than my aunt and uncle's home and sorely in need of attention.

Two cars were parked in the driveway, and three others lined the street in front of the house. What were they all doing here at this time of night? I was surprised to see drapes drawn across the large living room window. Haven House wasn't scheduled to be furnished and decorated until after the contractor and his crew had finished their work.

A bright light shone through a gap in the drapes. It was much too narrow a space for me to see anything from my car. Excitement built up inside me as I pulled in front of the lineup of cars.

"I'll be right back," I told Smoky Joe—quite unnecessarily since he was fast asleep. I closed the car door as quietly as I could and hurried toward the house, hoping none of the men would suddenly open the front door and find me lurking about. I dreaded to think what they would do if they caught me spying on them. I offered a silent prayer of gratitude that there were no streetlights near the house, and I wouldn't be visible if one of them were to peer out from the well-lit living room.

Still, I stepped carefully, avoiding patches of snow and ice as I crossed the shallow lawn, then crouched among the low evergreen bushes that fronted the living room window. I gulped in a cold rush of air as I peered inside. Eight men were sitting around an oval table, playing cards. Judging by the cash out on the table, it was a high-stakes game. I knew all the players but two.

Chapter Thirty-Two

Gerald, Ernie, Ben, Theo, Roger . . . and Harvey Kirk and two strangers were playing what looked to be poker. I pressed my ear against the cold windowpane to hear what they were saying. No one was talking. They were concentrating on the game and drinking from shot glasses.

I quickly ducked down when Ernie rose from the table. He headed for what I imagined was the kitchen and returned with a bottle of whiskey. He poured liquor into the glasses. "A toast to Trevor Glackens!"

Who is Trevor Glackens?

"A toast to *you*, Ernie!" Gerald shouted back, holding up his glass. "For dreaming up this lucrative, fail-safe scheme!"

"Yay, Ernie!" the others roared, like a bunch of high school boys at a football game.

"Let's not forget my friend in the state housing department!" Theo said.

"Yay!"

"And especially our helpful congressman for proposing a second grant," Gerald shouted. "He wanted to be here but had a previous engagement."

"Yay to our congressman!"

My mouth fell open, though I shouldn't have been surprised from what I'd heard about our local official.

I was so busy focusing on the scene before me, I nearly jumped when a car approached, its bright beams lighting up the street. I slid to the ground and wedged myself between the bushes and the wooden exterior below the window. I peered out from my hiding place as the driver parked on the other side of the street. A minute later a man walked up the cracked cement walk. It was Fred Hawkins.

I drew in my breath as he glanced to the right, to the very spot where I was lying on my side. Well hidden, I hoped. Then why was he staring? Had I made a sound? Was the light coming from the living room exposing me?

Fred shook his head, as though doubting he'd seen what his eyes told him he'd seen, and stared at the door. I was safe! He knocked four times.

Is that supposed to be a signal? I wondered.

The door opened. I heard Gerald greet Fred as he let him in. It took me a few minutes to work up the courage to move to a crouching position and peer through the window. Roger was pulling over a chair from the kitchen, and Ernie was pouring Fred a drink. Fred didn't look too happy to be there. Still in his parka, he sank into his seat and gazed down at the floor.

"Hey, why the long face?" Ben asked.

Fred shrugged. "I'm not really in a poker-playing mood."

"Have a drink." Ernie handed him a shot glass filled with liquor. "You'll get in the mood."

Fred put the glass down on the table. "I don't think I'll be staying."

"Of course you'll stay," Ernie said. It sounded like an order.

Leave! The visceral message came from the deepest part of my brain. I trembled as I rose from the window and ran to my car. I sped down the block as if the hounds of hell were chasing me.

Poor Smoky Joe! I'd woken him up. He let out a meow of indignation. I slipped my hand inside the carrier and stroked his back until he fell back to sleep. "Sorry, baby," I murmured as I slowed down to an appropriate speed and made the necessary turns to take us home.

I had to tell John. But first I wanted to ask Ken a question. I called him as soon as I stopped at a red light. "The Haven House ringleaders are holding a poker game."

Ken sighed. "Carrie, I thought you agreed—no more playing detective. And why are you calling me instead of John?"

"I will call him, but first I have to know—who is Trevor Glackens? Ernie mentioned his name."

"Trevor Glackens owned the house before that group bought it. He died a few years ago and left it to his nephew, Curtis Bradshaw. The name isn't familiar to you because Trevor's name isn't on the bill of sale that you looked up. Curtis lives in California with his family and wanted to unload the house ASAP. Pfeiffer got wind of it and made him an offer he couldn't refuse."

"I see," I said, impressed by Ken's knowledge regarding the sale.

I called John on his cell. He answered quickly. "What is it, Carrie? Are you all right?"

"I'm okay," I said, feeling a twinge of guilt for worrying the people who cared about me. "I—er—happened to be driving by Haven House. There's a poker game in progress."

"And you just happened to see it," he scoffed.

"Well, I noticed the cars, so I peeked in."

"I hope to God they didn't see you."

"Don't worry. They didn't."

"I'll look into it," John said. "And no more sleuthing, Carrie. I mean it."

"No more," I promised. "I intend to lead my quiet little life."

* * *

I turned on the local TV station as soon as I woke up the following morning, and was surprised that there was no mention of arrests made at Haven House. When I called John to ask what had happened, he told me that when he had entered the premises, there was no sign of cards or cash on the table.

"Couldn't you see the game going on through the space between the drapes?" I asked.

"The drapes were tightly closed."

Had Fred seen me, or were they just being extra careful?

"They're not fools, Carrie," John said wryly. "They know how to play the game, and I'm not talking about poker here."

When I spoke to Dylan and told him what I'd witnessed the previous evening, I was relieved that he didn't read me the riot act.

"I know it's frustrating for you because the law can't simply step in and haul them all off to prison. Building up a case like this takes time, Carrie. You need to learn patience."

I laughed. "Not my strongest suit."

"I'm afraid I'll be trying your patience even more. I had to change my flight to Saturday morning."

"Oh no!"

"Just think, though: Saturday I'll be home for good. And please—no more playing detective."

"A thing of the past," I said.

Angela also was glad that I'd agreed not to do any more sleuthing. "You've done all you possibly can," she said over lunch on Wednesday. "Besides, I don't want anything to happen to my maid of honor."

I laughed. "Always the wedding. You'd think that's the most important event in the world."

She shot me an inscrutable look. "Just wait. You'll find out one day what this is all about."

I quickly changed the subject to her new condo.

By Thursday afternoon, twelve patrons—all women—had emailed me to say they'd be interested in a knitters-crocheters group. Evelyn made an appearance as soon as Trish left for the day. I told her what I'd witnessed and my decision to let things be.

"So it's true—my nephew and Gerald are both up to their ears in this scheme." She tsk-tsked. "You'd think they'd know better than to get involved with Ernie Pfeiffer."

"I am sorry," I told her.

"They're fools!" she declared. "They'll end up in prison. I can only hope that Frannie isn't part of this."

"I honestly don't know. She got very upset the night of the dinner dance when someone backed out of the project, saying it was dirty."

Evelyn's expression softened. "Poor Frannie. She wants money and prestige but has no idea how to get it on her own. I don't remember her working a day in her life."

"She's been an active volunteer for Haven House."

"I can only hope she has nothing to do with their reprehensible scheme." Evelyn paced up and down the short length of my office.

"You're worried that when this all comes to light, Francesca might get swept up with the others and be charged with larceny or whatever the charge will be."

"I am." She paused. "I wonder if there's any way you can find out *if* Frannie has gotten herself involved in the criminal aspect of Haven House."

"I don't see how I can, Evelyn. I don't have access to their financial arrangements."

"No, but you can ask her."

"Are you kidding? No matter how I phrase my questions, they're bound to offend. Even worse, she'll tell her husband. Then someone in that group will come after me."

Evelyn wrung her hands. "You're right. I'm sorry I asked you to do the impossible. It's just that I'm worried about Frannie. Roger's a lost cause, but . . ."

She looked so sad, I found myself saying that I'd try to find a way to talk to Francesca but that I couldn't make any promises. As Evelyn faded from sight, I told myself I didn't have to contact Francesca today or tomorrow, or even over the weekend. To paraphrase Scarlett O'Hara, I'd think about it next week.

I drove back to my place, warmed by the thought that in just a few days Dylan would be home for good.

Chapter Thirty-Three

Something bad had happened. I sensed it the moment I entered the library Friday morning. I set Smoky Joe free and, instead of heading for my office, walked over to the circulation desk to question Angela.

"Fred Hawkins has been assaulted," she told me. "He's in the hospital. A concussion and a few broken ribs."

"Oh no!" A pang of guilt assailed me. "I told you he looked unhappy when he joined the others at Haven House on Tuesday night. I should have let John know."

"Now don't go feeling responsible," my best friend said. "Just because he didn't want to stay and play cards doesn't mean they were about to beat him up. For all you know, someone else attacked him."

"Like who?" I demanded. "Some angry person's going around hitting people just for the fun of it?"

Angela shrugged.

"When did it happen?"

"Last night. Around ten o'clock. Outside his house."

"The Haven House group met last night," I said, "I don't know where. And I have no idea if Fred attended the meeting."

"Carrie, it's not your fault he got hurt."

"No? Then why do I feel like it is? I'm calling John."

When John heard my voice, he was totally pissed. "Carrie. You promised not to do any more sleuthing."

"I didn't. I just heard that Fred Hawkins was assaulted last night. I should have told you that I saw him at Haven House on Tuesday night. He arrived late and said he wasn't in the mood to play cards. Ernie told him he had to stay."

"Really? For your information, he wasn't there when I stopped by."

"He must have left," I said. "I should have told you. Maybe if I had . . ."

"Carrie, please don't turn this into a guilt trip. Even if you had told me, there was nothing I could have done. Can you understand that? You didn't like how Ernie talked to Fred, but you had no proof they were planning to give him a beating. He didn't file a complaint against them. And even if he had, we don't have the manpower to protect someone twenty-four/seven."

"I hear what you're saying, but it doesn't seem right."

John's laugh held no humor. "Of course it's not right. But please understand, there was no way you could have prevented this. If Fred wanted protection, he should have come to us. But given his involvement with that crew, I was probably the one person he most wanted to avoid. And I probably would have advised him to leave town for a week or two."

"Is he at Conn South?" I asked.

"He is. Planning on visiting him?"

"Maybe I am."

"Be careful, Carrie. I don't want you ending up there too.

* * *

I cancelled lunch with Angela and drove to the hospital instead. Regardless of what Angela and John insisted, I couldn't shake the feeling that I was partially responsible for Fred's landing there. I

257

was angry with him too. Didn't he know that getting involved with someone like Ernie Pfeiffer would lead to trouble? And announcing that he wanted to back out of their arrangement—which was what I assumed he'd told them—was plain stupid. I shook my head in frustration. I didn't know how I could have prevented the situation— only that I hadn't acted, and Fred had gotten hurt. Not taking action seemed to be the rule of the day.

Between visiting Dorothy after her fall and my father's two stays in December, I had the route to South Conn down pat. I stopped at a small market and bought a pound of grapes and a bag of clementines. I parked and headed for the hospital entrance. The woman at the front desk gave me Fred's room number, and I waited for the elevator to take me to the third floor.

I found Fred sitting up in bed, a bandage around his head. Leila sat in a chair facing him. They seemed to be arguing.

"Look who's come to visit me!" Fred said, his voice hearty with bravado.

It was all show. I knew it, and so did Leila, judging by her pained expression. Still, I played along. "I heard you were here, so I thought I'd pay you a visit. Just a short one, since I have to get back to work. I hope you're not seriously hurt."

"Just a sore head and a few bruised ribs. I'll be out in a day or two."

"And then what?" Leila asked, her eyes blazing with anger. "How will you protect yourself?"

"Now, Leila, don't be like that," Fred said. "I'll be fine."

Leila pursed her lips. She turned to me. "Thank you for the fruit. I'll wash it as soon as I wrangle some paper plates from the nurses' station."

She left. I turned to Fred. "Leila's seriously upset."

"Uh-huh."

I sat down in the chair Leila had vacated. "Who did this to you, Fred?"

He cocked his head. "Why? Is someone going to arrest him? Keep him from doing it again?"

"Do you think you're safe by not telling the police?" I asked.

"I do. The point was made. I say nothing, I do nothing, and nothing's done to me."

I leaned closer to Fred. "Did Ernie Pfeiffer do this to you?"

"I'm not saying."

"Of course he's not saying," Leila said.

I gave a start. So did Fred. We hadn't heard her return.

"Honey, we went over this," Fred said. "The man's dangerous. He might come after you next."

"Let him try!" Leila said.

"It's for me to decide," Fred said. He turned to me. "Carrie, please don't say anything to anyone about this."

"I won't." I stood. "I'd better get back to the library." I bent down to kiss his cheek. "Heal quickly and stay away from that group."

"Don't worry. I intend to."

Leila slipped on her jacket. "I'm leaving too."

"Call me later?" Fred asked.

Leila nodded and led the way out of the room.

Neither of us spoke as we walked down the hall to the elevator. Leila pressed the "down" button and sighed. "He's impossible."

"Did he tell you what happened?"

"Oh yes. He left my house close to ten o'clock last night. He drove home, pulled into the garage, and took the garbage out to the curb. Ernie was waiting for him with a metal pipe."

I gulped. "My God."

The elevator arrived, a full car of visitors, doctors, and nurses. At street level, we let everyone get off and then walked to the parking lot.

"He managed to call nine-one-one, and an ambulance brought him here. He had someone call me."

I looked at her. "You've been here since—"

"Since last night." I studied her face, saw how tired and drawn she looked. "Lieutenant Mathers came by. He tried to get Fred to tell him who did this to him, but Fred wouldn't say."

I slowed down as I approached my car. "The police and other agencies know about Ernie Pfeiffer and his group's dirty tricks. They'll move on them when they have enough evidence."

"I hope you're right," Leila said, "but it's been my experience that people like Pfeiffer and that bunch get away with bloody murder."

I drove back to the library, musing over what I'd just learned. Fred had all but admitted that Ernie Pfeiffer had beaten him and put him in the hospital, and I had promised not to tell anyone. That included John. But now John knew what I'd witnessed when Fred went to Haven House on Tuesday night. He would question Fred again and hopefully, this time, manage to coax him to divulge everything he knew about the "other" plans for Haven House.

At any rate, my part in this investigation was over. As I'd told Leila, it was up to John Mathers and other law enforcers to make a strong case against Pfeiffer, Gerald, and their crew. I had to wait and see how it all played out.

Finally, I was learning the art of patience.

Chapter Thirty-Four

Saturday morning, Dylan called me at eight thirty to say he'd be arriving home a little after noon.

"I've shipped several boxes to my new office. They should be arriving by Tuesday," he said, sounding excited. "I'm conducting final office manager interviews on Monday and will officially open the office on Wednesday."

"How can you be sure you'll hire someone by then?" I asked.

"I've done several Skype interviews this past week. I've narrowed it down to two women and one young man."

"Sounds like you're ready for business."

"Am I!" Dylan sounded jubilant. "It looks like one of the leads John gave me last weekend is turning into a case, and there's the possibility of another one. I won't be sure for a week or two."

"Before you know it, you'll be hiring someone to help with the workload."

"I'm counting on that happening. I told you I want to cut down on my traveling in a year or two."

After lunch, Dylan surprised me by showing up at the library. I'd just left Sally's office, where we'd been discussing a few new ideas I had for future programs. He strode toward me and took me in his arms. Whistles and clapping broke out in the reading room.

261

I took Dylan's hand and led him to my office, where we enjoyed a welcome-home kiss.

Dylan only stayed long enough to inform me that he was going to his new office but would be back in time to pick me up at seven thirty for our dinner reservations.

"Where are we going?" I asked.

"A surprise."

It was difficult to concentrate on work the rest of the afternoon, but Saturday afternoons were laid back in their own weekend way. Except for the one o'clock movie and special events, there were no set programs. I hadn't considered a Saturday afternoon before, but despite Shirley's insistence on a morning slot, this might be the perfect time to schedule the knitting and crocheting group.

Five more women and one gentleman joined the list of those interested in the group. With Shirley and her two friends, the twelve that had already signed up, and these six, there were twenty-one patrons. I knew that, as with every other program and event, not everyone would show up or attend every meeting, but twenty-one was a great number to start a craft group,

I checked the schedule for the upcoming months. Sure enough, the small room on the main level was free from one until three on Saturdays. It was a nice setting, with a round table and good lighting. Of course, not everyone who'd indicated interest would be free to attend on a Saturday afternoon, but that was to be expected with every program. I shot off an email to Shirley.

"You got yourself a good-looking boyfriend. And he sure was happy to see you."

I spun around. Evelyn was in her favorite spot—perched on the corner of Trish and Susan's desk.

"Oh, Evelyn! I didn't know you were there."

"I came by before, but I left when I saw you were otherwise occupied."

I grinned. "I sure was. Dylan's home for good now. He'll be working out of his office in New Haven."

"He's a detective, isn't he?"

The calculating look in her eyes raised my antenna. "You know he's an investigator. Dylan retrieves stolen artwork and jewelry."

"Which means he has the skills to help you find out if my niece's involved in that crooked setup."

"Evelyn, it's one thing to ask me to help you, but Dylan's going to be busy working on his own cases," I said.

She sank into the chair behind the desk Trish and Susan shared, as downhearted as I'd ever seen her.

"I'm sorry to lay this on you, Carrie, but you're the only one I can turn to. I'm heartsick that Dorothy's killer is still wandering around free. My nephew's in deep with that lying, thieving gang. That leaves Frannie. She doesn't have the brains her siblings were born with, but I can hope she's not a thief like them."

I pursed my lips together. Evelyn was my friend. I had no choice but to help her.

"I'll speak to Frannie—Francesca next week. Though I can't promise she'll tell me the truth."

Evelyn smiled. "I have faith in you, Carrie. You'll get her to talk. And even if she won't tell you what you want to know, you'll know by her answers how deeply she's involved—*if* she is involved."

* * *

When I got home, I took a nice, leisurely bubble bath and put on one of my favorite sweaters and a pair of slacks. I took pains with my eye shadow, eyeliner, and mascara. I slipped on the only pieces of jewelry I owned—the gold earrings my dad had bought me for Christmas and the matching golden heart pendant from Dylan.

"Not bad," I said, after zipping up my favorite boots and admiring myself in my bedroom mirror. Then I burst into giggles. A year ago my Goth persona wouldn't have recognized the new me.

"Where are we going?" I asked Dylan an hour later as I buckled myself into his BMW.

"You'll see." He leaned over to kiss my cheek. "Did I tell you you look beautiful?"

I grinned. "Yes. Twice."

"Third time's the charm." He put the car into gear and we took off.

"I had a very productive afternoon," Dylan said, as he drove north on a main road. "But I still have items to buy and need to take care of a few things at the office. Do you feel up to spending the day in New Haven with me?"

"I'd love to. I'm off tomorrow."

We chatted about work—his and mine. There were a few pressing matters I wanted to discuss with Dylan, but they could wait.

As soon as we arrived at the restaurant, a valet opened the door for me. I stepped out of the car and found myself gawking at the view before me. The restaurant—a masterpiece of modern architecture—stood perched on a rise of land above a lake. Dylan reached for my hand, and we walked up the steps to the entrance. The dining area was shaped like half an octagon and was three tiers high, with each level receding so that every diner could gaze out at the lake through floor-to-ceiling windows that alternated with wooden panels.

"Wow! So this is The Precipice!" I said. "I've read about it in the paper. People come from all over to eat here. They're booked up months in advance." I cocked my head at Dylan. "How did you manage to get us a reservation?"

Dylan winked. "I have connections."

A solidly built man in a tuxedo greeted us with a smile and led us up to the third tier below the vaulted ceiling. Though all the tables were occupied, conversation was muted, convincing me even further that whoever designed the restaurant had considered the comfort and privacy of every diner.

"Beautiful, isn't it?" our escort said as he placed large menus on the table and pulled out my chair. "You must pay us a visit when the flowers are out in spring and summer." He chuckled. "Brides love the view. We have several weddings lined up for the next two years."

"I can only imagine what they must cost," I said when he had departed.

Our waiter appeared, and Dylan ordered a bottle of wine, which was swiftly brought to the table, along with two crystal glasses. The waiter uncorked the bottle and poured.

"To us," Dylan said, raising his glass.

"To us," I echoed.

We smiled at each other and sipped.

I sensed this meal was meant to be a celebration, so when our waiter returned, I ordered filet mignon, something I wouldn't ordinarily order. Dylan ordered haddock, and we decided to share a salad. That accomplished, we sank back into our comfy chairs and grinned at each other.

"Here I am, back home again, yet I feel as though I'm starting a brand new chapter of my life," Dylan said.

"It will be different, having your own office," I said.

He reached for my hand. "The best thing about coming back to Clover Ridge is knowing that you're close by. I have to admit, I'm relieved that you've finally stopped sleuthing. You sure took a chance, spying on Pfeiffer and his pals the other night."

"I know. Ken scolded me for doing it. And they mean business. Fred Hawkins is in the hospital with a concussion and broken ribs. Ernie Pfeiffer put him there."

"Really." Dylan's face took on a stern expression.

"Fred changed his mind about being part of that group."

265

Dylan laughed. "Backing out of a crooked deal comes with serious consequences."

"Fred's afraid to report what Ernie Pfeiffer did to him."

"And you know this how?"

I cleared my throat. "When I heard Fred was in the hospital, I paid him a visit."

"So much for not sleuthing," Dylan said dryly.

Our salad arrived just in time for me to change the subject. I asked Dylan what he wanted to shop for the next day, and he was happy to reel off his list. I smothered a gasp when our waiter brought out our main course. The portions were huge. I ate what I could and asked to have the rest of it wrapped to take home, though I managed to find room to share a slice of pecan pie with Dylan over a cup of coffee.

I was feeling sleepy and rather full when it was time to leave. Dylan withdrew a charge card from his wallet. Our waiter returned a few minutes later and handed back his card.

"The boss says it's on the house."

"Thanks, but that's not necessary," Dylan said. "You can tell Mr. Stavros I appreciate his fitting us in on such short notice."

"You can tell him yourself!" a booming voice answered. "And it's Pete, Dylan. I've told you that already."

A short, beefy man with a round bald head and a luxurious moustache approached our table, his right hand extended. Dylan stood and shook it warmly. The man pulled him close and embraced him.

"How was everything? Okay?"

"Delicious. Really great, Pete," Dylan said.

Pete beamed down at me. "And this is your young lady, I assume."

"Carrie, meet Pete Stavros. He owns The Precipice."

Pete laughed as he shook my hand. "Me and my brother and two cousins."

"This is the most beautiful restaurant I've ever been in," I said.

"Is that a fact? In which case, I hope you return real soon."

Pete put his arm around Dylan's shoulder and led him a few feet away, where they conversed in undertones. Pete was looking more serious when they returned to the table.

"Nice meeting you, Carrie." To Dylan he said, "Call me as soon as you find out anything," and then took off.

Dylan put away his charge card and left a generous tip for the waiter.

I waited until we were driving home to ask questions.

"Is Pete a client of yours?"

"My very first in the new office. John recommended me."

"Did someone steal his wife's jewelry or his coin collection?" I asked.

Dylan shook his head. "Neither. Pete's family owns five restaurants besides The Precipice. Two more in Connecticut, one in Manhattan, and two on Long Island. Pete thinks one of his cousins in skimming money from them all."

"Why did you take on a case like this when your specialty is art and jewelry?" I asked.

"Because Mac and I agreed I need to handle more types of jobs if we're going to make this office take off. It's not every day we're called on to find an art treasure or recover gems from a heist."

Suddenly butterflies were fluttering around in my chest. "I wonder if Pete's cousin carries a gun."

"Why? Are you afraid he might shoot me?"

"Well, if he's a thief, he'll want to protect what he's taken. And if he finds out you're checking his accounts . . ."

We stopped at a light. Dylan turned to meet my gaze. "There's always the possibility of danger in investigative work, but you knew that."

"I did—in theory. It sounded exciting and, I must admit, somewhat romantic. But now all I can think is that I don't want anything to happen to you."

Dylan began to laugh—a real belly laugh that ended in a coughing fit. "Carrie, my love, I appreciate the fact that you care about my welfare. But do you see how funny this is? You go off spying on homicide suspects. You question everyone and anyone connected to a murder and give little thought that they might be dangerous. Or consider that someone who loves you will worry about you."

I bit my lip. "I never thought of it that way. The fact is, I'm not used to people worrying about me. I get a hunch and I follow it up. But," I quickly added, "I have no more hunches, so there's no need to worry about me."

"Good to know," Dylan said. We drove on a bit, then he said. "You know, I didn't become an investigator overnight. I studied art, took courses in gemology and jewelry, and trained in martial arts and other fields I won't go into. I prepared for what I do. Then I went to work for Mac, and he taught me tricks of the trade that an experienced investigator learns over the years."

"I'm relieved," I said. "Somewhat."

"I'm relieved that you're somewhat relieved." Dylan chuckled. "And touched that you care."

Chapter Thirty-Five

S unday morning we started out early for New Haven. Dylan wanted to hit the stores and buy everything he needed to begin work on Monday. I found myself talking about Haven House.

"It's such a great project for the homeless people who have no place to go during the day," I said. "Too bad Ernie Pfeiffer decided to use it as a moneymaker."

"They'll get caught sooner or later and land a nice sentence in jail."

I thought of Evelyn's concern for Francesca. "Do you think spouses will be charged too? I mean, how can the police know if a wife was in on the deception if she was, say, only involved as a volunteer?"

"They have ways of finding out. Why?" Dylan shot me a piercing look. "Did you have someone in mind?"

"Francesca Benning, Dorothy's sister. Her husband Gerald is one of the ringleaders. I have no idea if she's involved in their dirty shenanigans or if she's willfully blind and simply refuses to believe he'd do anything illegal."

"Have you become friends with her?"

I laughed. "With Francesca—or should I say Frances? She's a shallow social climber. Not exactly my type."

"Then why are you concerned about her? Because I can tell that you are."

I swallowed. Having a boyfriend who was an investigator had its downsides. Like picking up tells I had no intention of revealing. "I might as well tell you now, since I have to tell you sooner or later. Her aunt is worried about her."

"And?"

How did he know there was more to the story? "Frances's Aunt Evelyn used to work in the library. She died some years ago but still visits the place. I'm the only person besides my little cousin who can see her."

The car swerved to the right, missing the bushes growing along the edge of the road by inches.

"Sorry, I didn't mean to startle you, but you asked and I had to share this with you eventually. No one knows about Evelyn. Dorothy did, but she's dead."

"This is for real?" Dylan said when he found his voice. "You're not pulling my leg? You're not hallucinating?"

"Yes, no, and no," I answered. "I first met Evelyn the morning Sally offered me a job. I was about to turn it down when Evelyn told me not to be a fool, but to tell Sally I'd think it over and give her my answer the following day."

"And no one else in the library can see her?"

"None of the librarians can. Only my little cousin Tacey. She tries to give Evelyn cookies. Tacey's mom is concerned that she has an imaginary friend."

"Has this . . . Evelyn helped you solve mysteries?"

"Sometimes. She eventually told me where Dorothy had hidden her list of blackmail victims. But Evelyn's not always as helpful as I'd like. She keeps plenty of her own secrets."

"I bet." Dylan let out a long exhale.

He drove on silently, shaking his head occasionally.

"Are you upset? Angry?" I asked.

"Not angry, but this is hard to swallow. And no one else in the library knows about this . . . Evelyn? Not Sally or Angela?"

"No one. Smoky Joe hisses when she gets too close to him, though I think he's getting used to her sudden comings and goings. I never know when she's going to appear."

Dylan let out a deep exhalation. "You'll have to forgive me, but it's going to take awhile for this to sink in."

I was glad to see we were approaching New Haven. Dylan concentrated on maneuvering through the buildup of traffic, and we drove the rest of the way to his office in silence.

Had I been wrong to tell him about Evelyn? I didn't want to keep secrets like that from him, and yet I didn't want to drive him away by giving the impression I was crazy or hallucinating. Dylan pulled into the parking spot assigned to him in the building's underground parking area. We waited for the elevator in silence. When the door opened, we stepped inside and began speaking at the same time.

"I'm sorry I told you while—" I said.

"I'm not angry, Carrie, just stunned."

Dylan wrapped his arms around me and held me close as the elevator doors closed behind us and carried us to the seventh floor.

The rest of the day was ordinary, thank goodness. The paint job and new furniture gave the office a fresh, appealing appearance. Dylan seemed to have shaken off the shock of my revelation as he walked me through the waiting room, office, and bathroom, pointing out everything that had been done since my last visit. He pulled out a list of items that he wanted to buy, and five minutes later we were back in the car on our way to the nearest mall to shop. Afterward, we stopped for lunch, then dropped off our purchases at the office and headed back to Clover Ridge.

My cell phone jingled when we were halfway home. It was Angela. "Steve and I were wondering if you'd like to go out for dinner with us tonight. Nothing fancy—just burgers at this place Steve loves. I know it's last minute, so don't feel bad about saying 'some other time.'"

"Er—just a minute. I'll check with Dylan."

I turned to Dylan and covered the phone. "It's Angela, asking if we want to have burgers with Steve and her tonight."

He bit his lip as he thought it over. I was certain he was about to say no. The guys weren't as social as us gals. That is, they might be social but preferred spending time with their own pals. Besides, Steve was in construction. He and Dylan traveled in different circles. The only thing they had in common was that Angela and I were friends.

"You don't have to—" I began, when he said, "Sure, I'd love to."

"Dylan said okay," I told Angela.

"I heard," she said. "Why don't you meet us at MacGregor's. Six thirty all right?"

"Six thirty?" I asked Dylan.

"Sure. Get the address."

When I disconnected the call, I saw that he was grinning. "You expected me to say I didn't want to go."

I shrugged. "Guess so. All this is new to me. I don't want to push you into something you'd rather not do."

Dylan patted my knee. "Carrie, I know how much Angela means to you. I expect we'll be going out occasionally with your friends and occasionally with mine."

"And occasionally with ours—like John and Sylvia."

"Sounds good to me."

* * *

Dinner went better than I'd expected. Dylan and Steve discovered they both loved hockey, and Angela and I caught up on things. I told her about Dylan's new office, and she told me about the latest wedding plans. We ordered burgers and beers and shared two desserts.

"Great guy you got there," Steve whispered as he hugged me good night. I was glad to see Dylan and Angela hugging too. After all, I wanted my boyfriend and my best friend to like each other.

It was ten past eight when Dylan drove up to the cottage. "Coming in?" I asked.

"I'd love to, but I have a long day tomorrow and every day this week," he said. "I'm working on Pete's case, which means going to some of the other restaurants his family owns, as well as to their offices. I'll be interviewing several people."

"Won't that tip off the cousin who's skimming off the top?"

"Word will get to him eventually. I say eventually because Pete says the guy isn't well liked, though he's sure to have people in each restaurant working with him."

"Won't they warn him?" I asked, suddenly nervous.

Dylan smiled. "Don't worry. Pete and I worked out a story that's plausible and won't tip off the cousin and his crew."

"I never realized how much goes into each investigation," I said.

"And this isn't even the half of it. A quarter of it." He leaned over and kissed me long and tenderly. Then he pulled back and said, "Carrie Singleton, I do love you."

"I love you too," I said, stepping out of the car.

"You can tell your ghostly friend that if there's no paper trail showing her niece is benefiting financially—that is, getting her own cut—from the Haven House scam, and if she isn't attending their private meetings, there's a good chance she won't be charged."

"Thank you, Dylan. For being so understanding and accepting."

He grinned. "Are you kidding? You bring the mystery and excitement in our relationship to a whole other level."

Chapter Thirty-Six

As I got ready for bed, I found myself humming "I'm in Love With a Wonderful Guy" from *South Pacific*. I *was* in love with a wonderful guy. Dylan and I hadn't done anything earthshaking that day—shopping and setting up his office, then having dinner with friends—but it was all brand new to me. Sure, I'd gone out with plenty of guys, but not one of them had ever told me that they loved me. Good thing, I supposed, since I hadn't loved any of them either. Dylan had warned me that things wouldn't always go as smoothly as they had this weekend. I should know since we'd experienced some bumpy times back in December. I especially appreciated that he hadn't mocked me when I'd told him about Evelyn, or said I was nuts for believing in ghosts.

My cell jingled. I grinned when I heard his voice.

"I wanted to wish you a good night and tell you I had a wonderful day."

"Me too," I said.

"Opening a new office is risky. I was glad you came with me today."

We chatted a bit before saying good-night. *Life is wonderful,* I told myself. *At least it is right at this moment,* I added, remembering how quickly things could change. I got into bed and read a few pages, with Smoky Joe nestled at my side. Ten minutes later I was fast asleep.

The next morning, I was singing along with the radio as I dressed for work, when my cell phone rang.

"Hello!" I said, expecting to hear Dylan's voice.

The sound of sobbing greeted me. For a moment I thought it was a prank call and was about to hang up, when a woman said, "Carrie, it's Gillian."

"Oh." I hadn't thought much about Gillian over the past week, not after she'd made it clear that she resented my advice about dating Roger Camden.

"I know," she said between hiccups, "you must think I'm an idiot for not listening to you. I mean, I knew he was married. But he was so damn nice and drop-dead gorgeous, I thought for once I'd hit the jackpot."

"What happened, Gillian?" I asked, though I already had a pretty good idea.

"I ended it with Roger." The sobbing began anew with fresh vigor. "And I'm soooo unhappy. I picked another rotten apple. How could I have been so *stupid*?"

I spoke as soothingly as I could and finally managed to calm her down. "Where are you, Gillian?"

"At home. I'm so upset, I don't know how I'll get through work today if I don't talk to someone."

And that lucky someone is me. "Sorry, Gillian. I'm about to leave for work myself. I can't talk now."

"Can we meet for dinner? I absolutely have to talk to you or I'll—explode!"

I had no idea Gillian was this volatile. But then how well did I really know her? We'd formed a quasi-friendship a few months before, when she was dating Ryan Foster, and Ryan's brother Jared and I had been trying to discover who had murdered their mother fifteen years earlier. I had wondered then how she could continue to go out with Ryan, who was sarcastic and nasty to Jared the few times we were all together.

"Gillian, why don't you come for dinner tonight? Say around six thirty. This will give me enough time to prepare something for us to eat." *Or to buy something in town.*

"Oh, no, Carrie. I can't impose on you to make dinner as well as listen to my pathetic tale."

"I think it will be better than meeting in a restaurant. This way we'll have privacy, and no one will be able to hear our conversation. Do you still have my address?"

"Of course. You gave it to me when Ryan and I came to your birthday party."

We said goodbye, and I started making a shopping list in my head. I could pick up a rotisserie chicken in the supermarket on the way home. I had plenty of salad, veggies, and rice as well as an unopened bottle of chardonnay in the fridge. Voila! Dinner!

"Good for you, Gillian!" I said aloud. "Too bad you got involved with Roger in the first place, but better late than never."

"Meow!" Smoky Joe said, agreeing with me.

I arrived at the library in good spirits. As I walked to my office, I admired the festive valentine decorations—Susan's artistic handiwork—that adorned the walls and bookshelves. February had begun only a few days ago, and while I knew spring wouldn't be coming to Connecticut anytime soon, I felt hopeful that at least it was on its way. I looked forward to seeing flowers and leaves on trees and the last of the snow. Uncle Bosco and Aunt Harriet would be flying home in a week. I could hardly wait, I missed them so.

Evelyn paid me a visit shortly after I arrived. "Did you get a chance to talk to Frannie?" she asked as soon as she materialized.

"No, but I've given it some thought. Honestly, from what I've seen of her at meetings, I don't think she's involved. I asked Dylan what he thought about her chances of going to prison. He thinks she'll be okay. They'll go after the ringleaders, not their spouses."

Evelyn shot me a look of pure admiration. "So you asked him after all! I thank you from the bottom of my heart. Frannie's a foolish girl, but I hate to think of her standing trial."

"I also told him that you often visit me in your—ghostly form."

"Did you?" Evelyn beamed. "And how did he take the news?"

"After nearly crashing the car, he took it pretty well. At least he didn't think I was nuts."

"He's a good man, Carrie. I hope you don't screw things up."

I put my hands on my hips and pursed my lips at her. "And why would you think that?"

"Forgive me, Carrie. I apologize for sounding so critical," Evelyn said. "I just want things to run smoothly for you and Dylan."

"Do things ever run smoothly, I wonder? We had the nicest day yesterday, but things crop up. Problems. Issues. Speaking of which, your nephew broke Gillian's heart."

Evelyn shook her head as she tsk-tsked. "What did he do this time?"

"I don't know. I'll find out tonight. Gillian was distraught. I invited her to dinner so she can get it all off her chest."

"Seems like he'll never learn," Evelyn said.

She had no sooner disappeared, when someone knocked on my door.

"Come in."

Doris Maris entered my office, her face wreathed in smiles. She was wearing lipstick and a touch of blush, and her hair looked as though it had recently been styled.

"Hello, Doris. I'm sorry I've been neglecting you lately. How are things?"

"I know how busy you are, Carrie, but I wanted to tell you—they've found an apartment for Shondra and me! We can move in next month. And I start working next week. In a shop in town. Isn't that wonderful?"

"It sure is. How's Henry doing?"

"He's a little more energetic, but the doctor says he won't get any better. He'll have to stay in the facility. Thank God there's a program that covers the cost." Doris shuddered. "I don't know what would have happened to him if he had to sleep in that shelter much longer."

"I'm so sorry."

She gave me a small smile. "There is one bright spot, though. Remember Jimmy Belco?"

"How could I not?"

We both laughed.

"I talked to Henry's doctor about him. A colleague of his is starting a group for young people—like Jimmy—who have ADD and can't control their impulses. The treatment involves group therapy and meds and hopefully leads to housing and employment."

"I hope Jimmy sticks to the program," I said.

Doris thrust back her shoulders and narrowed her eyes. "I told him he'd better or I'd be coming over to drag him to every meeting."

So this was Doris Maris before she'd lost her home and her business and ended up in a homeless shelter!

I hugged her tight. "I'm happy things have improved in your life. Stay in touch."

"I will, Carrie. I'll never forget that you cared and asked your uncle to help us."

I was still smiling when I went downstairs to the small storage room to examine the cooking equipment that Sally and I had bought a few months ago when I'd started scheduling our culinary presentations. This coming Wednesday evening, we were holding our very first cooking program. Chef Alfred, who owned a popular local restaurant, would be demonstrating how to make butternut squash soup, chicken medallions, and a surprise Valentine's Day dessert. Though he would be bringing the food, his knives, and his own pots and pans, I was determined to make sure we had everything else he'd need to make this a successful evening.

Dylan called me twice to tell me how his interviews were going. At three o'clock he called, sounding very excited.

"I've made my decision! I've asked Rosalind Feratti to be my Gal Friday. She's enthusiastic and bright and computer savvy."

"How old is she?" I asked, wondering what Rosalind looked like.

"Mid-forties. She has three kids—two in college and one in high school. And a husband." He laughed. "In case you were curious."

"Just wondering," I said, and then I told him about Gillian's phone call.

"The girl has problems. She saw the same warning signs you did and went ahead and dated the guy. Don't get too involved in her melodrama," Dylan said.

"I don't plan to," I said, somewhat annoyed by his attitude.

"I'm only saying it for your sake," he said, picking up on my reaction. "Sometimes people with emotional baggage lean on other people and drain their energy."

"Okay. I'll keep it in mind. Thanks."

* * *

At five o'clock I went looking for Smoky Joe and found him in the café. A teenaged couple was petting him as the girl tried to coax him to eat a piece of her muffin.

"Please don't feed Smoky Joe," I said, pointing to the sign on the wall.

"Sorry," she apologized.

"Told you," her boyfriend said, a smirk on his face.

"I know it's tempting, but think how fat he'd get if everyone gave him something to eat," I said.

I scooped up Smoky Joe, put him in his carrier, and carried him out to the car. "Now I have to pick up a few things for dinner," I told him as we exited the parking lot.

Besides the chicken, I ended up buying a frozen package of mixed veggies in a cream sauce that looked yummy, as well as a simple coffee cake. When I got home, I fed Smoky Joe and put the chicken in the oven at a low temperature to keep it warm while I saw to the veggies, salad, and rice pilaf.

The table was set and our meal ready to be eaten by the time Gillian arrived. She hugged me and handed me a cake box. "For dessert."

"Thank you," I said, very much relieved to see she'd calmed down and was once again her usual self. I poured us each a glass of wine and led her into the living room.

"I feel so foolish for the way I carried on this morning," Gillian said as she sank into the chair opposite me. "I almost called you back to say I'm fine. I did something stupid, but I sure won't make the same mistake again!"

I hope not. "Do you want to talk about it now or over dinner?"

"Now! I want to get it over with and forget Roger Camden as quickly as I can." Gillian sipped her wine, then placed her glass on the coffee table. "At first things were going well. Too well." She laughed, clearly embarrassed. "I suppose that in itself is a sign of worse to come."

"I certainly hope not," I murmured, thinking how yesterday had been as perfect a day as I could have wished for.

"Roger was charming and funny. It meant a lot to me that he wanted to please me. We had dinner out most nights. Nothing fancy—mostly subs and pizza or the diner—but that didn't matter to me. I figured money was tight. After all, he wasn't working and had to support his family."

She took a deep breath and continued. "And then he asked to borrow two hundred dollars—just for a few days. I wasn't happy about it since I don't think it's a good sign or a good idea to lend money to a guy you're seeing, but I gave it to him anyway. I was relieved when he paid me back. I must have looked surprised because Roger said, 'You thought I wasn't going to pay you back, didn't you?'

"But a day later, he asked to borrow a thousand dollars. I told him I didn't have that kind of money available, that it was all in savings. He persisted—couldn't I take it out for a week? I saw how he paid back his debts. I hemmed and hawed. Roger threw up his hands in disgust and stormed out. I thought I wouldn't hear from him again, but he called me later that week and asked me out, sounding cheerful, as though nothing had happened."

"Wow," I said, remembering that Evelyn had said her nephew was used to living off women.

"By now I was on my guard. I began to wonder if Roger thought I was an easy target. Someone he could sponge off of." She laughed, but it wasn't a happy sound. "As if he were a professional gigolo."

I started to cough.

"A few days later he asked to borrow money again. This time I was ready. I told him I didn't feel comfortable lending money to men I dated, and perhaps it was time we ended our relationship. Roger shrugged. 'Fine,' he said. 'Whatever you want.' He said it was my loss, and he took off."

"So that's how it ended?" I asked, knowing there had to be more.

"If only," she said bitterly. "Guys like Roger don't like to be dumped. They'll end a relationship on their terms, never yours." Gillian gulped down the rest of her wine. "Roger called a few times.

I stopped answering the phone when his number showed up. Then I got a few hang-ups from a number I didn't recognize. I knew it was him. The calls started to freak me out. The guy's devious. I started imagining all kinds of weird things he might do. I don't want to be on his shit list."

She was beginning to hyperventilate. I covered her hand with mine. "Gillian, don't let your imagination run away with you. So far it's only a few hang-ups. He's just letting off steam."

"There's more. This morning I got an email. It said 'You'll be sorry. Even sorrier if you tell anyone' in bold caps. What should I do, Carrie? How can I stop him?"

"First of all, I'd call the police."

"Of course I thought of that, but what can they do?"

"They'll look for proof that Roger's been harassing you. Threatening you, actually."

"I bet he made sure to cover his tracks. If they question Roger, he'll deny everything. And then he'll know how scared I am." She began to sob. "I don't think they have the manpower to protect me."

I put my arm around her. "I'm so sorry, Gillian. I know how scary this must be."

Her sobs grew louder. I ran into my bedroom for tissues and handed her a wad of them. She blew her nose.

"Your boyfriend's a detective."

"Investigator."

"Do you think he could trace the calls? Look into Roger's past? Maybe he's done this before."

"The police can look into it for you."

She sighed. "I've called them a few times about inconsiderate neighbors. There wasn't much they could do to help me. I need someone who will focus on my problem."

"Would you like me to go with you to speak to Lieutenant Mathers? He's a friend of mine, and I know he'll take this seriously."

Gillian sniffed. "I'll think about it."

We sat quietly for a few minutes. "Are you up to eating dinner?" I asked.

She smiled. "Yes. I'm hungry, and I refuse to lose my appetite over Roger Camden."

Chapter Thirty-Seven

G illian's spirits improved over dinner. I was glad to see her taking a second serving of everything. "This is really good," she said. "I must remember to buy rotisserie chickens. They're easy to heat up."

"And there's enough for a few evenings' meals," I added.

We chatted easily as we always had. I thought Gillian was feeling well enough for me to ask if Roger had ever talked about Haven House being used as a moneymaker for him and his pals.

"He never admitted that was the case. The one time I mentioned it, he said I shouldn't bother my pretty little head about business deals and should concentrate on setting up fun programs for the homeless."

"Hah! Business deals, my eye!"

"I hope the bunch of them get caught and thrown into jail!" Gillian said.

We both laughed.

I made coffee and placed both cakes on the table. We both had a slice of each. As soon as she finished her dessert, Gillian stood.

"Thanks for dinner, Carrie, and for listening to my sad story. I'll fall asleep on my feet if I don't leave now. I hardly slept last night, and I'm beat."

"I understand." I went to get Gillian's jacket from the hall closet and held it while she slipped it on.

"I'll think about your offer to go with me to talk to Lieutenant Mathers about Roger,"

"It's up to you," I said.

She gave me a sad-looking smile. "I'm considering calling a therapist and finding out why I keep on picking guys like Roger and Ryan."

"Not a bad idea," I said.

We hugged and I closed the door behind her.

I returned to the kitchen and carried our dessert dishes to the sink. What a rat that Roger had turned out to be! Poor Gillian had fallen for his "caring" act, but she was smart enough to call it quits when she saw he was after whatever money he could worm out of her.

I was loading the dishwasher when Smoky Joe woke up from his nap and came into the kitchen, meowing for a treat. I shook a few of his favorite brand into his dish. Then the phone rang. It was Dylan.

"I just got home," he said. "How did your dinner go?"

"Fine. Gillian's calmed down, but she's mad at herself for being taken in by Roger Camden. He asked to borrow money and got pissed when she turned him down. She dumped him, and he started pulling annoying tricks."

"Sounds like a prince of a guy. I'll talk to you later, after I grab something to eat, okay?"

"You're welcome to eat here. I have plenty of leftovers from tonight. And two kinds of cake."

"Thanks, but I think I'll make do with a bowl of cereal."

The doorbell rang.

"Uh-oh. Gillian must have forgotten something. Talk to you later."

I disconnected the call and ran to open the door. Big mistake. Roger stood in the doorway. I tried to close the door, but he shoved it open and stepped inside the cottage.

285

"What are you doing here?" I asked, doing my best to stop the quaking in my voice.

"What do you think? I'm really angry at you, Carrie Singleton, for telling Gillian all kinds of lies about me." He spoke slowly and distinctly, a sure sign that he was drunk.

"I didn't lie, Roger. I told Gillian the truth—that you're married."

"Gillian knows I'm sep-ar-a-ted from my wife." He dragged out the word and grinned at me. "And soon to be divorced. I'd have my sweet Gillian at my side, if it wasn't for you."

I had no idea what Gillian might have said in the heat of an argument—probably in an attempt to get rid of him.

"I'm sorry you think I ruined things between you and Gillian, but I hadn't spoken to her in weeks until she called me this morning."

Roger shook his head, the macabre grin still frozen on his face. "I know you turned her against me." He strode forward, forcing me to step backward into the living room. "And tonight she came running straight to her good friend, Carrie, Miss Librarian."

"She was upset." My eyes darted around the room, looking for something to hit him with when I got the chance. The table lamp was too large. Too unwieldy.

"I'm upset, but who gives a damn about *me*? Who treats *me* with respect? My brother-in-law—Mr. Big-Shot Lawyer—treats me like dirt. My own sister doesn't support me."

I opened my mouth but couldn't find any words that might help the situation. Roger was too far gone, mired in drink and the depths of self-pity.

He jabbed his index finger at me. I ducked just in time to avoid getting stabbed in the eye. "And you were Dorothy's friend, the worst of the lot. How could you stand her?"

"We weren't exactly friends. I was only there—"

"She browbeat me every chance she got. She not only refused to lend me money the few times I asked, she took pleasure in kicking me when I was down. Some big sister!" He snickered. "Dear Dorothy got exactly what she deserved."

He moved closer. I fell back into a chair. "Someone did the world a favor and got rid of her. Someone very clever—don't you think? The police never caught him and never will."

I stared at Roger as I stumbled to my feet. He'd all but confessed to killing Dorothy. Roger—so devoid of ambition. The person I'd least suspected.

"You murdered your own sister."

"Surprised you, didn't I?" The grin was back. "I see it in your face. You didn't think I was capable of putting an end to her malice."

"What about your Aunt Evelyn?" I said, not knowing where I'd gotten the nerve to ask the question.

"Auntie Ev? She was another skinflint. And planning to leave all her money to Dorothy. It wasn't fair! I went to talk to her one night as she was about to drive home from work. She wouldn't listen. I barely touched her to get her attention, and she fell down." He shrugged. "So I took off."

"How could you?" Unbidden, the question shot out of my mouth. "They found her dead the next morning."

Roger's eyes were those of a madman. "You're all in a plot to keep me down!"

He lunged toward me, his hands outstretched. Terrified, I looked left and right. No place to dodge. The hands came closer. Going for my throat.

A hiss sounded as a flash of gray flew at Roger. He faltered backward as Smoky Joe landed on his shoulder.

"Get this devil cat away!"

Are you kidding? I raced to the guest bathroom, the closest room with a lock, and pressed the button in the knob, knowing it wouldn't hold the madman for long. *What to do? What can I do?*

"Open that damn door! I'm not finished with you!"

I reached inside my pocket for my phone. Dylan was home. He'd come. Only there was no phone. I let out a sound of frustration. I'd left it on the kitchen table.

Roger pounded on the door. I heard him trying to twist open the doorknob. It was only a matter of seconds before it gave way. I looked around for something. Anything! I yanked open the cabinet door beneath the sink and grabbed the can of Lysol. I had my finger on the nozzle and waited for the door to swing open.

I aimed for his eyes. He roared curses as he rubbed them and only managed to worsen the effect of the spray. I ran for the front door, not knowing what I'd do if he followed me. I was counting on his drunken state and hoped he'd slow down until I reached the manor house and Dylan.

Dylan stood outside the cottage, startled by my sudden appearance. I threw myself into his arms.

"Roger Camden's inside! I don't know if he's armed. He killed Dorothy. How did you know . . . ?"

"I decided to take you up on your offer."

The front door flew open. "You won't get away—" Roger began, then let out an *oof* as Dylan grabbed him. He put up a brief struggle until Dylan caught him in a headlock.

"Go inside and call John," Dylan said.

I didn't need to be told twice.

*   *   *

Minutes later I heard the welcome sound of a police siren. I opened the front door as John Mathers and Danny Brower were exiting a police car. Blue and red lights spun round and round, casting grotesque shadows on bushes and trees.

"Here we go again." Danny grinned as he walked past me.

"Yeah. She can't stay out of our investigations," John said. He wasn't grinning.

"I certainly didn't invite him over," I said to John.

"Save it," he said as he strode into the kitchen, where Dylan was guarding a dejected-looking Roger Camden.

John spoke to Dylan for a few minutes, asking him if Roger was armed and other questions that I thought he should have asked me. He read Roger his rights and told Danny to escort him to the precinct. Then he turned to me.

"Carrie, do you want to tell me what took place tonight?"

"Okay." I led him into the living room and sank onto the sofa. Dylan joined us a minute later with a glass of wine in his hand. He gave it to me.

"You're out of all the stronger stuff, so drink this."

"I will," I said, but I set the glass down on the table. For now, it was enough that he and John were with me in the room where Roger had terrorized me just minutes earlier.

"Did he have a weapon on him?" I asked.

"No," Dylan said.

As if he knew what I was thinking, John added, "That doesn't mean he wasn't a danger to you. And from what Dylan just told me, he entered the premises against your wishes."

"He certainly did." I gulped down a healthy amount of wine and welcomed the warmth that circulated through my body. "And he meant to kill me."

"Why don't you start from the beginning?" John said. "You could do this down at the precinct when you're calmer, though I'd rather hear it now while it's still fresh in your mind."

I told them about Gillian's phone call that morning and why I'd invited her for dinner.

"So she broke up with Camden because he turned out to be a deadbeat, and then he started his scare tactics?" John asked.

"Yes. She was terrified, but she didn't want to call the police—you. She didn't think there was much you could do to make him stop."

"Humph," was all John said.

"When the doorbell rang a few minutes after she left, I thought it was Gillian. Only it was Roger. He forced his way in here and rambled on about no one caring about him or giving him credit for anything."

I drew a deep breath. "He confessed to killing Dorothy and knocking down his Aunt Evelyn and leaving her to die."

Dylan's eyes widened. "He used the words, 'I killed Dorothy Hawkins?'"

"Not in those words, but he admitted he murdered his sister."

"And why did you bring up his aunt?" John asked. "As I recall, she slipped on ice outside the library six or seven years ago on a cold February night and remained there through the night. We ruled it an accident."

"Because at one point Dorothy thought that her husband had killed Evelyn and was about to kill her. A crazy thought—probably a result of her trauma—and an irrational connection that proved to be half-right." I clenched my hands into fists. "Roger said, and I quote, 'I barely touched her to get her attention, and she fell down.' Then he left, leaving her lying on the ground. He killed Evelyn as surely as if he'd put a bullet in her head."

John smacked his thigh. "This helps but unless he confesses to me, we'll need a hell of a lot more evidence if we're going to bring him to trial for two homicides."

I thought a moment. "Do you think Roger would be more cooperative if he believed he'd get a better deal by turning on Ernie

Pfeiffer and the others? He must have plenty of insider's knowledge of how they plan to use Haven House to make money."

John grinned. "I can encourage him to do so, though it won't cut him any sentencing time he'll get for murdering two people."

"Still, it might help your case against Ernie Pfeiffer and his gang when you have enough evidence to charge them."

Dylan hugged me. "Sounds like you're learning the ways of the law."

Chapter Thirty-Eight

"Carrie, dear, I'm afraid I ate too much of your delicious dinner." Uncle Bosco muffled a burp as he pushed back his dining room chair.

"Glad you liked it. It's Aunt Harriet's meatloaf recipe." I dropped a kiss on his bald spot as I collected dishes and carried them into the kitchen.

"With a few additions," Aunt Harriet said. "I must include basil and mushrooms the next time I make it. They add great flavor and texture to the meatloaf."

When she started to rise, I put my hand on her shoulder. "No need to help. You must be exhausted after your flight."

"Let's not forget the three-hour delay," Uncle Bosco groused. "If we'd known there was a delay, we could have eaten on the way to the airport instead of at one of their fast-food kiosks."

"Please, Bosco," Aunt Harriet chided. "That's the third time you've brought up the delay. It's over and done with."

Dylan and I exchanged glances. I bit my lip so I wouldn't burst out laughing.

"Did you enjoy your stay in Florida?" he asked to change the subject.

'It was lovely," Aunt Harriet said. "The condo was roomy and well appointed. We're thinking of staying there longer next year."

Dylan helped me clear the table. I put on a pot of decaf coffee and brought a small pitcher of milk to the table.

"I'm glad all that bad business has been resolved." Uncle Bosco frowned at me. "Though I wish you hadn't gotten into the middle of things as usual."

"Smoky Joe saved me," I said.

"Exactly!" my uncle thundered. "I hate to think that your life rested in the hands of a cat!"

"Paws," I corrected.

"Humph!"

"Sorry, Uncle Bosco. I'm only making light of it because I was terribly frightened. The only reason Roger Camden came here was because I'd invited Gillian to dinner."

"I think I can speak for us all," Dylan said, "when I say how glad I am that Smoky Joe attacked Camden."

"He'd never attacked anyone before," I called from the kitchen, where I was placing slices of cake on a platter. "My little protector."

"And that was quick thinking—spraying Camden with Lysol as soon as he broke open the door," Dylan said.

"Dylan, thank God you arrived in time to make sure that man didn't harm Carrie." Aunt Harriet tsk-tsked. "To think he killed members of his own family."

"John said Roger confessed to murdering Dorothy Hawkins but insists his aunt's death isn't on him," I said. "He figured she might have hurt her head when she fell, got a little dazed, and would get up when she was good and ready."

"And for what!" Uncle Bosco demanded. "Money? Out of spite? Maybe there wouldn't have been any murders if the man held down a job like the rest of us."

"Once news of his confession became public, Fred Hawkins filed a complaint against Ernie Pfeiffer for assaulting him," Dylan said. "He's been telling the authorities everything Pfeiffer, Gerald Benning, and the rest of their crew had planned to make money off of Haven House."

"Which stops them in their tracks," Uncle Bosco said, "but provides little reason to put them behind bars." He pursed his lips. "The original plan to let them continue until they did something illegal would have brought prison sentences."

I set the cake platter and dessert dishes on the table and sat down. "So I suppose that's the end of Haven House before it even got started." I sighed. "It was a great idea."

"It's still a great idea." Uncle Bosco ignored Aunt Harriet's frown as he reached for the largest slice of cake and slid it onto his plate. "I've been talking to our mayor about Haven House."

"You have?" I stared at Uncle Bosco. "But you've been in Florida. You just got home."

"Carrie dear, haven't you heard of the telephone? Email? Texting?"

"Really?" I stared at my great-uncle. "Now you text?"

"Your uncle spent the past week holed up in our bedroom, which he'd turned into his office," Aunt Harriet said. "Our Florida friends asked me if he'd taken ill because they never saw him from one day to the next."

"I had more important things to do than play cards at the pool every afternoon." Uncle Bosco turned back to me. "Anyway, I thought it was a good project and offered to put my money where my mouth was. I even offered to take charge of the project."

I wrapped my arms around his neck. "Uncle Bosco, what wonderful news!"

I brought the carafe of coffee in from the kitchen, then sat down and ate a forkful of cake. I was happy to have my aunt and uncle back home with me, and delighted that Haven House was finally in honest, responsible hands. How sad that Dorothy's killer had turned out to be her own brother; even sadder that he was also responsible for Evelyn's death.

Poor Evelyn. I'd seen little of her this past week, ever since I'd told her how she died. It seemed that even a ghost needed time to recover after receiving bad news.

I watched Dylan chatting comfortably with my aunt and uncle. I was so very lucky to have him in my life. Fifteen minutes later, he was ushering them outside to drive them to their lovely home on the Green.

I was putting the last of the dishes in the dishwasher when the cottage phone rang. I wondered who it could be since the people I spoke to most often—Dylan, my aunt and uncle, Angela, and Sally—usually called me on my cell.

"Hello?" I said, glancing down at the long distance number I didn't recognize. Of course it could be someone trying to sell me something or wanting a donation.

"Carrie, dear, it's Brianna! I'm so glad I reached you."

"Hello, Mom."

She laughed. A fake laugh. "I think you're old enough to call me Brianna."

"But you're my mother. And Brianna isn't your real name."

"It is now, formally and legally." She sounded testy. "Carrie, I didn't expect the first words you've spoken to me in months to be an argument."

I waited, having learned not to rise to the bait. Sure enough she caved and let out her trademark trill of a laugh.

"Anyway, I called to tell you that Tom and I are coming to Clover Ridge."

"You're coming for a visit? The cottage isn't very large—"

"We wouldn't dream of staying with you and upsetting your little routine."

Little routine? My stomach started to churn as it usually did when my mother called and shot off one of her barbs.

"Then where will you stay? In a hotel?"

"No, dear. We'll rent a house. Actually, the film company's sending a large crew to make Tom's movie, so I imagine they'll be renting several houses." That trill again.

"Tom's in a movie?" I asked. "That's wonderful."

"Have you forgotten he's an actor?"

"I know but . . ." *But he's only managed to snag a few commercials and a tiny role in one film that no one ever saw.*

"And the wonderful thing about this movie," she gushed, "is Tom has a very large role—practically the lead. The movie takes place in a small, picturesque town. Naturally, I suggested Clover Ridge. The director checked it out and agreed it would be perfect."

I closed my eyes, imagining the havoc a movie filming would bring. "When are you coming?"

"They're thinking the beginning of April. As soon as your New England winter starts to thaw."

"Uh-huh. How long will the filming take?"

"How can I know, Carrie? Weeks. A few months, maybe. Just think. I'll be very busy on the set, keeping up Tom's morale and helping out as needed, but I'm sure we'll get to spend some quality time together. Won't that be fun?"

"Of course." I gulped. *Weeks? Months?* "Let me know if I can help with anything."

"I certainly will. Must fly now. We'll talk soon." The sound of two noisy kisses.

I hung up the receiver and called my father.

"Hi there, Caro. What's up?"

"Dylan and I picked up Bosco and Harriet at the airport. We had dinner here, then Dylan drove them home. The good news is, Uncle Bosco is taking over the running of Haven House."

"And the bad news?" When I didn't answer, he urged. "Come on. I can hear it in your voice."

"It's nothing, really." I shouldn't have called Jim to complain about his ex-wife.

"You don't sound very happy, darlin'. Is your boyfriend giving you *agita*? If you like, I'll fly there and give him what for."

I tried to laugh but didn't quite make it. Dylan and my dad were good friends. "My mother just informed me she and Tom are coming to Clover Ridge. Tom's making a film here."

"A film, did you say? Someone actually cast Pretty Boy in a movie?"

"So it seems. And *Brianna*, as she now expects me to call her, will be staying here the entire time. Not here in the cottage, thank God. They'll be renting a house."

"Oh, honey, don't let your mother upset you," Jim said. "She can't help putting on airs. It's in her DNA."

"I know. That's what I keep telling myself."

"If you like, I'll come up when she's in Clover Ridge—to diffuse things."

"Diffuse things? Dad, no! Don't even think about it."

"Whatever you say, Caro. Whatever you say."

We spoke a few minutes longer, then said goodbye. All my good feelings from the earlier part of the day had evaporated with the news that my mother was coming to Clover Ridge.

Part of me understood she'd had a tough time raising my brother and me because my father was never around. Being married to a professional thief couldn't have been easy.

Still, part of me resented her for not being more loving, more maternal. Last spring when I'd been at my lowest point, I'd called to ask if I could stay with her and Tom in Hollywood. She'd made up some feeble excuse why they couldn't have me come, and so I'd gone to live with Bosco and Harriet. Of course that turned out to be the best thing I could have done, but it didn't excuse my mother's ungracious behavior. And now she expected me to call her Brianna! A name she'd pulled out of a hat.

Why had she bothered to tell me about the film months before shooting began? I suspected it was to brag about Tom. To let me know he wasn't the wannabe actor he seemed to be.

And why had she suggested Clover Ridge as the film's locale, of all places? She'd never lived here. And the few times she'd driven Jordan and me to the Singleton farm outside of town where we'd spend our summers, she couldn't leave fast enough.

I drifted into the living room and curled up on the sofa. I couldn't stop her from coming, but I refused to be affected by her presence. I was a grown woman with a responsible job and a boyfriend who loved me. I would *not* let her erode my self-confidence, as she'd done so many times in the past.

Smoky Joe wandered over for some attention. I lifted him onto my lap. "Smoky Joe, old pal, we're in for a rough month of two."

"Meow," he said, agreeing with me.

Acknowledgments

I want to thank everyone at Crooked Lane Books who helped turn my manuscript into a book my readers will enjoy. A shout-out to my editor, Faith Black Ross, and to Sarah Poppe, Jenny Chen, and Ashley Di Dio; to my copywriter, Jill Pellarin, and to the Griesbach/Martucci team for another wonderful cover for the Haunted Library mystery series.

I am ever grateful to my indefatigable agent, Dawn Dowdle, and to the Sachem Library, where I've learned a good deal about the workings of a library. Sachem Library has been chosen the best of Long Island for five years in a row because of its terrific programs and events—always an inspiration to my sleuth, Carrie Singleton, who is head of programs and events of the Clover Ridge Library. In fact, my dear friend, Anne Marie Tognella, who retired from her position as Public Relations Specialist of Community Services, and Lauren Gilbert, who was Head of Community Services when I wrote this book, inspired me to create Carrie Singleton.

Read an excerpt from

CHECKED OUT FOR MURDER

the next

HAUNTED LIBRARY MYSTERY

by ALLISON BROOK

available soon in hardcover from
Crooked Lane Books

CROOKED
LANE

NEW YORK

Chapter One

"More coffee?" I asked Dylan as I got up from the table to pour us both a refill.

"I'd love some, babe, but I'd better leave now if I'm going to squeeze in a few important phone calls before my ten-thirty appointment." He stood and planted a kiss on my lips. "Traffic's bumper-to-bumper this time of the day."

I wrapped my arms around his waist. "All the larceny out there sure is keeping you busy. I'm glad you had time to stop by for breakfast."

"My pleasure. The eggs were prefect, Carrie. Just the way I love 'em."

Dylan shrugged into his leather jacket and I walked him out to his car, making sure that Smoky Joe didn't follow me. It was the first week of April, and the balmy weather and budding trees and bushes were sure signs that spring was on its way. My gray feline had a bad case of spring fever and was doing his best to escape the confines of my cottage to explore the great outdoors. But I couldn't allow that, not if Smoky Joe and I were going to get to work at the library on time. As the head of programs and events, I needed to be punctual, and the library patrons would be wanting a friendly visit from their library cat.

Dylan slid into the driver's seat of his BMW. "Have fun. I'll call or text when I have a free moment."

I smiled as I watched him drive off. Dylan was an investigator— a new partner in the company where he'd been working for years recovering stolen art and jewelry. A few months ago he'd opened his own office in New Haven, where he was investigating all sorts of situations. His first client had been a member of a family of restaurateurs who suspected that one of his cousins was skimming money off the top. Dylan had proved his client's suspicions correct, and now the thief was cooling his heels in jail. Dylan Avery was clever and handsome, and I considered myself lucky that he'd fallen in love with me.

I was lucky in many ways, I thought as I reentered my cottage, which stood at the end of the Avery property and faced the river. I had my wonderful job at the library, and good friends and loving relatives nearby. Of course, there were some less-than-wonderful aspects of my life—like my mother and her young husband, who were about to descend on Clover Ridge because Tom was going to be in a movie they were filming here in town. But I had a week until they arrived, so there was no point in dwelling on how Brianna, as my mother now called herself, was going to drive me crazy.

I stacked our breakfast dishes in the dishwasher, glad that Dylan and I had been able to have this hour together. We both had busy work schedules that rarely left us time for each other outside of weekends. Still, it was better having him living in the manor house a quarter mile up the private road than in Atlanta, Georgia, where his company headquarters were located.

Twenty minutes later, I put Smoky Joe in his carrier and brought it out to my car. I talked to him as I drove to the library.

"The trees have sprouted their light-green leaves and the forsythia is out. But maybe I shouldn't be telling you this. You'll want to go frolicking in the woods, where you can pick up ticks and fleas."

I made a mental note to stop at the vet to buy medicine to ward off ticks and fleas. Just in case Smoky Joe managed to get outside. Thank goodness he had been altered the month before, so there was no chance of his racing into the street chasing after female cats in heat.

Ten minutes later I pulled into the parking lot behind the library. Like the other centuries-old buildings bordering the Clover Ridge Green, the library had once been a large private residence. And like the other edifices, many of which had been converted into restaurants, shops, and art galleries, the library retained its white, wood-framed exterior. Across the Green, which was squarish in shape and roughly two small blocks wide in every direction, my Great-Uncle Bosco and Great-Aunt Harriet lived in one of the eight original homes still used as private residences.

As soon as we entered the library, I set Smoky Joe's carrier on the floor and slid open the metal door. He took off like a bullet.

"Someone's feeling his oats," Max, our senior custodian, commented as he halted the dolly cart he was using to move three large cartons.

"I'm afraid Smoky Joe has spring fever," I said. "I have to watch him at home and make sure he doesn't sneak out to explore the countryside."

"We wouldn't want him to run out of the library and into traffic. I'll keep an eye on him when I can. I'll mention it to Pete as well."

"Thanks, Max. I think I'll put up signs so patrons will know to watch out for him near the exit doors—at least for the next few weeks."

"Good idea, Carrie. We'd all be heartbroken if anything happened to our little friend."

I continued to my office, reflecting on how Smoky Joe had become a fixture in the library in just a matter of months. Last fall he'd ventured through the woods to my cottage from a nearby farm. He'd jumped into my car, and I'd ended up carrying him into the library for safekeeping. Smoky Joe had proved to be a very social creature. Patrons loved to make a fuss over him, and he enjoyed the attention of young and old alike. I loved him fiercely, and I knew that the many people who frequented the library would be distraught if anything were to happen to their little mascot.

I sat down at my desk and turned on the computer to find several emails waiting for me. I was responsible for making sure our many activities ran smoothly. Given the variety of programs we offered, with new ones being added each month, my job kept me on my toes. My goal was to entertain and educate our patrons, and so far I'd been pretty successful. Sally, my boss, gave me a good degree of freedom and flexibility—as long as I didn't go crazy moneywise.

I pulled out three sheets of printing paper. With a blue magic marker, I wrote on each of them:

When exiting the library, please make sure that Smoky Joe, the library cat, isn't leaving with you.
Thank you,
Carrie Singleton, Head of Programs and Events

I drew the outline of a cat with a bushy tail on each note. Scotch tape in hand, I set out to post them—one in the coffee shop, another in the reading room, and the third beside the circulation desk.

At the circulation desk, my best friend, Angela Vecchio, glanced up from the book she was checking out for a patron and waved to me. "See you at noon!"

I gave her a thumbs-up. Whenever Angela and I had the same lunch hour, we ate together, usually at the Cozy Corner Café a few blocks away. I'd just stepped back inside my office when a ping sounded from my cell phone. I read the message. *Thinking of u. XOXO.*

Me 2. I smiled as I texted back.

I glanced at the schedule of the day's activities. An exercise class, a current-events discussion, and a writers' workshop. Then in the afternoon, a book discussion, a lecture on "How to Remain Beautiful as You Age," and a food presentation of spring desserts.

I heard a knock on my door and looked up, expecting to see Sally or Angela or Marion, the children's librarian.

"Come in," I called.

A woman who looked a few years older than me—maybe midthirties—stepped into my office. Her jacket, pants, and boots nicely set off her shapely figure. Well-styled wavy brown hair framed her pretty face. Her smile was tentative, as though she was expecting a rejection of some kind.

"Hello. I hope I'm not interrupting. I'm interested in giving a library program, and the girl at the circulation desk told me to speak to the head of programs and events and directed me to your office. Am I in the right place?"

"You are—in the right place, that is." I stood and held out my hand. "Hi. I'm Carrie Singleton."

She shook my hand briefly. "My name is Daphne Marriott." She gave a little laugh. "No relation to the hotel chain. But I know the name Singleton."

"My family once owned what was the Singleton Farm outside of town. My uncle's on the library board." I rolled out the only other chair in my office from behind the desk my part-time assistants shared. "Please have a seat and tell me about the program you'd like to present."

"Of course." Daphne cleared her throat. "I recently moved to the area. I'm starting over, so to speak. New location, new career, new life."

I laughed. "I can relate to that."

"Really?" Her eyes lit up. When she realized I wasn't going to elaborate, she cleared her throat again. "Before I moved here, I had a near-death experience."

"Oh. I'm so sorry to hear that."

"I'm all right. I'm only mentioning it because, after I kind of blinked out for a short time, I discovered I had psychic powers."

I nodded, wondering where this was going. Did I have a nutcase on my hands?

Daphne must have realized my discomfort, because she continued, "I know this must sound weird to someone who's never had an experience like this, but after I recovered from my injuries, I discovered I knew things about people and situations—things that no one told me.

"I started giving readings. My clients found the information I shared with them to be authentic and helpful. I'd like to do that here, and I figured the best way to introduce myself to the people in the area would be to offer programs in the local libraries." She smiled. "And the Clover Ridge Library is the prettiest library around."

"You mean like a séance?" I asked. "I don't think—"

"No." Daphne laughed, all signs of her nervousness banished. "I don't communicate with the dead."

I do, I thought.

Daphne's eyes widened with surprise, as if she'd read my thought. Thank goodness she didn't pursue that. Instead she said, "I'd like to talk about the many different types of psychic abilities there are. Some psychics have the gift of divination and can foresee the future; others can heal; still others are mediums and are able to speak to the dead."

"And what type of psychic ability do you have?" I asked.

"Telepathy. Clairvoyance. They put me in touch with a person's innermost thoughts, fears, and occasionally his or her future. Honestly, it varies and depends on the person and the situation."

"So it depends on various factors?" *How convenient.*

"I know." Daphne smiled. "It sounds self-serving to say it depends on the person and the situation. Gives me an easy out if I'm unable to read someone who asked for my help with a problem. Did you ever watch the TV show *Medium* with Patricia Arquette?"

"I've seen a few episodes," I said.

"Then you probably know the show is based on the real Allison DuBois, who claimed she helped law enforcement agencies solve crimes."

I nodded. "She got her information about killers through dreams."

"That's right," Daphne said. "But if you'll remember, the dreams were never straightforward. They never revealed the entire picture or situation. They presented themselves as puzzles that Allison had to figure out in order to help her boss, the DA, ID the killer and go after him."

"I get it. It works sometimes."

"A good deal of the time," Daphne said. "For example, I've gotten a pretty clear picture of you in the few minutes we've been talking. You've had your position here in the library a short time, and you thoroughly enjoy what you do. You're in a loving relationship with a man you knew briefly as a child. Your parents are divorced, and your older brother died in a car accident."

My mouth fell open. "Everything you say is true, but it's also common knowledge. Clover Ridge is a small town. We all know quite a lot about our neighbors."

Daphne pursed her lips. "That may be so, but I swear no one ever told me anything about you or your background."

Is she telling the truth? Before I could decide how to answer, Evelyn Havers, the library ghost, began to manifest a few feet from where Daphne and I were sitting. Weird! Though my little cousin Tacey and I were the only people who could see and communicate with Evelyn, she never showed up when I had someone in the office. But here she was, with a Cheshire cat grin on her face, looking extremely pleased with herself.

"Oh!"

I turned to Daphne. Her hand was pressed to her chest, her body still as a statue.

"What's wrong?" I asked.

"I sense the presence of an entity from another plane."

"Really? You mean a ghost?" I had no intention of explaining Evelyn to someone I'd just met.

"Yes. An older woman, I believe, who died close by."

Bingo! Right on target! I pursed my lips together so I wouldn't burst out laughing at the sight of Evelyn thrusting her fist in the air. So unlike her!

Daphne must have thought I was frowning at her, because she said, "You don't have to believe me. Many people can't accept what I know to be true." She stood. "Well, thank you for hearing me out."

"Wait!" I called as she opened the door, eager to make a quick getaway. "I think our patrons would enjoy hearing you talk about the different psychic abilities."

Daphne turned. "Really?"

I nodded. "You're in luck! A presenter had to cancel his program a week from next Tuesday evening. Are you interested?"

"You bet!" She grinned. "If time permits, I'll be happy to go around the room and give what I call minute readings."

"The patrons will love that." I handed her a form. "Please fill this out ASAP. You can return it via email or bring it back here."

"Thank you! Thank you, Carrie."

For a moment, I was afraid she was going to hug me, but instead she held out her hand. As we shook, a small shock ran up my arm and I had a divination of my own—that Daphne Marriott had a troubled past, which was about to spill over into my life.